Book III of the Austen Gaskell Series

Triumph & Tragedy

A 'Pride & Prejudice' and 'North & South' Variation

NEY MITCH

TRIUMPH & TRAGEDY
Copyright © 2025 by Ney Mitch

ISBN: 979-8-88653-378-1

Published by Satin Romance
An Imprint of Melange Books, LLC
White Bear Lake, MN 55110
www.satinromance.com

Published in the United States of America.

Cover Design by Caroline Andrus

Hello Readers! Welcome to Book III of the Austen Gaskell series.
I hope that you enjoyed the previous books in the series, and I'm not wasting another minute by delaying you. You are the reason this third book is possible. And that's what makes you quite spectacular.
May this next part of the series be worthy of you again. Special thanks to family, friends, publisher, and all who helped bring this book to the world.
And a noted dedication must be given to Helyn-Roberts Vickers, A. Madison, and Miss Novo. Thank you for being you!

Book I

The Longest Day

Chapter 1

Flashes

The Afternoon Ride

Half an hour before the riot, Plato Pitcher was riding along, headed towards Frances Street to visit the Bennets and see if his sister was there, when he came upon a strange sight.

Nothing.

In all his time in Milton, he had never come upon the street where there was no one walking about. For reasons that he could not deduce, he was filled with an extreme foreboding, for the silence hung about his instincts with an intense darkness.

Something was wrong.

He could not account for his rash assumption, but something was very wrong indeed.

Dismounting, he knocked on the Bennets' door and received no word.

"Miss Bennet?" he called. "Miss Elizabeth, Miss Kitty?"

"Mr. Pitcher!"

Plato turned to where his name was called, and he saw Mary Higgins rushing toward him from her doorway. Despite all logic, Plato couldn't help but view this as the second sign that something was irregular. Mary Higgins barely ever spoke, and when she did, it was rarely ever so loud.

"Miss Mary?" he asked, "What's wrong here?"

"Have yer heard, sir?"

"No, I haven't. Something feels strange, and I don't like it."

"Yer one of those second sight fellas, eh?" she asked, her voice a little winded. "Did yer hear about the riot tha' might be happenin' at Marlborough Mills?"

"Riot?" Plato repeated, his eyebrows scrunching together in surprise.

"Many of the workers found out about the Irish that Thornton brought in to end the strike and they are marchin' there."

Putting his arm on her shoulder, concerned, he lowered his voice.

"Crowds like that have been known to get violent. Did Thornton send for the officers?"

"Don't know 'bout that," Mary pressed, "but Plato...the ladies are there."

"Ladies? Mary, what ladies?"

"Yer sister, Plato. She went there with Lizzy, Margaret, and Kitty. They went to warn Thornton."

The third sign had come and now his forebodings had come true.

Over Mary's shoulder, Plato saw Bessy Higgins leaning weakly in her doorway, a heavy shawl around her shoulder and her face sickly.

"Yea, Plato," Bessy supported, "they went. We're scared."

"Oh god," Plato said. Without thinking another minute, Plato climbed on top of his horse and looked to Bessy and Mary. "Stay inside until this is ended. Commoners don't want to be on the street if a riot breaks loose. Soldiers won't be able to tell the difference between an innocent and the guilty running for their lives."

Egging his horse on, he rode away and headed to Marlborough Mills. Filial duty and devotion took over his instincts and he didn't take heed to being one man versus a mob.

As he dashed away, Mary went to her doorway as Bessy watched him go.

"What can he do?" Mary asked.

"Help, I guess," Bessy said. "Then again...he could get hurt, couldn' he?"

"And we told him to go there."

"Rasby is his sister. We did right, Mary. Aye, we did."

***

"Thank you," Mr. Darcy said as he purchased some meat from the best butcher in Milton. Time had taught him not to bring flowers to the Bennet sisters. After all, they lived in a way where practical gifts meant much more. He grinned down at the side of pork that he had purchased, for the times had dramatically shifted. One poor sonnet would not suit Lizzy. One set of flowers would satisfy her eye, but not her needs. One purchase of ribbon or sheet of music just would not do!

If Elizabeth Bennet were to fall in love with him one day—which he believed that there was a chance of—then he could shower her with all the more traditional ways of doting on a proper lady later. However, her station in life, at present, had obliged him to think very differently, and he wanted to show her how much he was trying.

How much he was taking notice of the shift in her life.

How he was enhancing his outlook on people of profession.

How he wanted to help.

Slowly and surely, he was finding more pathways into her mind and soul, and that was the source and means through which he could finally enter her heart.

He put the meat in his leather bag, slung it over his shoulder and got onto his horse. The state of his being was that of comfortable ease and a sense of self-assurance when he turned onto another street and was surprised when Plato Pitcher was racing down the road, shocking all the passersby. His riding was neither practical, nor prudent for a man who was riding along public streets.

'Plato,' Darcy thought, 'what the devil are you about?'

Realizing that he could not let such reckless riding go on, Darcy rode his horse through the traffic and intercepted Plato.

"Plato!" Darcy roared, about to grab Plato's reins, 'slow down, man!"

"I can't!" Plato cried as Darcy rode alongside him, "They're in danger, Darcy. I have to help them."

"Danger? Who?"

"My sister, Kitty and Elizabeth!"

When hearing Lizzy's name, Darcy's eyes widened. His spirit transitioned from reprimanding to inquiring.

"What's happened to Lizzy?" Darcy cried.

"They went to Marlborough Mills to warn the Thorntons about rioters who were coming there. They might be trapped!"

The powers of implication and imagination! Mr. Darcy's mind jumped from an image of Elizabeth, to seeing her locked in a room while rioters broke in, to get to the family. Then the hungry and enraged faces of the rioters pressed against her beautiful countenance—and any violence that could occur afterwards.

His blood was on fire. His heart raced. For when the unknown attacks the desire to protect someone, a flame ignites from within.

Elizabeth had to be kept safe! Nothing else in the world mattered besides that.

Both men raced along and eventually they reached Marlborough Mills.

Margaret's Declaration

After Elizabeth, Kitty, and Rasby had left to calm down the Irish workers, Margaret watched their progression from the window.

Every instinct to join them was awake, but Lizzy was right. She had to remain there, in case Mr. Darcy returned, and he had gotten caught up in the mob. Either way, she was helping and this way, she could see if any threat were to enter the Mill's courtyard. And she was correct to.

"Oh my god!" Fanny Thornton cried, "they are here! They're at the gates!"

"Fanny," Mrs. Thornton declared as the three women pressed their faces against the window and saw the angry crowd bash against the gates, trying to get to the poor Irish workers who were huddled up in the mill. "Fanny, call John in from the Mill!"

"He might be safer there than out in the open!" Fanny cried. "Look! They might get in!"

Mrs. Thornton gave her daughter a harsh look, Fanny relented, and she left.

"True," Margaret said, gentler. Her eyes were wide in alarm and also filled with empathy when she looked down at the crowd. She recognized some of the people who were rushing in. Among them was Boucher. Next to him was Custer, the man that Thornton dismissed from his service for being neglectful in the sorting room.

Why did Boucher have to get involved in this? In fact, by the way that he was climbing the gate, he might have even been the one who was leading the mob.

"My word!" Margaret uttered as she watched the crowd push their bodies against the gate, to get inside. "they are using their bodies as battering rams. And retreating a short space, only to come with more united steady impetus against it."

"And it's working," a servant cried. "Look! The gates are giving way!"

Margaret watched Fanny as she left the house, but she didn't have to go far. Thornton had exited the mill all on his own and had been coming to the house. When Fanny met him, she jumped when she heard the mob roar out, still pushing themselves against the gate. Thornton held her and

helped Fanny back into the house. Despite her best intentions, Margaret couldn't help but resent Fanny's want of
courage. She seemed to be too delicate for her liking—afterwards, she dismissed her harsh judgments. Fanny Thornton
was not her favorite person, but the scene was a frightening
one, and perhaps Fanny couldn't help but be terrified.
Many people would feel the same sort of trepidation.

"Foolish child," Mrs. Thornton hissed, nearby.

Now that was going too far. Even though Fanny's feelings did not have any special place in Margaret's heart, but
Mrs. Thornton ought to have understood that this whole
experience was scary to her daughter.

They heard the door open and close, rushed footsteps,
and they turned to see Fanny bursting into the room, her
cheeks red from the hysterics.

"They hate us!" Fanny cried. "They want to kill us!"

Mrs. Thornton rushed to her and held her as Fanny
was on the point of collapsing on the floor.

Mr. Thornton had entered and had approached his
mother and sister, ignorant of Margaret's attendance, for
she was still at the window, half-hidden by a curtain.

"The gate holds for now," Thornton uttered, looking at
the yard.

"But not for much longer," Mrs. Thornton responded,
helping Fanny to the sofa. "How soon will the soldiers get
here?"

"Perhaps in a quarter of an hour or twenty minutes. Just
in case, remain here."

"Miss Hale," Mrs. Thornton called to Margaret, "come
from the window, in case they break in and throw stones at
the glass."

"Miss Hale?" Thornton questioned, unaware that she

was present. He turned around and his face grew flushed when he saw Margaret there, peering around the curtain. As if things were not horrible enough! She already had much against his profession and habits, and now she was going to see this? This was more confirmation and more against his favor. He had been progressing at making himself more endearing to her, and now he felt the drawbacks of the reality of his life.

He looked in Margaret's eyes, and he saw the disturbance that lay there. She didn't look resentful at him, but the tragedy of the starving workers naturally would draw her sympathy toward them, and apathy toward himself. This was everything that he didn't want. Would their dance at the dinner party now mean nothing?

"Mr. Thornton," Miss Hale said, "Lizzy, Rasby, and Kitty sought you in the factory. Did you find them?"

"I did." He breathed. "They are safe in there, I promise. That door is heavily solid."

"More solid than the gate?" Margaret questioned, ignoring Mrs. Thornton's words, and remaining at the window. "Mr. Thornton, I think they are making progress, sir. Look!"

Happy that she was talking to him with nothing more or less than bravery and tolerance, he joined her at the window and did indeed see the gate buckling under the mob's progress.

"I am sorry," Thornton apologized, "that you have visited us at this unfortunate moment, Miss Hale. I fear, you may be involved in whatever risk we have to bear."

Margaret looked at him, resolute.

"Sir, I am here. And I am not afraid."

They both looked into each other's eyes and there was

an intensity. However, that connection came from two different perspectives that both thought they shared but really didn't.

On Margaret's side was the feeling of triumph. She dreaded that her courage should fail her in any emergency, for she feared being a coward. But now, in this real great time of reasonable fear and nearness of terror, she forgot herself, and felt only an intense sympathy—intense to painfulness—in the interests of the moment. She conquered any fear and wanted this to be evident.

On Thornton's side, he felt that their souls had connected, and she was supporting him. She would not buckle and break under the weight of the moment but stand by him and rally to his side. In that moment, she was everything that he ever wanted.

He desired her. In ways that he could not ever utter.

Tearing his eyes away from the depth of hers, he turned to his mother.

"Mother! You should go to the backrooms and take Fanny with you. Whatever happens, you both will be safer there than in here." He turned to Jane, the servant. "Jane, go!"

Jane and some other servants left the room, with Fanny crying.

"Not me, John," Mrs. Thornton said, turning to her son, determined. "I stop here! Where you are, I'm staying."

Margaret watched as both mother and son looked on each other, with a strong understanding of family loyalty. Whatever she felt for Mrs. Thornton, Margaret could not help but appreciate the protectiveness she had for her son's life. Their silent strength clashed with the cries and shrieks of the servants in the house, and it reminded Margaret of the hysteria. She looked away from them and back to the factory.

"Lizzy, Kitty and Rasby," Margaret whispered, "please be safe."

When hearing Margaret's whispering, Thornton turned back to her and watched her countenance. There she was, standing still at the window that was nearest the factory. Her eyes glittered, her color was deepened on her cheek and lip. She was beautiful!

"Your friends will be safe in there, I believe," Thornton assured her, "the door is strong."

"I hope so. I don't want anything to happen to them or your new workers. Mr. Thornton, the gate is breaking!"

"Shut the windows!" Thornton cried, "shut them, Miss Hale and mama."

Margaret did so, then helped Mrs. Thornton, whose hands were trembling. While doing so, Mrs. Thornton didn't look gracious, but contemptuous. Margaret understood her well. Mrs. Thornton was not happy that Margaret saw her showing any sign of weakness. And for Margaret to see it, of all people! The pride of the matter!

Then came the dreaded sound. Of wood creaking, suffering under the weight of bodies pressing against it. Through the window, they saw the mob's progress. The gates had now broken and fell over.

The angry mob, mad and starving, had come pouring into the courtyard. They raced in, roaring violently.

"Oh, no!" Fanny cried. "We are going to die. We..." She collapsed in her mother's arms. Mrs. Thornton, with the help of another servant, picked her up and carried her up the stairs.

"Miss Hale, it would be best if you went with my mother," Thornton said.

Even though Margaret would have said no at the order, she was too busy focused on the angry voices and stomps that filled Marlborough Mills. She remained by the window, watching the crowd.

"What is to be done?" Margaret said. "How can we calm them?"

"The soldiers will be the chief influence."

Margaret's eyes widened at the implications of this.

"Soldiers?"

"Yes. Let them yell! I hope the Irishmen are not terrified by this."

"They've gotten to the door and are banging against it," Margaret observed, horrified, for her friends were also in there. "That door must hold."

"Keep up your courage for five more minutes," Thornton pressed.

"I am not afraid, nor be afraid for me. But five minutes? For the soldiers to come here? Can you do nothing to soothe them, to calm them down? They are poor creatures."

"The soldiers will be here directly, and that will make them see reason."

Margaret was horrified. She knew that Thornton had a harsh outlook on his workers, but how much colder was he?

"To reason!" she spat. "What kind of reason?"

"The only reason that does with men that make themselves into wild beasts."

"Mr. Thornton," Margaret declared, emboldened, "go down there this instant. Do not be a coward. You are better than this if you just tell yourself so. If you go down there, face them like a man, and listen to them, there will be no need for the officers to exercise your idea of 'reason'. Speak to your workmen as if they are human beings, for they are! They are starving and driven mad from an inability to support their families. They have been driven to this. Please, show your quality. If you have any courage within you, go out and speak to them, man to man. This will keep them from the mill door, where I am sure that my friends are defending your Irishmen. Protect them and listen to your workers."

Every word that she said touched him and even went so far as to drown out the enraged voices that rang throughout the mill yard.

"You are right," he uttered. "When I am outside, do me the courtesy of bolting the door behind me."

Turning his heel, he left her. Once he disappeared, Margaret immediately regretted her passionate words. What if she was wrong? What if the mob hurt him?

She looked at the crowd again and saw that the mob was bashing themselves against the door. They were going to make their way into the factory, where her friends and the Irish were.

Elizabeth, Kitty, Rasby, the Irishmen, and Mr. Thornton—all of them were in danger.

She would not have it!

"Nothing must happen to them," she declared. "Nothing must happen."

She rushed down the stairs, to see Mr. Thornton open the door. With one last look at her, he exited. Margaret did as he instructed and fastened the door behind him.

She leaned against the wood, closing her eyes as she rested her forehead against the door, steadying herself.

Lizzy, Rasby, and Kitty were in the mill house.

Thornton was outside, under her instruction.

She was the one who had not joined her friends.

She was the one who sent Mr. Thornton out there—and placed him in untold danger.

The weight of responsibility, duty, and compassion rose within her.

The workers had the right to voice their complaints.

But Thornton had the right to be protected.

Just as she needed to do whatever she could to keep them from breaking into the mill and attacking her friends and the Irish.

May my courage never leave me, Margaret thought to herself as she became resolved. She unbolted the door, breathed in one last time, opened it, and felt the light overwhelm her as she stepped out of the house and joined Mr. Thornton on his stoop.

And she could not have come out a moment too soon. She was met by a sea of angry men who were shouting, roaring out frantically, rebelling against Mr. Thornton, who they felt committed the worst crime of all by sending for the Irish. In their eyes was the fiery passion that sweeps over anyone when they are possessed by the mania that occurs when you decide to become an angry mob. Individual and independent thought dies, and you all become one collective. When looking on the mob, Margaret saw how young many of the men were. Most of them were teenagers, mere boys! They had turned cruel and thoughtless. Some were men, gaunt as wolves, and thirsting for their prey. Like Boucher, they had starving children at home, and they had been driven mad from hunger, an inability to receive higher wages, provide for their families and also were starving themselves. Circumstances maybe had turned them into wild creatures. But reason could bring them back. She had to hope.

"Miss Hale!" Thornton cried, worried about her being out there with him. Margaret, however, was not going to shy away from her purpose now. Raising up her hands, she appealed to the crowd.

"Please!" she cried to the crowd, "do not use violence! He is one man, and you are many." She raised her voice even more. "Go! The soldiers have been sent for and they come now. Go peacefully. You shall have relief from your complaints, whatever they are. If you will only appeal calmly from this day forth!"

Boucher came forward, roaring to Thornton.

"Will you send the Irish away?" Boucher cried, threatening and with a fiery rage.

"Never!" Mr. Thornton roared, standing next to Margaret.

Internally, Margaret felt defeated. This last declaration would be the final straw that broke the mob's mentality. And it did so. Thornton's staunch defiance instantly led to an uproar. The storm clouds fell over the crowd, the angry shouting filled the air, Margaret saw the mob pick up objects, threatening to throw them at their stubborn master. She knew the meaning. Thornton was in danger, and it was all her fault.

Only one thought came to her: she must save him.

Wrapping her arms around his neck, she placed her body in front of his, as a shield. Instinctively, Thornton held her around her waist and then remembered himself. She was endangering herself for him.

"Go inside!" he cried.

"No, I will not leave you here to be harmed! They might not harm a woman. I can protect you."

She shielded him again as some clogs began to fly their way, from the bitter throng. Out of the corner of her eye, she saw that one of the men who were throwing things was Boucher. But there was another man, one particular young man in the crowd, driven by their love of cruel excitement and sadistic mentality, who threw a clog and Margaret only had the ability to close her eyes as it hit her forehead.

White!

All that she saw was white as the pain overwhelmed her, she struggled to remain conscious for a few seconds, and then her eyes closed, overcome by the blackness. She fell against Mr. Thornton, who held her in his arms.

"Fools!" Thornton cried. "You want my death! Kill me then! But see the truth of your evil in where she now lies!"

The Fiery Ladies of the Mill

As this all occurred, the other part of the mob had bashed through the mill door and had attacked Lizzy, Kitty, Rasby, and the Irish defenders. While Margaret was collapsing in Thornton's arms, Elizabeth was leading her sister and friend... and they were fighting back their own neighbors, being overcome by the mob, their reckless passion carrying them so far that they lost any sense of morality or chivalry. To them, any opposition was their enemy. Elizabeth, Kitty and Rasby, were their friends, their fellow beasts of burden, women who were made to toil and labor as they had done so. All of that was forgotten. These three women dared to stand against them, dared to protect the Irish, and so, they were not these ladies' allies. They were the adversaries.

Bashing against them, their mad energy overcame the women, knocking them with vehement blows and sending the ladies to the floor, unconscious.

As Elizabeth saw Kitty and Rasby on the floor, their eyes closed before hers did, she felt so foolish for bringing them into the situation, as Margaret had felt when sending Thornton to the wildness.

Regrets! Regrets! Regrets!

From inside the mill and outward, ladies of resolution were collapsing under the callousness of the contemptuous crowd.

The Calvary Coming In

It was in this precise moment that Mr. Darcy and Plato had rashly driven into the courtyard. They saw Thornton holding Margaret Hale in his arms and they felt the horror of it. Violence had happened there.

When seeing his two friends race through the court-yard, Thornton's eyes were insistent, and his tone was strong.

"There! In the mill! Save the Bennet sisters and Rasby!"

Needing no other encouragement, Mr. Darcy and Plato rode up to the mill door, scaring any workers out of their way with their powerful steeds. When reaching the door, Plato had his horse rear up on its hind legs. When the horse's legs came rushing back down to the earth, it knocked the villains who lingered in the doorway to the ground and barred any more workers from entering the place. Both men, of strong height, strength, and powers of intimidation, dismounted and rushed into the mill.

When they entered, it was to a horrible sight. Seeing over the crowd, they saw Elizabeth, Kitty and Rasby lying unconscious on the floor, along with an unconscious Irishman. Two other Irishmen were standing protectively over them. When seeing Plato in his regimentals, the Irishmen knew that they had allies who came for them.

"They attacked the women!" An Irishman cried, but Mr. Darcy did not need encouragement, nor did Plato. Removing his musket from his side, Plato used it like a staff. Darcy found a block of wood along the wall and picked it up.

Darcy was silent rage.

Plato was of a verbose battle cry.

After all, one was a gentleman, and the other a soldier.

With his strength, Plato widened his arms and shoved seven of the people backwards against the wall. He was truly frightening to the workers.

"Animals!" Darcy wailed, hitting them all with his block of wood, with an anger that overwhelmed all before him.

When Plato roared at the crowd, they began to recoil, out of pure terror of him. As Darcy swung the wood and wounded many in his path, Plato aimed his musket at the throng, and that's when they all froze.

"Disband and retreat, fools!" Plato roared, and his

words were hypnotic. Seeing Darcy wholly unafraid was not surprising, but Plato, who was not the sort to be so fearless in their presence, was altogether a surprise to them. Also, despite the mob mentality of blind rage and resentment, a musket can be very enlightening and remind someone of their individual fears of mortality. When facing the other side of a gun barrel, you cease to be one entity and you regain your own sense of self, self-preservation, self-awareness, humiliation, conscience, and dare it be said, mortification. Everyone in the crowd remembered themselves, or at the very least, remembered their fears. They filed out of the mill like drowning rats, who were scuttling through a small hole that could not fit their great escape. They fell over each other, in their attempt to exit, and Mr. Darcy, blinded by his rage, grabbed the nearest man who was trying to retreat, wielding him around with a fury.

"A woman," Darcy cried, letting the wood down and beginning to strike the man with intensity. "You call yourself a man, sir!"

The man buckled under Darcy's blows, almost becoming unconscious. Through the window, Plato could see that the calvary had come. The soldiers had arrived, and arrests could begin to be made.

The Arrival of Aid

Along the streets, Colonel Forster led thirty soldiers in his regiment. They rode through the street quickly, but not to the point where they caused any danger to passersby.

As he rode along, every now and again, he turned to his

left, where Colonel Fitzwilliam rode alongside him. It had been some time since Forster was aware about Fitzwilliam's attachment to Kitty Bennet and his connection to Marlborough Mills. In Colonel Fitzwilliam's eye was apprehension and slight alarm.

"Never fear," Colonel Forster roared over their riding. "We will get there in time."

"I hope so," Colonel Fitzwilliam replied, warily. "The Bennet sisters have been known to visit that factory."

This idea had never occurred to Colonel Forster, and the notion of it affected his sensibility.

"What?"

"Yes, Colonel. And I never am aware of their movements, so I have no notion of if they are there or not."

"It is very unlikely. One cannot fully determine the unknown."

"Precisely," Fitzwilliam said to him, his expression even more unsettled, "one cannot. I believe in exploring all possibilities. Colonel, can we not ride faster?"

Colonel Forster understood the impulses of the young, and of the heart. For whatever Fitzwilliam was feeling, was perhaps equivalent to what Forster would have felt if he knew Mrs. Forster might be in any danger.

Ah, Mrs. Forster!

How delightful it always is when we place our situation in another person's predicament. We see. We empathize. We understand. And we learn to believe. If Colonel Forster even knew that there was the slightest possibility that his wife would be in a place that was stormed by an angry crowd, he would race all the way there, even if his solitary person could do little to assist. It is the nature of any true man when his beloved is in danger.

Now he understood.

Now he believed.

"Company!" Colonel Forster roared, "ride faster!"

Eagerly, Colonel Fitzwilliam urged his horse to quicken. Daedalus, his noble stead, understood his rider all too well, and hastened onward. Together, horse and man became one: on a mission of urgency.

When they arrived at the mill, they rode through the gate and saw Thornton on his doorstep—with a woman laying unconsciously at his feet. Colonel Fitzwilliam recognized her immediately.

Miss Margaret Hale!

Then if she was here, what were the chances...no, it was too terrifying to confront. And yet, confront the possibilities, he must.

Colonel Forster sounded his alarm and led the attack on disbanding the workers. The officers rode through the crowd, driving the mob off, sometimes smacking them in their heads or arms with their clubs. Among the bunch, Colonel Fitzwilliam recognized Boucher and felt an immediate rage at the man's betrayal.

As the other officers chased the crowd off, and also made arrests, Colonel Fitzwilliam rode his horse up to the front steps, just as Thornton lifted Margaret up and held her in his arms.

Colonel Fitzwilliam stared at her lifeless body, dangling in Thornton's embrace, and feared the worst.

"Is she..."

"She's alive," Thornton pressed, heavily, "but I must send for the doctor, to make sure that she remains such."

Colonel Fitzwilliam breathed a sigh of relief.

"But Lizzy, Rasby and Kitty..."

When hearing Kitty's name, Colonel Fitzwilliam's eyes shot open wider.

"She's here! Where are they?"

"Darcy and Plato went after them in the factory," Thornton gestured to the mill door. "Bring them inside immediately!"

Colonel Fitzwilliam did not need to be told such before he rode his horse up to the mill door, jumped down immediately and entered to see Mr. Darcy with a man, limp in his arms.

The Falling Moments

Seeing that Darcy was on the point of possibly killing the man who lay trapped in his clutches, Plato rushed forward and grabbed his arm before he struck the worker again.

"Darcy!" Plato cried, "you are killing him. You must stop or be it forever on your conscience!"

Plato had seen such behavior before, where the wildness overtook a man who was driven to the point of grief, chivalry, and protectiveness. It led to a passionate rage, where he forgot himself and the monster that lurked underneath took over. The beast within every human soul, became alive. And the man's morality lay dormant until the creature was finally subdued. There was only one thing to do; Plato grabbed Darcy's face and made him look into his eyes.

"Darcy, look at me, man!" Plato hissed, and finally Darcy did so, freezing before he struck the limp worker again. "He is subdued; he will be arrested. We have won.

You can stop now. We have to get the women to safety. Elizabeth needs you."

Hearing Elizabeth's name gave the desired effect, Darcy's eyes transformed from a wild man, bent on revenge, to an expression that was softened with compassion, care, and consideration. His soul returned to him.

"Elizabeth," he sighed, releasing the weak creature from his grasp, and letting him fall to the floor, his eyes fluttering, in and out of focus. This was the precise moment that Colonel Fitzwilliam entered and saw the last moments of Darcy's rage.

"Darcy!" Colonel Fitzwilliam cried, "where is Kitty!"

"Here," an Irishman said, picking up Kitty and holding her in his arms. "She needs a doctor."

"Dear god!" Colonel Fitzwilliam hissed, rushing up to the Irishman and taking Kitty from his arms.

"She's alive," the Irishman stressed, "but she suffered a great blow."

Meanwhile, Darcy rushed to Elizabeth and Plato tended to his sister.

Leaning down, Darcy saw that Elizabeth's face was covered by her hair, which had come undone. He leaned down and removed it from her face. Seeing her there, with blood trickling down her cheek, made his stomach churn over, feeling sickened.

"There will be blood," Darcy hissed, revenge overcoming him again as he picked Elizabeth up, "there will be blood spilled for this."

Darcy turned to the Irishmen, angry.

"How could you let them fight?" He declared, enraged, "they were women!"

"We couldn't stop them," another Irishman stated,

unashamed and bravely, "they would not shy away. They came to defend us."

"Darcy," Colonel Fitzwilliam said, cradling Kitty in his arms, "you know Elizabeth: would she have stood by?"

Seeing the sense of this, Darcy relented and felt a little ashamed of himself. He knew that he should have apologized for accusing the Irishmen for negligence, but his pride was somewhat affected.

"I understand," was all that he could muster.

"Come," Plato demanded, unafraid of being authoritative, "let's get the women inside." Plato turned to the Irishmen. "Go upstairs and assure the others that the worst is over. Officers will remain at the doorway so that the crowd won't return again."

All three men left, with Lizzy, Kitty, and Rasby in their arms.

When they emerged into the sunlight, they moved around the officers, who were making arrests of the people they had managed to capture.

"Colonel," Denny cried, riding toward Darcy, Plato, and Fitzwilliam. Looking down, he saw the three women in their arms. "Oh, god," Denny gasped.

"They are alive, Denny," Colonel Fitzwilliam said, "remain for further instruction as the doctor comes. I don't want to alarm Mrs. Denny until we know that it's not serious."

"Yes. Lydia would be horrified."

"Bring the ladies in," Thornton cried to the three men. They looked up at him, and he was holding Margaret Hale in his arms, who was also unconscious.

Four women overcome by the same vehemence.

They carried the ladies into the house, and Mrs. Thornton overtook the situation.

"Take them upstairs to one of the spare bedrooms," she declared.

"My bedroom will suffice," Mr. Darcy stated so strongly that it would not be denied. "The bed is large enough for them four." All the men carried the ladies upstairs, into Darcy's room and began to lay the women down on it.

"Lay that Raspberry girl on the floor," Mrs. Thornton ordered to Plato. The distinction was too marked to be mistaken. Plato, however, was not one to fear much. He turned to Mrs. Thornton with a cold firmness that was over-powering.

"My sister will lay on the bed, or no woman will."

"Lay her down next to Margaret, Plato," Mr. Thornton replied, overturning his mother's orders. Plato laid Raspberry down on the bed, next to Margaret Hale.

Mrs. Thornton went up to her son.

"John, what are you doing?" She asked him.

"Being master of this house," he replied. He touched her arm, "please, look after these ladies with the men. I have to go down and see to the Irish. These men can't be left with the women alone, or the servants will talk."

"Aye, there will be talk indeed," Mrs. Thornton replied, forgetting her momentary moral lapse—then again, she did have many of those, which she either forgot about, or excused in her character, as many of us are wont to do. "Send Hannah up here to assist me."

Thornton went downstairs and ordered Hannah and his sister upstairs to assist his mother.

"You don't need to be here," Mrs. Thornton told the

men, moving about the room to remove the ladies' outerwear from them, "this is ladies work now."

"I know how to dress wounds," Plato said, removing his regimental coat so that he could assist the ladies more easily, "I will tend to them until the doctor arrives."

Hannah entered and Plato turned to her.

"Miss Hannah, I will need some warm water, clean white linen rags, smelling salts and if you have any yarrow plants, goldenrod, or aloe plants about the place, bring me them."

Hannah looked at him, confused.

"What?" She asked.

"Do what he says, girl, and don't stand there, looking stupid!" Mrs. Thornton declared. Mrs. Thornton's sudden reversal of attitude only overwhelmed Plato for a few seconds before he accepted that dramatic shifts from prejudice to compassion swung from side to side with this strange woman.

Fanny Thornton entered, and she gasped when seeing the unconscious women. Seeing that her daughter would be no help, Mrs. Thornton ordered her as well.

"Fanny, go and help Hannah with the herb retrieval."

"Me?" Fanny asked.

"Yes, you. Or am I speaking to another daughter that I have, who I have never met until today?"

Fanny bit her lip and followed Hannah.

As Mrs. Thornton continued to remove the ladies' cloaks, the men looked queerly at her.

"Too much outerwear can be trying for a sick person," She explained, "their bodies need to breathe, especially with how confining ladies apparel is." She handed Darcy and Colonel Fitzwilliam two fans. "Fan them so that they can get more air on them."

Darcy and Colonel Fitzwilliam did as they were bid, as Mrs. Thornton looked at Plato, still with a critical eye.

"Are you telling the truth, sir, and know a little about medicine?"

"Not a little, madam," Plato said, rolling up his sleeves. "And I may have my defects but lying about my knowledge of wound-tending is not one of them."

"Very well."

Mrs. Thornton went to the door and called for another servant, named Jane. As she did so, she glimpsed out of the window and saw that the officers were making proper arrests, the mob had fully broken up, and her son was talking to the officers.

She breathed a sigh of relief.

All was over. In more ways than one.

Chapter 2

The Calm After the Storm

Now that all commotion had ended and her son was safe, Mrs. Thornton was at ease. Or rather, as much at ease as a person like her could be. Being a remarkably strong woman, she was filled with strong prejudices, and those prejudices were felt so keenly, that they were irrevocably a part of her character. Her mean understanding gave her strength and helped her feel justified in anything she said and felt. It is a strange sort of truth, philosophically discovered, that our more imperfect sides give us our strength, and our moral sides are more passive, and have less willpower. Our flawed sides give us self-confidence, and our better sides give steadiness, moderation, modesty, and morality to our imperfect halves.

The chaste regulates the wanton.

The purifier calms the passionate sinner.

The good redeems the bad.

The indiscriminate enlightens the inequality.

The restful reconciles with the restless.

The laborer understands those who enjoy leisure.

Therefore, as much as it is to say that this next moment in time helped Mrs. Thornton overcome the baser sides of her character, the part of herself that needed to release being a woman of mean understanding and fear of anything that could upset the tranquility that she had found... but that is not reality, nor was it likely. For what can you do when the vices and virtues are so very much linked in a person? Not much. For their stubbornness is what gives them strength. Mrs. Thornton's strong and stern outlook in life is what gave her solidarity and made her a steady and solid maternal figure who raised her son above his past circumstances and made him into a great man.

When looking on these four unconscious women who remained on the bed, she did feel a sense of obligation and respect for their sacrifice. But only in a general sense. Another part of herself felt that they were presumptuous for their speaking on her son's behalf, making it appear as if he could not defend himself and protect those who were in his care. Of course, there was a hint of jealousy involved; these ladies defended him in the way that a mother would have—and she now felt that she should have. But she was not ready for such self-awareness. She was a woman torn between her better and worse sides and both would have to remain as they were: divided.

Soon, Jane entered, followed by Hannah and Fanny Thornton, who came with the water and rags.

"We didn't have aloe plants or yarrow, madam and sirs," Hannah said, "but we have plenty of goldenrod."

"Good enough," Plato said, going over to the desk and taking Darcy's brush. Darcy watched him. "My apologies, sir, but the bottom of your brush will be very good at mushing down the goldenrod and making into a balm."

"Very well," Darcy declared, "go to it, man."

Plato poured a little bit of water into a basin, while Mrs. Thornton went to Jane, the servant.

"Jane, you must fetch Doctor Donaldson," she instructed.

"Beggin' your pardon, ma'am," Jane said, "but I can't."

"What do you mean that you can't?" Mrs. Thornton snapped.

"Not me, ma'am, if you please," Jane said, shrinking where she stood, "Them rabble may be about. I don't think the cuts and blows are so deep, ma'am, as it looks. And Mr. Plato seems to know what he's doin'."

Mrs. Thornton looked at her, scoldingly.

"I will not run the chance of not saying that I didn't call for another doctor in here," she replied, embarrassed at her own servant's weakness. "She was hurt in our house. If you are a coward, Jane, I am not. I will go then."

"Mrs. Thornton," Darcy objected, "it may be dangerous. I cannot permit it, in your son's absence."

"Precisely," Colonel Fitzwilliam supported, wiping down Kitty's face with a wet rag and handing one for Darcy to wipe down Lizzy's forehead scar. "pray ma'am, let me send Denny or Carter. There are many soldiers down there to do the service."

"Aye, that's a good thought," Jane supported, "they can do it. It's their duty."

"And yours is to help," Mrs. Thornton hissed to her. "And yet, you are afraid to go. I will not have the officers' time taken up with our errands. They'll have enough to do to catch some of the mob. No, we have just as much courage here as any other lady." She turned to the men. "Never fear for me. I have a way of surviving a great deal. Tend to the ladies till I return." She turned to Fanny and Hannah, "make sure that the ladies always have a chaperone."

"We are safe to be around, Mrs. Thornton, I assure you," Darcy said.

"I know, but I don't care. I will do things right, or I will not do things at all."

Turning her heel, she left the room, left the house, and went to retrieve Doctor Donaldson.

And thus, Mrs. Thornton's character was brought to completion: a spiteful antagonist in one moment, and a stern heroine in the next.

After wiping the injured women's injuries, Plato began to administer the goldenrod ointment on the wounds and scars while Hannah and Colonel Fitzwilliam administered the bandages over the ointment, to help it heal. While he did so, Plato turned to Fanny Thornton.

"Miss Thornton, do you, perchance, have any spare nightgowns? All four of these ladies appear to be around your height. They might be able to fit your garments."

"Yes, I do," Fanny said, a little peevish, but that was not her intention. She was actually concerned, but her voice, being naturally nasally, gave off the 'annoyed' tone. "Why would they need them?"

"Being a man, I am only allowed to inspect their facial wounds. But I have to acknowledge that the Miss Bennets and my sister may have wounds in other places that are not my place to inspect. If that is the case, then they cannot be moved, at present. They might need to remain in this room for some time."

"Oh. If Doctor Donaldson says so, then I will get some nightgowns for them."

"Thank you, Miss. That is very kind of you."

Once Plato finished placing the balm on Kitty's forehead and arm, Hannah wrapped the bandages around those places.

"Darcy," Plato's voice implored, for Mr. Darcy was looming over Lizzy. However, Plato's voice might as well have been of a whisky spirit that was barely uttered along the winds, for all that Darcy had heard him.

There Elizabeth Bennet was, laying down before him, unconscious under her heroic efforts. He could easily have envisioned her, standing among the Irishmen, protecting the innocent. Her strong heart, her unfailing courage, and her will to persevere must carry her through this time. He feared the worst. For what if there was internal bleeding? What if she suffered a blow that would affect her mind? Darcy had seen wounds—specifically head wounds, do terrible things to the human spirit. Head wounds had been known to lead to character changes, memory loss, loss of physical functions, and the worst... death. What if it were so now?

How selfish he was being, he knew. For he thought of the loss of her when it regarded himself. But it was no fault of his own. For when one is in love, the loss of that love cannot help but be in the forefront of one's mind.

Here, at the beginning of their newly found romance, and him coming so close to achieving her affections, she might be snatched away from him. He could not bear it! In that moment, he was surer than ever...their lives were linked. If she would be lost to him, he would lose a part of himself. Feeling the tugging away at his heart, the weight that was holding his soul down, and he feared what this all would do to him. He had found his second self in Elizabeth Bennet and knew very well that he could walk the entire earth and perhaps not find another.

Externally he was still as stone, but internally, he was a storm that was reaching its apex, with no new dawn in sight.

"Darcy!" Colonel Fitzwilliam said, grabbing his arm. This forced him out of his revelry. But his internal anger was not fully abated, and when he turned to his cousin, his eyes still flashed. This expression did not alarm Colonel Fitzwilliam, because he understood Darcy all too well.

"Plato needs to tend to Elizabeth's headwound," Fitzwilliam said to Darcy, "he needs you to lean back. Don't worry, cousin. You can stay in the room."

Being driven out of his inner musings, Darcy's animal instincts died and were replaced by understanding and rational acceptance.

"Very well. Yes."

Mr. Darcy stood back and remained sentinel, as a guard, watching Plato attentively as he administered the ointment on Elizabeth's face, followed by Hannah bandaging it up. Darcy watched most acutely, because he felt, if he could remember everything, then he could eventually tend to Elizabeth himself.

After all, she was now in his bed. Perhaps, he could always have her so.

Soon, Margaret Hale began to show signs of waking up, but she did not fully do so. Her head wound was successful at making her feel too unsteady to move and she remained there. But through the slits of her eyes, she saw Elizabeth, Kitty and Rasby lying next to her, in a bed. She saw Plato tending to Lizzy, but the image was blurred, and her pain was so much throbbing that she could not fully make sense of anything she had just seen. She closed her eyes again, wondering if she had seen fact or fiction, for she was so often slipping into consciousness and then subconsciousness, that she couldn't attend to anything. Giving into slumber, she did not try and rally herself but knew that it was best to give into rest. Soon, she was another resting lady that was upon the bed.

But one thought she had before her eyes closed once more was knowing that she probably had been dreaming when seeing her friends beside her. Lizzy, Rasby, and Kitty surely were safe. Nothing had come to harm them.

When Hannah finished dressing all the wounds, she stood next to Fanny, who could only stand against the wall and observe everything. Being a sickly sort of creature herself, Fanny was very selfish when it came to her symptoms. She needed attention whenever she was feeling ill, but when others were infirm, she had no knowledge of how to tend to them.

However, what she did possess was a desire for intrigue, and now was as good a time as any.

"How did this all happen, I wonder," Fanny said, fanning herself.

"She'd have been safe enough," Jane, the servant, explained, who stood on her other side, "if she'd stayed in the drawing-room, or come up to us. We were in the front garret, and could see it all, out of harm's way."

"She had gone outside, I know, but from my view, I couldn't see what fully happened. But all the servants did?"

"Aye, Miss, we did."

Fanny's face altered from alarm at seeing the ladies, to desire to know all the gossip that she may have missed.

"What did you see, Jane?" She asked.

"Just before the front door...with the master," Jane said significantly.

"With John? What did she do?"

"Sarah had the best view of it. Mind you, she could have been mistaken. She said that she saw Miss Hale with her arms around the master's neck, hugging him before all the people."

Fanny Thornton gasped.

"I don't believe it," Fanny declared, but it was more so in a way that it gave confirmation to Jane's words. "I know that she cares for my brother; anyone can see that. And I dare say, she'd give her eyes if he'd marry her, which he never will. I can tell her. But I don't believe she'd be so bold and forward as to put her arms around his neck."

"Miss Thornton," Darcy responded, "While it can be considered inadmissible to contradict a lady, but if Miss Hale did such a thing, it was done out of a general sort of concern, and not out of any particular affections. Miss Hale has always struck me as the sort who is of a philanthropic way. Her instinct is to protect. I do not believe that her actions were romantically ambitious, but merely selfless and protective."

"Oh, Mr. Darcy, you do not know that," Fanny said. "I have seen the way that she looks at my brother."

"How does she look at him?"

"As if she is angry when he does something that she does not agree with. And she often observes him and analyzes his character. I know a lady who is seeking a good match when I see it."

"Miss Hale is not the mercenary sort," Plato supported. "It is not her way."

"You would be surprised, I believe. But between all of us, Jane, Hannah and I are the best at knowing what's in the heart of a woman."

The men did not bother to argue with Miss Thornton, because they were aware that she would believe whatever she would.

At last, Doctor Donaldson entered, followed by Mrs. Thornton. The men moved out of the way and stood in the hallway as the Doctor tended to the four wounded ladies.

"Miss Hale's headwound is more fortunate," Doctor Donaldson said within, "it looks worse than what it is. By the looks of it, there is no true damage. The wound is superficial. As long as we keep the bandage on for as long as we can, then it will heal. This ointment that has been placed on these women...is it goldenrod?"

"Yes, it is, sir," Hannah responded, "Officer Pitcher added it himself."

"Pitcher? Well, whoever that is, he did good work of it. Goldenrod helps with wounds. I will add my yarrow plant ointment to the injuries that are along the women's arms and legs. Both plants will help close the wounds faster. Now, Mrs. Thornton, you said that Rasby and the Miss Bennets were wholly attacked from the mob."

"Yes, Doctor."

"Well, I shall need to interview anyone who was there

to see it all. Are there any witnesses? If I learn the extent of where they were attacked, I will know more about what to treat. Miss Hale's head injury is self-evident and there is no cause to worry of there being injury anywhere else. But with the other three ladies... no, it could be much worse."

"The Irishmen would know," Mrs. Thornton said, "for they were with them the entire time."

"I should like to hear their statements."

"I will return with the Irishmen who fought with our women," Colonel Fitzwilliam stated to his cousin, departing as soon as he said it. "Tell that to Donaldson."

"Right," Darcy responded, looking at the wall, still mentally preoccupied. But he still had the presence of mind to warn Plato. "I'll tell Donaldson. He might not be so amenable to paying attention to you."

"I had the notion," Plato said casually, "I have very little allies in this place."

Darcy turned to Plato and was seeing him in a different light. He was so taken up with his own woes that he didn't realize that everyone in this world, in one way or the other, had their own tragedies that had to be often faced. Obstacles, as it were. But Plato looked so indifferent, so above everything in his mood and manner, that he gave the impression that nothing of agony ever affected him. Even his last sentence uttered was spoken in a way that indicated that he was a solid sort of character, so little affected by the pettiness around him.

"I look at you like an oak, don't I?" Mr. Darcy asked Plato.

Plato turned to Darcy, his eyes still twinkling.

"You look at me that way because I make certain that people do. We all have our superpowers, as it were. Especially since I have the notion that people look at you in a similar fashion."

Darcy thought on it, and his past and present life swept over his mind.

He befriended Bingley, with an express instinct to look after this young man who was novo riche and needed a guide to steer him in the right directions.

He spent his time assisting Colonel Fitzwilliam, whenever he needed help with his finances. His cousin was economical, but sometimes, his income did not allow him certain liberties that was needed for a young man.

His honorable father died, and Darcy immediately had an estate to look after, and tenants to reside over. From tenants to servants, so many were under his care.

He had a sister that he had to safeguard, because she had been duped by Mr. Wickham before, and he vowed that such a circumstance would never happen again.

He came to Milton to recover from Elizabeth's refusal of his proposal, and Mr. Thornton immediately needed a friend to be a constant support to him.

Even when Darcy needed leisure, he had to be the one that was needed. Plato's point was valid.

"Yes," Darcy sighed, "perhaps so. I never had time to even think of the weight of things."

"Men such as us never do. It is not our habit or right to indulge the idea of it."

"But that is the problem. We are meant to be depended upon, and that is the way it is. Yet, what happens when men like us break?"

"Then everyone breaks around us."

"Then we are not allowed to break at all. That is the solution."

"No, we are not. But that's the *problem*. Everyone has no choice but to break eventually."

"Precisely. We are human. Coming undone, every now and again, is inevitable. What do we do when that inevitability happens?"

"I figure that we only have two options," Plato offered.

"What would those be?"

"We come undone and face the consequences. Or we manage to fall in love with a woman who is stronger than us. Therefore, when we break, they can patch us up again or carry on where we broke off. My father often broke under the weight of the world's view of him. What person wouldn't? But somehow, our mother always managed to pick up where he fell off. Rasby is like her."

"Rasby is pretty. Your mother must have been lovely."

"Oh, she was. Enough for captains to take a fancy to her and allow me into the army."

"Oh," Darcy said, his eyes widening.

"Beauty is either a blessing to a woman or a curse to her. For my mother, it was a blessing, and she knew how to use it to save us. Why do you think I have gotten as far as I have?"

Plato chuckled.

"Father married the right woman."

"And all this time, I thought your circumstances were because of your lack of fear. I've noticed that about you. You don't fear much."

"No, I don't," Plato said, smiling, "I learned a long time ago that there was nothing to be afraid of. Especially people's opinions of me, any coldness they express because of their misplaced pride, or their harsh words and actions inflicted upon me because of their prejudices. I suppose it's because I never feared death. I just fear being in a cage. But even then, I would find something about that worth rising above. A long time ago, I refused to let mankind's foolishness get the better of me. But having a sturdy mother did help it. Father was strong, but the world broke him eventually. Somehow, mother knew how to patch up the wounds."

"But what about you?" Darcy asked. "I never saw my father crumble, but perhaps it was because mother might have saved him from doing so. If you believe that your mother helped your father, then is that what you wish? Do you wish to get married?"

"You would think so, but I couldn't fathom it. First, I am too career driven, and second, I have never been in love."

"Really?" Darcy asked, thoroughly aghast. "Never?"

"Not to my knowledge. I've been in lust with many women, and had dreams of them, but I'm not certain that it was ever love. Perhaps it's because I attribute love with marriage and children. I wouldn't know how to be a father just yet, and also—I have never met a woman who fancied me who I could see being stronger than myself. You see, that is the problem with having a superior mother. You can't settle for anything less. Since my mother was strong enough to endure the worst in life, I need a woman who can do such. She has to be stronger than me, to patch me up when I break. And break, I must do eventually and inevitably. Nothing less will suffice for me."

"I suppose that I understand," Darcy acknowledged. "We all are chasing something that is the best sides of the woman who raised us. Maybe that's what I've been looking for... all this time."

"And you found it, in the room behind us."

Darcy looked pointedly at Plato. Until that moment,

both men had not been looking at each other. But hearing Plato reference Elizabeth made them face one another at last. His instinct was to reprimand Plato for speaking too boldly, but Darcy did not feel that it made any sense to avoid the discussion. After all, despite decorum, he did want to talk about it.

"Yes." Darcy turned away from Plato again and looked ahead. "But it may all come to nothing."

"Why would you say so?"

"When it comes to love, it is not just about the man's heart, but the woman's as well. Whatever I feel will not determine anything, if the woman refuses."

"You have doubts?"

"I have reason to have them."

"Ah. Well, as I always say, 'only one thing is certain: death'. Everything else shall always be up in the air and fall where they may."

They were interrupted when Doctor Donaldson exited the room and both men turned to him.

Chapter 3

Soldierly Assistance

"We overheard you tell Mrs. Thornton that you wished to interview the Irishmen that were there when the mob broke into the factory," Darcy began, "we wish to tell you that my cousin, Colonel Fitzwilliam, has gone to retrieve them."

"Good, good, good," Doctor Donaldson responded, making sure that his sleeves were properly rolled down and that his jacket was straight. "The sooner the better. I am of the suspicion that they have many more wounds than meets the immediate eye, excepting Miss Hale."

"It's best if we wait downstairs, in the drawing room," Darcy said. "Colonel Fitzwilliam would bring the Irishmen in that way through the front door."

"Well, you know your cousin better than I."

Doctor Donaldson followed the men downstairs and was not waiting for more than a minute before Colonel Fitzwilliam entered with four of the Irishmen.

"Forgive me if I kept you waiting," Colonel Fitzwilliam

apologized, ushering the men in. "but it took a while gathering them."

"No matter," Doctor Donaldson said, taking out a notebook and adjusting his pen. "What are your names, sirs?"

"I'm Robert, Doctor," the first Irishman said, "Robert McFlannery."

"I'm Liam McMillan."

"I'm Colin Townsend."

"I'm John O' Donohue."

"Were any of you close to the ladies when they were struck down?"

"Aye," Colin confirmed, followed by the Irishmen affirming this.

"Do any of you recall if the ladies suffered any wounds on their bodies, on their persons, and not just their face?"

"Aye, they did." Liam added, "I saw the lead one get hit across her arm and then trampled over by the crowd—it would have hurt her legs."

Darcy ground his teeth when hearing this.

"Very good," Donaldson said, writing this all down. "But what do you mean by the lead one?"

"Well, she was the one who led the resistance. The one in the blue dress."

"Miss Elizabeth Bennet?" Darcy clarified.

"Aye, that be her," Robert confirmed.

"And I was close to her sister at the time—or at least, I think it was her sister," John added. "Name like a cat."

"Miss Kitty Bennet," Colonel Fitzwilliam confirmed.

"She got hit in her stomach as well as her face, I swear it."

"Her stomach!"

"Aye, she got kicked there."

Colonel Fitzwilliam's eyes turned hollow. His rage wasn't expressed, but it was evident.

"The darkie got the worst of it, from what I saw," Colin continued.

"What happened to my sister?" Plato asked firmly. This knowledge made the Irishman's eyes widen.

"She's your sister?" Liam asked.

"Yes, lads, she is. It would do well to tell me the extent of her injuries. Do not shy away from the truth. The more that you tell, the more that I can treat."

The Irishmen looked a little dumbfounded.

"Come man, find your tongues," Donaldson stated. "Speak up."

"It's just that you may not like to hear it," Liam said.

"The sooner the better," Plato stated.

"Well, they weren't as considerate of her, you see? I think she was pushed against the wall and injury must have happened to her back and right leg in the process. As well as her facial wounds."

"Where are the ladies?" John asked. "Wherever they are, they can't be moved, that's what I think, at least."

"They won't be," Donaldson assured them. "They will be tended to."

"Well, can we see them at all?" Robert asked. "We should talk to them."

"They are unconscious and are in bed at present."

"Unconscious?" Colin asked, seriously. "They haven't woken up yet?"

"No, they haven't," Mr. Darcy said to them.

"But they need to, if you don't mind me advisin' you lot," Liam counseled, "sometimes when you let someone remain that way for too long, resting can make them fall into a deeper unconscious—and they could die."

"He's right," Plato confirmed. "I've seen that happen."

"I know a little bit about treating wounds, I think," Donaldson snapped, feeling offended that his medical expertise was being doubted. "It is a difficult business to determine when to have someone wake versus when to let them rest. It must be considered with great care."

"Sir," Colonel Fitzwilliam smoothed over, "we are not questioning your professionalism, but speaking of what must be done out loud. Now that these gentlemen have told us everything, we know that the ladies must be woken up and changed into nightgowns and have serving women inspect their wounds, so that we can properly have them treated. Plato is very good at treating war wounds, and these women have been in combat."

"This is not a battlefield."

"It was to us!" John declared, passionately. His sudden exclamation made the reality become so very real, and the tragedy of the encounter now was laid bare for it to not go ignored. When seeing that no one would interrupt him, John continued. "Have you ever had a mob attack you just because you exist? You never done anythin' to them, but they look at you with such hate. Such anger, wrath, and resentment, because you represent a 'wrong' idea. A wrong idea, that is only wrong because they are wrong to look on you so? To come to this land, brought by one man's request, and then attacked by many other men and women's vicious ways? And all you had were three women who protected you and look what happened to them? No one cares. When no one cares about you—that is a battle. Don't tell me that it's not somethin', just because you didn't live it!"

46

Doctor Donaldson didn't respond, due to the world living in the age of subtlety and emotional responses not always being considered professional. However, he did remove his spectacles and began to clean them.

"I do not mean to belittle the situation," Donaldson uttered, "I just don't have the luxury of getting emotional. It does not lead to accurate reports."

"What cannot be denied is that these ladies have suffered a great deal," Mr. Darcy determined, his strong voice putting an end to all misunderstandings, "and they have endured a battle-like situation. Therefore, we will treat their wounds like the battle scars that they are."

Plato looked at the Irishmen.

"Were either of you hurt at all?" He asked.

Liam, Colin, Robert, and John all looked at each other.

"Just a few cuts, soars, and bruises for my part," Liam said, "but nothin' that a few days won't get the better of."

"Sufficient."

Robert chuckled.

"What is funny?"

"Nothin'. It's only that you are the first person to ask us how we are."

The weight of this revelation was heavily placed on everyone's shoulders.

"I'll take you back to your wives," Colonel Fitzwilliam said. "We can tell them that the worst is over."

Colonel Fitzwilliam led the four men out and back to the factory.

Donaldson turned to the servant, Jane.

"Miss Thornton was said to have extra nightgowns. Have the servants place them on the ladies, so that we will be able to tend to their wounds easier. I'll return in a few hours, with more ointments and to make a closer inspection. The Bennets and Rasby cannot be moved from the bed they are in. They might have to remain as such for another few days, at least. Margaret is another matter. If she recovers, she should be allowed to return home."

"Yea, sir," Jane confirmed. Next, Donaldson turned back to Darcy and Plato. "I understand that the Miss Bennets have two sisters. They should be notified. But I would recommend that the Hales not be informed on the matter just yet."

"Why not?" Darcy asked.

"The mother, Mrs. Hale, is suffering from illness. Receiving bad news about her daughter would not be beneficial to her health. Mark my words, sir, sometimes bad news and bad health do not go together very well. *Mark my words.* When Miss Hale is ready to stand up, she will be happy that I recommended such a thing."

Doctor Donaldson put his hat on.

"I shall return in a couple of hours. Please, make sure that the ladies are prepared for me."

With that, he left.

Chapter 4

Awake

After Doctor Donaldson left, Darcy and Plato climbed the steps, to give the news to Miss Thornton.

"To change the women, they would have to be woken up," Mr. Darcy noted.

"Believe me," Plato stated, "it is a good thing. They need to wake up for a brief while. Their roused spirits would confirm that they are not taking a turn for the worst. Also, an unconscious patient is not an informative one. When they wake up, they can tell us what they are feeling and what hurts where. *Mark my words*, it's better that they wake up."

When they went to Darcy's bedroom, they were alarmed when the door opened, and Fanny Thornton exited out of it.

"Well, of all the presumption," Fanny extoled, "she actually wants to leave. Can you believe it?"

"What is the matter?" Mr. Darcy asked.

Fanny lowered her voice and spoke conspiratorially.

"When Doctor Donaldson tended to Miss Hale, she woke up and now she is declaring that she must return home. He gave her permission, and now she is set to do it, despite that she is recovering from a headwound. Speak to her."

"Are the other ladies awake at all?" Plato asked.

"No, they still have not woken up."

"I'll go and speak to Miss Hale," Plato said, turning the knob.

"You?" Fanny asked.

"Yes. Me."

He opened the door and met the scene where Margaret Hale was leaning over the three other women, inspecting her fallen comrades. When seeing Plato standing there, she looked at him, sympathetic.

"Plato," she gasped, "poor Rasby."

While Plato walked up to her and leaned over her shoulder, Darcy turned to Fanny and told her everything that Doctor Donaldson had instructed.

"Oh, there's no need to remind me," Fanny said, "we've got three invalids now, in Marlborough."

Mrs. Thornton exited the room, ordering Hannah and Jane to fetch more nightgowns and blankets.

Mr. Darcy passed them and entered to see Plato talking with Miss Margaret Hale and inspecting her face.

"You cannot go home without me checking the cut on your head," Plato stressed.

"Doctor Donaldson already did so," Margaret said, "He took my pulse and all. There needs to be no fuss over me."

"Look upward," Plato said, inspecting her eyes, "now downward. Now sideways. From side to side."

When she did as he instructed, he released her chin.

"All that time that your eyes were moving, did you see double of anything, even for a second?"

"I saw everything with perfect clarity."

Plato raised up four fingers.

"How many fingers am I holding up?"

"Four."

"Recite your parents' names and any close relatives."

Margaret did so.

"Margaret," Mr. Darcy asked, "tell me, why must you feel like you must go home? We can always send a message to your parents."

"You must not do that, Mr. Darcy," Margaret Hale pressed, appealing to him, "My mother is very ill, presently, and cannot be imposed upon with bad news. Especially when regarding us children of hers. If she were to hear anything terrible that may have befallen me, it can overwhelm her. I fear hearing this might overcome her sensibilities, and it might make her illness worse."

Donaldson was right. It was what Margaret wanted.

Margaret turned back to Elizabeth, Rasby, and Kitty.

"Does Jane and Lydia know what has happened to them?"

"Denny will inform Lydia," Darcy said, "and I will send a message to Mr. Bingley."

Margaret looked heavily at them.

"What if..."

Mr. Darcy read her expression.

"I believe that they will wake up soon."

Margaret looked at herself in the mirror and saw how the plaster was covering her cut.

"I don't want mama to see this," she said, and began to

adjust her hair so that it covered the bandage. "She mustn't see..."

When it was fully covered, she turned to the sleeping ladies again.

"I don't want to leave them, but I must." Margaret turned to Plato, demandingly as she touched his arm to press the matter, "When they do wake up, tell them that I will return to see them eventually. Will you?"

"When they wake, they will know."

"Thank you."

"But you must not go," Mrs. Thornton cried, impatiently, "you are not fit to go. I planned to send for the surgeon, Mr. Lowe, and he will be here within the hour."

"Thank you, but I must go, and Doctor Donaldson said that I was fit before he left."

"I really believe she must do as she says," Elizabeth said, from the bedside.

Her sudden waking up startled everyone.

"Elizabeth!" Mr. Darcy cried.

"Yes," Elizabeth sighed, "I am awake."

Chapter 5

Words That Were a Long Time in Waiting

When hearing my voice, they all turned to me with alarm in their faces. I had woken up to the strange sight of being in a foreign bed, with ladies to my left and right. I didn't have the ability to move around and look at who they were, because I was met with a sharp and searing pain that raced along every aspect of my body. I gritted my teeth at it.

But I heard voices, and they were all familiar to me. Loud and clear, I heard Plato, Mr. Darcy and Margaret Hale discussing her going home, for she didn't want to alarm her mother. Then I heard Mrs. Thornton speak.

While I didn't want to lift my head, I could roll it on my pillow. I was able to turn my head just enough to see Darcy, Plato and Margaret talking and Mrs. Thornton objecting to letting Margaret go. Before I knew it, my instincts led to me adding my voice to Margaret's view.

"I really must believe that she must do as she says."

They all turned to me.

"Yes," I whispered, my voice hoarse, "I am awake."

"Elizabeth!" Darcy cried, rushing to me, and grabbing my hand. "You wake! You wake."

"Yes," I said, reading his expression. Despite all the pain I felt, my will seemed to override it. All seemed not important now that I could see Mr. Darcy with perfect clarity. I felt his fingers cover mine with such deep assurance. "You found me."

"I worried," he declared, desperate, "We were worried."

"Did I scare you? I didn't mean to."

"It doesn't matter now. As long as you are here, and you are awake, that's all that I care for."

"Margaret?" I asked, looking around Darcy and casting my eyes on her.

"Yes," she replied, her face sedate, but her eyes were heavy, "I am here, dearest."

I saw the plaster on the side of her face.

"What happened to you?" I asked her.

"Nothing of consequence," she said, "and we'll say none of that, because it was nothing when compared with what you, Kitty and Rasby have undergone."

"Kitty and Rasby? Where are they?"

"They lay behind you."

I tried to move my neck, but it hurt so significantly that I winced and shut my eyes.

"That action hurt you?" Plato observed.

"Yes, it did. I can't move my neck just now. So, tell me, how do they look? Tell me they are just resting."

Darcy and Plato gave each other a look.

Margaret leaned forward and took my hand.

"Whatever happens," she assured me, "they were very brave. Lizzy, I promise, I will return when I can. I will."

"Yes," I said, "and when you do, you have much to tell me about Mrs. Hale. You've been keeping things from me."

"I didn't want to upset you. It all seems so foolish now, doesn't it?"

"Yes, it does."

"I will return soon."

Margaret turned to Mrs. Thornton.

"Lizzy knows me better than anyone," Margaret said. "She knows that I do not belittle my condition and that my mother will be worried when she hears about the strike and doesn't know where I am."

"At least let me fetch a cab for you," Mrs. Thornton said.

"Oh, thank you. It will do me more good than anything. The fresh air might help me."

"Very well."

Margaret gave me one last look, kissed my forehead, and followed Mrs. Thornton out of the house.

***

"Well," Plato said, looking between Darcy and I, "I shall go down into the courtyard to see what instruction that Colonel Forster will give me."

"Thank you," Darcy said, knowing the real reason that he was leaving. Plato was perceptive; he knew that Darcy and I needed time alone. Internally, I thanked him for his discerning nature, as well as comprehension of discretion. I wonder at my mind, sometimes. I woke up from being attacked, and the first things that I thought of was discretion and the valor that rested behind it. Ah, the intricacies of the Victorian mindset!

Once the door was closed behind us, Darcy was the only man in the room.

"Happy accident," I voiced, still hoarse, "with all the comings and goings on, they didn't notice that you are the only male in the room, without supervision. What would Lady Catherine de Bourgh think of me?"

"Elizabeth, don't do that."

"Don't do what, pray?"

"Don't jest to hide the pain that you are in."

My expression sunk, not from the agony I was experiencing, but the insecurity that comes from being so easily found out. How much did he know my character that he was able to dissemble my instincts and intentions? At what point, between our first acquaintance in Hertfordshire, to our last meeting in Milton, that he began to understand the recesses of my mind?

"How did you know?" I asked him.

"You are brave in front of a mob," he explained, "so of course, you would be brave in front of me. Elizabeth, tell me truly? Are you in much pain?"

I sighed.

"I hate sounding so weak."

"You do not have to be ashamed of it. I know you are strong. Everyone does."

Closing my eyes, I rested my cheek against the pillow. Now it was time to give way in full.

"My whole body, Darcy. I feel as if I had been bashed against a rocky precipice. Everything hurts."

"The surgeon is coming soon, and Plato has knowledge in these matters. Elizabeth, please promise me that you will allow yourself to remain here. The Thorntons have arranged for you, Kitty, and Rasby to stay in this room, until you are fully recovered."

"Don't worry," I said, chuckling through the agony, "I am not that proud to ignore my body when it shouts at me, with every move I take. A part of me is happy that I cannot move my head at all. If I do, I will turn around and see Kitty and Rasby lying there, won't I? After all, they are the ones who are laying behind me."

"Yes, they are."

I breathed in heavily, clutching my chest from guilt.

"Darcy, you do not have to be kind to me now. I am prepared for the truth. How are they?"

"They haven't woken up yet. Margaret was the first one, for she suffered the least awful of it. Then you woke up."

"Did it make you happy?"

"Of course, it did," he urged me to believe.

"If it were just me, then I would find joy in that. But this is all my fault. I led them into this. I should be the last one to wake up, by rights."

"They are breathing steadily. They show no signs of it being fatal."

"But I don't know that. None of us know that."

I tore my eyes away from his and looked over his shoulder.

"Guilt," I sighed. "Do you know how it feels, Mr. Darcy? To be so possessed by guilt over something. I cannot tell you if it is a selfish emotion, or a selfless one. Do you do it because you care only about how the matters affect your own heart, or because you care so very much about those who were casualties who got in the way of your actions? But then there is regret. Ah, that word! Regret, now that is a more selfless word. Perhaps I do feel both. If only it had been me that I put in harm's way, then I could be proud of every wound on my body. But they suffer for it, and there, the hammer stroke may fall hardest on them."

"You must not blame yourself for standing up against violent behavior. It was brave."

"I do not regret the action—I regret not thinking of them while I did it. They should not suffer for my audacity."

"I do not think they will wake up regretting it. Do not give way to despair, Lizzy. It will not help you recover. And it will not help them now."

At last, I looked back at him and marveled at the man before me. How resolute and resilient he was. The very philosophy of life is that perseverance is a virtue, but how few of us maintain that. Often, at first when we do not succeed, we cower and run away. After all, the pain of failure and disappointment can be too trying to endure, again and again. Many of us lack the constitution for it. However, Mr. Darcy was constantly surprising me with his ability to try again—even when success was not a definite thing.

I smiled sadly.

"You are determined to not let me hate myself, nor give into foolish displays of despair. Shame on you, sir. How dare you not let me be like a woman?"

He chuckled. "Even when you are in pain, you jest."

"When you can barely move, jesting can be your best source of recovery."

"To add to your remedies, the Irishmen were proud of you."

"The Irish!"

Finally, falling away from my self-contempt, I was able

to stumble back into the reason behind the confrontation. After all, we had been fighting for something all along.

"How are the men who fought with us?" I furthered. "If they are hurt, did the doctor see to them?"

"They did not suffer any serious lacerations or injuries. With the exception of a few bruises, that can be remedied with time, they assured us that they are well."

"When I recover, I would like to speak to them."

"I am sure that they will find it to be a great honor."

"At least they are well. There is that to alleviate any woes. Now, I'm going to ask for a favor. It will be most ungentlemanly of you, but it will be the best thing in the world."

"I am here."

"I need you to help me roll over. I need to look at Kitty and Rasby. I need to face them."

"Are you sure?"

"I faced a mob. I had better face who I went into the fray with."

"Very well."

I tried to roll over myself, but it was proving so difficult, so Darcy assisted me and rolled me over, on my other side. When I did, I saw Kitty and Rasby's limp forms on the bed next to me. When seeing the bandages on their arms, Rasby's black eye, and the bruise on Kitty's cheek, the tragedy became too raw—too real! Ah, the reality of it! Closing my eyes, I took in a sharp breath of grief.

"Look at them," I whispered harshly, "oh, look at them."

I began to take in sharp breaths. For, despite all the air in the room, the sensation of feeling as if I was drowning had overcome me.

"You can look away now," Darcy insisted, but I was determined.

"No," I said, "what has been done is my doing, and I ought to feel it. I ought to..." when looking at them again, I was adamant. I would not lose them. No one should suffer more than I, out of us three. "I will not lose them. They will not be lost for the world."

Ignoring every sharp pain that was in my arm, I reached out to them and brushed my hands across their cheeks.

"Kitty and Rasby, please," I begged, "wake up."

I pushed my body against Kitty's back and pressed Rasby's shoulder.

"Dears, do not die. Do not do so. It would not be fair! It—"

Kitty began to stir and Rasby's eyes began to flutter.

Making miracles was not my habit. But whether it was from prayers being answered by the Great Redeemer, or because of the fire that rests within any of us that wills us to keep on living—faith or science—whoever was the hero, I was indebted to. And I would do everything to promote its progress.

The pain in my arm was immense and I cared for none of it. Pressing their cheeks each, I whispered their names.

"Kitty and Rasby, please wake up. For yourselves, please, I must see you wake up. Wake up! And live."

Little by little, Kitty and Raspberry's eyes fluttered more and then they opened.

"They wake," I cried, overcome with joy, "Darcy, do you see? They wake!"

"Yes, they do."

Kitty turned her head slightly.

"Elizabeth?"

"Yes. I am here, dearest."

"Are we alive?"

"Yes. We are still here."

I looked over at Raspberry, who began to try and find her voice.

"She needs water," I said to Mr. Darcy. "Please, Darcy, get them something to drink. Water helps everything."

Mr. Darcy went to the nightstand, where there was a pitcher of clean water. He poured a cup and first gave it to Rasby, who he had to raise the cup to her lips and help her drink it. Next, he got a glass for Kitty and helped her drink it as well. What a dignified display he presented as he did so. The proud and revered Mr. Darcy, of Pemberley, Derbyshire, assisting in the nursing of three savage daughters—who dared to run barefoot, cursing sharp stones.[1] Ladies who dared to not cut their hair, but let it blow in the wind, and not lower their voice when the world said that they had nothing to say. And here he was, caring for Kitty, a woman who he once chastised, for she bordered on impropriety.

He had changed. Very much, he had changed. What a beauty he was. And always would be, in my eyes, from this day forth. Wherever he would go, I would go with him. Be it into a warm dawn with a swift sunrise before us, or a stormy evening where the wind threatened any felicity. I would go with him. If he would still have me. But I flattered myself...that he still did.

---

1. This passage is inspired by the song 'Savage Daughter'.

He turned to me. "Lizzy, you must drink as well."

"I would be happy to if you will help me. See? Not too proud to ask for help."

His eyes twinkled.

He got water for me as well and I let him press the cup to my lips and pour the water down my throat.

"Does that help?" he asked.

"Yes, nurse. I thank you."

"Teasing me? Another part of your remedy?"

"Perhaps."

The door opened and Mrs. Thornton entered, followed by the servants Jane and Hannah, who had night garments to put us three ladies in.

"Mr. Darcy?" Mrs. Thornton declared, "what do you do, sir? Were you in here with the ladies, quite alone?"

"Mrs. Thornton," Mr. Darcy said, "you must forgive me, but I felt that the ladies needed someone to remain with them, and I was the last to do it. Erring against decorum seemed like the proper thing to do, though improper it was."

"Well, the ladies must be changed out of their clothing, and baths prepared for them once Mr. Lowe comes and sees to them. Can you please wait in the hallway, and my son will come and speak to you about where we can place you? I'd say wait in the parlor, but I am of the suspicion that you prefer to be a sentinel and remain near the ladies."

"Yes, madam. Thank you for being discerning."

Mr. Darcy stood up to go, but my current condition had made me bold. Sometimes, when being so close to death, you realize how trivial waiting is. How much a current sentiment must not be put off for another moment—after all, another moment is not always a guarantee. Mr. Darcy must know...he must.

Ignoring how it would make me appear, or how the servants would talk and gossip about my character was of no importance. Truly, too much of life was dictated by us caring about the good opinion of those who did not care a fig about ourselves. I grabbed Mr. Darcy's hand, determined.

"Sir," I urged, my voice still raspy and low, "I must tell you—you must know."

He leaned down so that I didn't have to speak louder.

"What is it, Lizzy?"

"I love you."

Expressions can be the opposite of what one expects.

While my eyes were a little heavy, I could see his face become suddenly so very serious, so somber, and utterly unreadable. Jolly and pleasant men wear their emotions on their cheek and chin, but a man of such complexity cannot always be dissembling his character in such a fashion. Rather, he has that of a face that can easily convey the opposite of what he means.

"So serious," I whispered, "what does Mr. Darcy think? Are his thoughts dark or light? Do they still agree or is he afraid?"

The words arrived, at last, and they came tumbling out of him with a sincere steadiness that always became the Master of Pemberley.

"Afraid?" He finally voiced, "you translate my silence for fear? Dearest Elizabeth, what sort of weak creature do you suppose me to be? To run away from the very object that I have been seeking all this time! I was only silent because I feared that it wasn't real. Lizzy, could you really mean it?"

"When have I ever struck you as the sort to lie on such matters?" I asked, fighting through my pain, and trying to be amusing. "No, Elizabeth Bennet will never lie to you, when it comes to love."

He held my hand tighter.

"Oh, Elizabeth, dearest, you really love me?"

"I do. With all my heart do I profess it!"

With a heavy and happy heart, I felt the sensation of the space closing between us, as Mr. Darcy became quickly overcome by his passions. His face was stern, and the sensuality was underneath, as it was evident that he was about to press his lips against mine. Then he halted, remembering himself and where we were. How easy it was to forget propriety when one's heart was finally alive and awake. Our present circumstances should have restrained our revelry on the matter, but even the past tragedy felt so trivial, so inconsequential, when in the face of the urgency of the matter.

"Mr. Darcy," Mrs. Thornton urged, "you must leave, sir. I appreciate your company, for my son's sake, but don't think I won't throw you out of the room, under the circumstances."

"You would be perfectly correct to do so," Mr. Darcy said, still staring at me. "I must remove myself, Lizzy, but I'm not leaving the house."

"Looking after me, are you?" I whispered. "Are you to be my guard?"

"And I always will be, from this day forth."

He kissed my hand, and I watched him as he departed.

The pain of being changed into night garments was

excruciating, for we had to be moved. Yet we didn't complain through it all, but only groaned, for there was nothing more liberating than being released from the confining clothing of our gowns and stays. Now our bodies could breathe.

When we laid down on the bed, Jane and Hannah laid the blankets over us, to keep us warm. As they tucked the top around our necks, I closed my eyes, cheerfully.

However, I was stricken with a sudden curious scene when I opened my eyes again and Miss Fanny Thornton was standing in the doorway. Her eyes were tear-stained when she looked on me. It wasn't a sad sort of cry, but an angry one. She looked on me with a fiery fury, a staunch resentment, and I was able to discern the matter.

I always considered her to be like Miss Bingley, except Fanny had a less robust constitution and lacked Miss Bingley's health. But other than that, the similarities were too keen to be felt. Too blatant to be ignored. Even in my agony, I still was determined to be a keen observer. To willfully be such a studier of character right up to the very end...that was I. And, from what I discerned, the two ladies were similar in emotion and attachment.

She knew.

Fanny Thornton knew that Mr. Darcy loved me...and therefore, would never choose her.

While I was certain that he probably never did anything to ensnare or entice her, in the same fashion that he never did anything to enrapture Miss Bingley, but it was what it was. His handsome features, his noble mien, his awe-inspiring countenance, and his fortune would naturally lead to a lady seeking a fantasy from a man who was worth fancying. Their affection was only natural. Their preferences were explainable and displayed their excellent taste. However, that very desire that probably kept them warm at night is now what slashed a sliver of ice into their hearts and wounded it. The drudgery of disappointed affections!

When I widened my expression and she saw that I was observing her, embarrassment overcame her, she left the doorway and rushed down the hall.

For one brief moment, I did feel heartily sorry for her. However, that empathy did not live long, I confess, when I considered all the biting words that she might possibly say about me, from anger. Miss Bingley—if we ever were to see each other again—did not incite my compassion, because she had made it impossible for me to feel anything for her. I suspected that it would be the same way with Miss Thornton.

Before I closed my eyes, Kitty was looking at me, her eyes half-open, but she was solidly conscious.

"Well," she whispered, "you told him?"

"Yes, I did."

"About time, is all that I can say."

"Yes, Kitty, I suppose it is about time."

Chapter 6

Sound Advice

When leaving his bedroom so that the ladies could get changed into better apparel, Mr. Darcy's woes transformed to ecstasy.

Elizabeth loved him!

She finally loved him. All his efforts, his choice to not give up on obtaining a deep love that affected him to his very core, had finally been rewarded. Delving under the surface of every intention that he ever had on that score, of running to Milton to recover from his broken heart, only to rediscover it under the dust and smoke of the Milton skyway, and the snow white of the cotton that hung about his friend's mill. No, all those days and nights of agony would not be forgotten—not out of any stubborn resentment for her waiting so long. Of course not. But rather, it was remembered as a foil to set off this happy moment. It was a reflection on the rewards that came from struggling and wrestling with one's heart, head, and habit. Of accepting that a young lady must not accept any man simply because he wants to marry her but rather accepting a man when she finally loves him.

Elizabeth's love for him was earned, and it was worth the earning.

When going downstairs, he had a light air about him, and it was impossible to be ignored by those who knew how to discern properly.

When coming back into the house, Colonel Fitzwilliam encountered him and saw the dramatic shift.

"You look happy," he observed.

"Do I?"

"Yes," Colonel Fitzwilliam said, his scrutiny becoming keener as he watched Darcy most acutely.

Darcy's spirits were so much raised, that he didn't see how his behavior was somewhat agitated and his mood uneasy.

"But more than that," Colonel Fitzwilliam continued, "you look as if...well, cousin, there is no other way to say it. It's as if you are glowing."

"They are awake," Darcy uttered, "all three of them are very much awake."

Colonel Fitzwilliam grabbed Darcy's shoulder, insistent.

"Kitty is still awake? Is she well? Come man, give me some more information than simple answers. She, Rasby and Lizzy?"

"All three of them were awake when I left them. And they looked like women who would recover. They will not be snatched from us, Richard. By god, I swear, they will recover, and they will not be taken from us!"

Colonel Fitzwilliam's whole countenance swelled and then released from the loss of anxiety and the escape of apprehension. He released Darcy's shoulder, turned away, holding his waist as he continued to breathe out and in, steadying himself.

"For one second in time," Colonel Fitzwilliam confessed, "for one horrifying second, I believed in the worst. I gave way to gloom, despair and loss."

"So did I, for a time."

"And to know now that she will not be ripped away from me—Darcy, would that I could marry her!"

Darcy breathed in heavily.

"I know," he assured his cousin, "I wish that you could. In this moment, my heart goes out to you, Richard, for this way, you, Bingley, and I could all be happy at once."

"Yes," Colonel Fitzwilliam responded, but then he thought on Darcy's last sentence. What did he mean by all three of them being happy? Turning to Darcy, he took in his cousin's glowing countenance and began to make deductions. "What did you mean by us all being happy? Bingley has Jane's heart, but..." He squinted at Darcy. "Elizabeth woke up and she said something, didn't she?"

"Yes," Darcy said, breathing heavily. For a brief second, his passions overcame his prudence, and his stoicism gave way to emotional display. "She has discovered her love for me, Richard. She has announced her heart and unfolded it in such a way that it...she loves me in return. She loves me in return." Darcy half-smiled. "Who was to think that would ever happen? Even in the wake of the horror that has just happened, I cannot help but be so much light as a feather. I know that I don't display it, but you know me quite well."

"Yes, I do. You are happier than you perhaps have ever been in your entire life."

"I am."

"You have Elizabeth now, and I am happy for you."

"Thank you, cousin."

Love was now the province of one cousin.

Logic thus was the province of the other.

Colonel Fitzwilliam marked Darcy, and felt joy for him, yes, but he also was more able to analyze the situation from a wider view. A more objective one. How he was to despise the service that he was about to render. One never wants to ruin a loved one's happy moment. However, he thought it was best to protect his cousin, offering him the best counsel that he could provide. After all, Darcy had been hurt by Elizabeth's first rejection—it would be a terrifying experience for him to be set down again.

"Darcy," Colonel Fitzwilliam said, sitting down, "This is a great day, but I must advise you to tread carefully, and consider the situation before fully accepting Elizabeth's confirmation."

Darcy turned to him, his eye cold as he was beginning to fall away from the romantic revelry that his spirit had fallen into.

"What do you speak of, Richard?"

"Elizabeth is a strong and determined woman," Colonel Fitzwilliam elaborated, "she is of fire and earth. Air and water runs through her as well. She knows her own mind, and I admire her for it, but she is still human. I am going to tell you something that I know might disturb your happy state and enthusiasm. But it is not meant to do that. I want you to be contented and revel in this happy moment. I only do this to put you on your guard."

Darcy did not reply but patiently prepared himself. Colonel Fitzwilliam was a steady and pleasant companion, therefore, he waited for an explanation.

"Any chance that you will not despise me for giving you this warning?" Colonel Fitzwilliam asked.

"You know that I will not. I prefer the truth, of all things, especially if that truth will benefit me."

Colonel Fitzwilliam sighed, relieved, and he began distributing his advice.

"It is something that I have often noticed, when leading soldiers into battle, or in speaking to naval officers. When a soldier or sailor undergoes traumatic experiences, and they have brushes with death, either three things happen: the horror drives them mad, and they must alleviate their grief, be it from drink, reading, or seeking the company of fancy ladies. Some just give into despair and give up on life altogether. Or they go in the other direction: their situation leads to them not running from life but clinging to it all the more. They go out, and make decisions, quick decisions, because they know that their lives can be cut short at any moment. This leads to them falling in love quickly, marrying quickly, or wanting to have children—something for them to be remembered by. I know that it seems that I am rambling, but there is a point to this advice."

"I know there is," Darcy replied heavily. Being a man of keen insight, he was seeing where Richard's story was leading but knew that it was best to still listen. "Pray, continue."

"What I'm saying is, these soldiers had no choice but to live for the moment, yes. And mostly, they are right to.

71

Action is the province of the doomed. But also, I have deduced more. These men don't rush into life, because they are reckless, but something in their mind shifts. Their brush with death makes their emotions speed up or creates emotion where it did not used to be. Death gives them a perspective that they might not have had before. Now, usually, this works out for them a great deal. Other times, they realize that their sentiments were the work of a moment, and then they enter an arrangement where the love will not last."

Darcy went to the fireplace and looked down at the flames.

"Darcy?"

"I know what you are saying. You are implying that, perhaps Elizabeth's declaration is a result of her brush with this experience. And that it has altered her mind so much, that it's led to either speeding up her feelings for me or creating a deeper affection that might not have existed had not death come near her."

"I do not wish to tell you this."

"I'm happy you did."

"But I don't want you to feel as if this is not a special time for you. She probably does feel for you in that regard. I only say it, just in case the situation proves to be the reverse."

"You are trying to protect me."

"Yes. With all my instincts. Elizabeth is worth loving, and worth marrying. I don't want you to speak to her with a sullied feeling. That happiness that you have found, cherish it. When you see her again, be as blithe and blissful as you present. I am merely advising not to marry her immediately. Talk to her as she recovers, enhance your acquaintance, and then, give her a couple of weeks. Observe her, see if her affections hold, and when you are certain, then make her a full offer. Let her come to you when she is not overcome by the sensibility that occurs from almost dying. That's the only way that she will not have fallen prey to the mistake, and you will not take advantage of her during her troubling time. This way, neither of you will be hurt by the other. You're a strong man, but I don't want to see you get hurt again."

Darcy still looked into the fire, letting the advice wash over him.

"And I've ruined your euphoria," Colonel Fitzwilliam stated.

"No, you didn't. You are right. Her words could be the product of emotional irregularity, or it could be genuine. Only time would tell. Should I tell her, or not tell her?"

"I never thought of that. It either might help you both, or it will lead to her delving too far into the history behind her emotions, and she will result in analyzing every aspect of her mind—and never feel anything organic again."

"Elizabeth is brilliant. She is not the sort to fall prey to doubting herself."

"Yes, she is." Colonel Fitzwilliam thought of this, and his tone lightened. "Yes, she really is. Talk to her about it. It might make you both stronger for it. Besides, Elizabeth has confidence in her thoughts. She is not easily brushed about by mere suggestions."

They were interrupted by Mr. Thornton.

When seeing the two men, Thornton appealed to them immediately.

"How are the ladies? Have they woken up?"

"Lizzy, Kitty and Rasby woke up," Darcy explained, "and your mother and servants are helping them get into nightgowns so that the surgeon can come and treat them."

"But...what of Miss Hale?"

"Doctor Donaldson saw to her," Colonel Fitzwilliam explained, "and when she declared that she wished to walk home, he allowed her the right to do so, and your mother ordered a cab for her."

Thornton looked surprised and gravely alarmed.

"What do you mean that she's left? She suffered a terrible blow. She should not be moving suddenly at all, but resting." He stepped back, covering his mouth, and beginning to talk to himself, as all are wont to do, every now and again. "What was my mother about, letting her go in her condition? Excuse me, gentlemen, but I must get to the bottom of this all."

With stern energy, he walked up the steps and went to speak to Mrs. Thornton.

"He's in love with Margaret Hale, isn't he?" Colonel Fitzwilliam whispered.

"Yes," Mr. Darcy replied, speaking equally as low, "and he is trying to resolve that fact inside of himself."

"The poor man."

"I know. We should not be in the house when he speaks to his mother."

"Yes, let's go out into the courtyard."

"Very good. I am in need of a walk anyway. Anything to

take my mind off current matters and reflect on what I must do next."

"I have to see if I can send Denny to tell Lydia and she can send a letter to Miss Bennet."

"You won't have to. In half an hour, I will send a letter to Mr. Bingley. When he reads it, I'll let him know and he will tell Miss Bennet himself."

"Right."

Both men left, but in two different directions.

Colonel Fitzwilliam went to see if Colonel Forster would release Denny, and Mr. Darcy walked around the courtyard. Then, he entered the mill, moving around the officers and police who were making inquiries.

When doing so, Mr. Darcy moved among the carding room, the machinery, seeing flakes of white cotton that rested on the floor. All the machinery, silent and still, presented a peace to his fevered heart. There was something serene about the image of the business that lay quiet, as if it was the calm that ended after a dark storm.

Despite his apprehension of industry, he could not help but cast his eye on everything he saw and found a beauty to it. Here, amidst the tradesmen and the laborers, Darcy's ideal answer for happiness in the South had been rendered unto him.

Irony.

Beautiful irony.

Chapter 7

Daughterly Concern

As Margaret Hale was sitting in the cab, she felt an occasional bump in the road, from the unevenness of it.

As she did so, she could not help but let her mind roam over the past events that had occurred.

Of when she, Lizzy, Kitty and Rasby had arrived.

Of when they separated, and each were on a mission: she to the Thorntons, and the others to assist the Irish.

Of the mob that rushed through the courtyard and stormed the gate and the factory.

Of ordering Mr. Thornton to go out and meet the angry crowd.

And of grabbing Mr. Thornton, to shield him.

"Of course, I did it," Margaret said to herself, "for I would have done the same for any other man or woman if they were in the same predicament."

But only then did she wonder how it must look in his eyes, and the eyes of others. After all, she and Thornton had an uneasy friendship that swung and swayed between kindness to a sliver of dislike. Their history was complicated, and underneath all those complications was a loose alliance that always was threatened by their next encounter.

But of all people for her to endanger her life for, it was a man who she had resolved to not like for the longest time. But that is the strange thing...could she now go on not ever liking him again? After all, she risked her life to preserve his. When that occurs, strange thoughts and instincts overtake the mind.

First, you cannot help but contemplate your own mortality, and what does your one character signify in the grand scheme of existence? Margaret Hale was one for inner reflection, as well as for outward observation. She was never unwilling to consider her own person, her own thoughts, and her own actions.

Second, she was willing to risk her life for someone else, and this knowledge of compassion swelled her pride, and cemented every feeling of her own views and veracity. At the last moment, where there was so much anxiety and animosity facing her, her courage did not escape her. Such knowledge must fortify her sense of self!

But in the next moment, it also cemented her longing and love for the South. If she had only had the chance to remain in Hampshire, she would not have to encounter such experiences. After discovering a love of home, a desire for provincial peace, and able to be a part of the common laborers' lives, she had been thrown into a world of such conflict, contrariness, and constant cloud and smoke. From the left to the right, and to the center, there was nothing but room for argument, strife, provocation, inequality, distance between master and laborer, and now belligerence.

She longed for Hampshire, and its simple ways. Therefore, she also felt that pang of regret that occurs when losing something that was so very dear to you.

And then there was the last revelation: she had possibly saved John Thornton's life: manufacturer, and magistrate of Milton Common. The last sort of man that she had any inclinations to be dashed against the shores of acquaintance with, the sort of character that she had no desires to be so constantly thrown in the way of, but she had been. For quite some time, she and Mr. Thornton had friends and acquaintances that made it impossible for them to avoid each other. From her home, to social life, he was always there. Ready for them both to provoke each other and, occasionally, detest the other one.

And now she had saved his life. Without speaking it, or ever uttering it, she was aware that she and Mr. Thornton had reached a great change. When you save a life, there is a shift; the paradigm must give way to something new. Whether she liked it or not, she had protected him and shielded him. The principal reason was because she had been the one to order the man into the very danger that she wished to save him from. Thornton was set on waiting inside for the soldiers and police to arrive, but she, Margaret Hale, had urged him to go down and speak to the mob. She was the reason behind him being put into danger. Thus, he became her responsibility.

And that was the word for it: responsibility.

'He was my responsibility,' she thought in her mind.

What a frightening thing!

Any person, who possesses any proper sense, becomes aware of the significance of that. For, there is a true horror in being responsible for someone, especially when it is someone that you never wished to be responsible for.

Usually, a person feels as if they are indebted to you when you save their lives. But often the reverse happens: you saved their life, and therefore, you owe them, because now, you are their guardian. You become their shield, their hero, the one who they can rely on, count on, and be responsible for them.

Margaret Hale, a young woman, who possessed a desire to be the best she could be, was very much capable of such a philosophy. Not because of choice, oh no, but rather out of instinct. There was a voice that called out within her, making her aware of these two conflicting ideas that now attached themselves to her selfless act.

She didn't want either of those roles.

But another thought arose in her mind that it didn't matter whether she wanted it or not. The fact remained, there was something now that made her responsible for Mr. Thornton. Or rather, he would feel, in one way or another, that he had to repay her. And, in some strange way, she worried that he might know that.

And then came the last of her worries: the fact that her actions might be misconstrued. She had wrapped her arms around a man, who she was not married to, and protected him in such a public manner.

People talk.

People misinterpret.

People see what they wish to see.

Or what they can make into a story, no matter how little they know of the situation.

How easy it is for rumors to spread of you.

Everyone saw her holding Thornton, protecting him

even unto death. How long, or how short, would the time be before everyone accused her of being in love with him? Of displaying herself in a way that indicated that she desired him?

With the way that Mrs. Thornton, Fanny, and the servants looked at her, she did not need to hear any words. Their looks were enough. They believed her actions to be romantically bent—or mercenary at worst. That ugly dream of insolent words spoken about herself could never be forgotten.

"We've arrived, Miss," the cabby said to her.

His voice made her start. She had been so much engulfed by her inner reflections, that she didn't even notice that the cab had arrived at Crampton Crescent, and she was at her front steps.

"Thank you," Margaret said, paying him for his service. She opened the door, exited the cab and it departed as she looked up at the steps.

Now it had come down to it. She had to lie, doing her best to make certain that her mother never discovered what happened. Any hint of what had occurred, and it might affect Mrs. Hale's nerves.

Breathing inward, she went inside, and soon came upon her mother and father, who were speaking casually by the fireplace. There they were, innocent and unsuspecting.

"Oh, Margaret," Mrs. Hale said, removing a handkerchief from her dress pocket, "you are returned."

"Yes, I am, mama," Margaret said, a little subdued.

"You look pale and almost white," she observed. Mr. Hale looked more pointedly and agreed with this.

"I am well enough."

"You look tired," Mr. Hale noted, "is the weather outside uncongenial?"

"Yes," Margaret responded, "very much so, and the streets are rather rough with the strike."

Margaret passed a mirror and saw that she did look quite done for the day.

"But I do come with news," Margaret said, standing behind her father's armchair, "Mrs. Thornton will send the waterbed, mama."

"Oh, that is very kind of her," Mr. Hale said, "isn't it, Maria?"

"Yes," Mrs. Hale said, coughing a very little into her handkerchief, "very kind of her. I should send a letter of thanks. Oh, Margaret, I almost forgot." She reached into her basket and produced a letter. "Bessy Higgins sent you a letter, asking you to go to her. If you wish to go, my dear, I would advise not doing so, currently. You look so very tired —too tired to go anywhere."

"You see me clearly, and better than I see myself perhaps. Yes, I am tired. I cannot go. Would you mind if I go to my room?"

"Yes, of course. I'll have Dixon send you some tea."

"Thank you."

Margaret went upstairs, removed her dress, and lay down in her bed.

While staring up at the ceiling, she had more time to reflect, to recall every incident of her actions at Marlborough Mills.

Who could she turn to? Who could she speak to who would be too far away to be removed from it all, but also be able to speak to Margaret in confidence?

Needing to profess her thoughts, she came to the revelation. Going to her desk, she took out a pen and paper and began to write to Edith. She begged her to keep this letter in confidence or even burn it when she finished reading it. Since she was aware that Edith had a wonderful ability at keeping a secret, she knew that she was safe to continue.

She conveyed all the events that had occurred when she had faced the mob at Marlborough Mills, and then she commented on her reflections:

> *I, who hate scenes, I, who have despised people for showing emotion—who have thought them wanting in self-control—I went down and must needs throw myself into the melee, like a romantic fool! Did I do any good? The mob would have gone away without me, I daresay.*
>
> *But this is me over-leaping the rational conclusion —because I have no way of knowing. No, perhaps the crowd would not have disembarked. I hope I did do some good. But what possessed me to defend that man as if he were a helpless child? Ah! It is no wonder those people think I might feel a tenderness for him, after disgracing myself in that way. I in love? And with him too? Dear god, that is the last thing that I wished for anyone to believe.*
>
> *Oh, how low I am fallen that they should say that of me!*

I could not have been so brave for anyone else, just because he was so utterly indifferent to me—if indeed, I do not positively dislike him. It made me the more anxious that there should be fair play on each side, and I could see what fair play was. It was not fair that he should stand there—sheltered, awaiting the soldiers, who might catch those poor maddened creatures as in a trap—without an effort on his part, to bring them to reason. And it was worse than unfair for them to set on him as they threatened.

Edith—I regret nothing now.

For I would do it again! Let who will say what they like of me. If I saved one blow, one cruel, angry action that might otherwise have been committed, I did a woman's work. Let them insult my maiden pride as they will—I walk pure before God!

My serenity would be returned to me, if my worries of Lizzy, Kitty and Rasby were not alive. But they are. I feel that they will recover, they must! But if their wounds were to impair their minds, vision, hearing, or lead to them walking with a limp for the rest of their lives—I would never forgive Milton. How I wish to spare them from this place now.'

She was about to continue writing, with her pride intact and her prejudice to Milton still a little set in its place, when there was a knock on her door and her mother entered.

"Mama," Margaret said, putting the letter away.

"I knew it," she said, shaking her head, "I had a feeling that, rather than laying down, you would be occupied with some sort of activity. I came to check on you, in case you were doing that, and I was right."

"Mama, I didn't intend to—"

"No excuses. I may be an invalid, but I am still the mother here. Put down the paper and pen, and lay down in the bed, Margaret."

Willingly giving in, Margaret did as she was bid, lay down in the bed and Mrs. Hale began to tuck her in.

"I haven't done this to you or your brother in years," Mrs. Hale said wistfully.

"I missed that, when I went to London."

"And all that time I spent, thinking I had done right, to send you away to have a better life than you could have had in Helstone."

"And all that time, I wanted to come home," Margaret sighed, "and be close to you and father." Mrs. Hale's expression changed from bittersweet memories to regret and self-contempt. Able to see that she had incited these emotions in her mother, Margaret immediately sought out to reassure her. "You must not think I was miserable. While I did not favor the pretense and constant diversions of the cosmopolitan life, I regret nothing of my time in London. I loved Aunt Shaw and Edith, and there were many happy memories in that life. I just wish that I had been allowed to be with you both more. But never feel any anger toward yourself, on my account. You and father gave me a good life. I appreciate it."

"I just wanted to do right by you."

"You did," Margaret assured her. "You did."

She began to cough, and Margaret immediately tried to rise out of her bed.

"I shall get you some water and Doctor Donaldson's tonic."

"On no account," She insisted, "it is just a cough. No more."

Margaret was a little anxious as she lay back down.

"Mama, you promised me that I would be allowed to look after you more. I know that Dixon loves you, but—"

"Margaret," she assured her, "it's not that. I am willing to have you care for me. But right now... let me care for you. Let me be the mother. Especially since I have not had the chance to be such since we came here."

Looking at her mother, Margaret was humbled. Seeing what this meant for her, Margaret gave way. Every now and again, a parent needs to be allowed to be such, even when their child is full grown.

Margaret rested her head against the pillow and stared up at Mrs. Hale.

"Thank you. I worried, since I spent so many years in London, that we would never find our way back to being close again."

Mrs. Hale kissed her on the cheek.

"Every now and again, I surprise people."

"You will let me look after you tomorrow, won't you?"

"Yes, you may, dearest. I am not fighting anymore. Nor am I hiding."

"Thank you."

Mrs. Hale left Margaret alone, to rest.

Margaret may have been exhausted, but sleep doesn't always come to those who have just undergone such a conflict. Rather, the reverse occurs. The mind dwells on things and goes off in the oddest of directions.

Having exhausted all thought on the morning's events

and having poured all her feelings in the letter to Edith, Margaret's mind fell back into the past.

Rather, her thoughts landed on another moment in time, weeks ago, where she first discovered a person who she needed to protect...

Dr. Donaldson had come to their house, to check up on Mrs. Hale. When doing so, Margaret was excluded from the room, while Dixon was allowed to remain. Naturally, this vexed her, because though Margaret was not a ready lover, where she did love, she loved passionately. Therefore, being not considered to remain with her mother while Donaldson inspected her, was trying to Margaret's sensibilities.

She paced back and forth, awaiting the end of the doctor's visit. When she heard him finish, Margaret went to intercept him before he left.

"My father is not at home, Dr. Donaldson," she announced. "He has to attend a pupil at this hour. May I trouble you to come into his room downstairs?"

This had been Margaret's attempt to learn of what her mother had been suffering under for the last few weeks. For, up until Donaldson's visits, she and Mr. Hale had only attributed Mrs. Hale's lack of health to the change in climate and the arduous journey to adjust to a new life. The fact that it could be anything else other than that was a daunting prospect.

Donaldson accepted her invitation, and Margaret was uplifted in that she would learn what was ailing her mother, despite Dixon's efforts to leave her in ignorance.

Once they were in her father's study, Margaret appealed to Donaldson immediately.

"Sir, I must ask you to tell me. What is the matter with mama? You will oblige me by telling the simple truth."

"Well, I confess that I did not expect to inform you of certain matters. Your mother is apprehensive about you being made aware."

"Doctor, please, I implore you. I am the only child she has here. My father is not sufficiently alarmed, I fear. Therefore, if there is anything truly serious about my mother's ailment, he must be told the news, gently. I can do this. Also, I can nurse my mother. If you worry about the news overwhelming me, it would be quite the contrary. Being ignorant on the matter does me more harm than good. Besides, I can withstand any news, and you will get no acts of fainting or sensibility from me."

Donaldson analyzed her and knew that she was sincere. But he had his orders.

"My dear young lady, your mother seems to have a most attentive and efficient servant, who is more like a friend—"

"I am her daughter, sir," Margaret had replied, heatedly.

"But when I tell you she expressly desired that you might not be told—"

"I am not good or patient enough to submit to the prohibition. Besides, I am sure you are too wise—too experienced to have promised to keep a secret."

Donaldson marveled at her, especially since she had seen so far into the truth.

"Very well, there you are right. Besides, I fear the secret will be known soon enough."

That last sentence uttered aroused Margaret's apprehension, but she did not show it. She only waited for him to continue.

"I am prepared," she uttered.

"You mother is very ill. You must prepare yourself for any tragedy that might—most likely, occur."

While Margaret's expression did not alter very much, Donaldson was able to detect the horror that filled her eyes when he said it.

"Truly?" she asked.

"Yes."

"And all this time all our hopes were that this was a passing ailment. That mother would recover. But I suppose that another part of myself dreaded this." She turned back to him. "I thank you most truly, for your confidence."

Worried that emotion might betray her, Margaret walked to the window and looked out of it. Donaldson watched her, aware that she was trying to maintain her composure.

At last, she spoke.

"Will there be much suffering?"

Out of the side of her eye, she saw Donaldson shake his head.

"That we cannot tell. It depends on constitution, on a thousand things. But the late discoveries of medical science have given us large power of alleviation."

With every word that he uttered, it all became more real.

"I mean, it is difficult to give advice," he continued, "but I should say, bear on, and be able to give what comfort you can to your father. Before then—my visits, which of course, I shall repeat from time to time, although I fear I can do nothing but alleviate. He will be alarmed, at first, but over time, he will learn to bear it."

Now, Margaret could not restrain weeping. She trembled as she held onto the windowsill.

"Please, do not look on me now," she stated. "Please, do not look on me."

"Miss Hale, it is natural."

"Yes, it is, I daresay. I just...worry for my father and am sorry for mama. Thank you for telling me, doctor."

"I am sorry that I could not tell you good news."

"You were honest with me; I could not ask for more than that."

She showed the doctor out.

When Doctor Donaldson had left, Margaret was pensive. There had been so many things to consider and fortify herself against. Her heartache was not just her own to endure, but her father! Mrs. Hale had walked by him for so long now. Even when they disagreed on things, he loved her, undoubtedly. And that was love; even when two persons did not get along, the mere presence of them in each other's life was like a balm of comfort. When each woke up to see the other's face, they felt an immense ease, as if all was right in the world, even when they knew, very well, that there wasn't. Whatever disagreements that her father and mother had, it didn't stop the fact that they had married for love, and underneath it all, they still were in love.

But as for being on the outside of her mother's ailment, where only her mother and Dixon were allowed to share in the burden, that was when Margaret had become adamant. She would not be on the outside of the situation. Her mother was ill, and she would care for her, right to the bitter end.

Going upstairs, Margaret had made her way to her mother's room. When she entered, Dixon was not there, but her mother was lying back in her easy chair, with a white shawl wrapped around her shoulders, and with a cap on her head. Margaret noted how her face had a little faint color to it, and she looked peaceful.

"Margaret?"

"Oh, yes. I'm just...forgive me, I'm just so surprised that you look so calm."

"Oh. Well, I suppose that would account for it. For how strange you look! What is the matter?"

Now that the moment came down to it, Margaret's desire to conceal emotion had quite abandoned her. Mrs. Hale was able to read her daughter's expression very quickly. Her shoulders slackened, disgruntled with the secret being exposed. How disappointing it was for her confidence to be betrayed!

"You have been talking with Doctor Donaldson, haven't you?"

"Yes, I have."

"You've been asking questions?"

"Yes, I have. And I've gotten answers as well."

Mrs. Hale didn't need to hear any more.

"He broke his word to me..."

"It was not his fault," Margaret replied, defending Donaldson, "I made him. It was I."

Out of urgent supplication, Margaret walked up to her mother, knelt down and sat on the floor, by her side.

"Blame me, and not him," Margaret urged.

"Margaret," Mrs. Hale said, sighing wistfully, "it was

very wrong of you. You knew that I did not wish for you to know. Oh, my poor girl, I did not want you to suffer from this." Reaching out, she grabbed Margaret's hand, sympathetic.

"I am happy that I did, or I would not have known the gravity of the matter. I like knowing. Why shouldn't I be the one to know? I'm your daughter. I ought to be the one who nurses you. You really ought to let me be that."

"My dear, caring for invalids is a grave and tedious business. I don't want you to ruin your youth over me."

"What sort of daughter would you have me be?" Margaret protested. "One of flimsy principles and weakness of feeling? I am your child, and I do think I have the right to do everything for you."

"And I am your mother! You don't understand, Margaret, what it's like, to see your child have to look after you, when you want to be the one who is strong and the reverse." Mrs. Hale sighed once more, closed her eyes, and leaned back against the chair. Here she was now, preparing to reveal the great weight of affectionate and genuine parenthood. "When you are the mother, your instinct is to shield your child from the evils and ugliness of the world. You want them to have the best of life, even when you did not have it."

Now the confrontation of intentions and well-meaning was displayed at Margaret's feet.

"Is that another reason for why I was sent to live with Aunt Shaw? I thought it was because Edith needed a companion, but was there more to it?"

"I wanted the best for you," was her mother's reply, and that said it all.

"And now we are here, in this very strange situation,

where things might have been different, if you had only asked me how I felt—and what I wanted. Then again, you probably never would have considered it. I loved being with Edith, and I love Aunt Shaw. But I wish that I had never gone to Aunt Shaw's and spent all those precious years away from you. And now that we are united, you will be snatched from me and Father! You and this deadly disease. It will hurt him when he must learn of it. But for now, do not send me away, but let me have more time with you. I will be your nurse."

How different her daughter proved to be than what Mrs. Hale had presumed.

"Oh, dear me," she sighed, "this is wholly unexpected. Do you know, Margaret, Dixon and I thought you would quite shrink from me if you knew—"

"Dixon!" Margaret declared, a little bitter, "Dixon does not know the depths of my feelings. Did she think, I suppose, that I was one of those poor sickly women who like to lie on rose leaves, and be fanned all day? Don't let Dixon's fancies come any more between you and me, mama. Please don't allow it."

"Do not be angry with Dixon. She loves me."

Margaret calmed down, understanding this.

"Yes, I know she does. Sorry for speaking rashly."

"It is also easier for me, you must understand. Dixon has been looking after me even before I married your father. When someone has been looking after you for so long, that is your relationship. She is not only my servant, as well as dear friend—but she is my protector. I can look at her, for nursing me, because she's always been my nurse, before I turn to you. Because it is I, the mother, who's instinct it is to nurse and care for her child. Sometimes, it is hard for the roles to be overturned in such a way. I don't want to burden you, because I am the one who is supposed to be the foundation on which you depend on."

"I understand," Margaret said, "I will not be angry with Dixon. But I would like to learn her ways of how to help. Will you let me?"

Unwilling to argue, Mrs. Hale agreed, because she knew that it would make Margaret happy.

"Well, Miss," Dixon had said as she was cooking in the kitchen, "I hope the truth satisfied you."

Thinking it wise to inform Dixon of this change in the running of the household, and how she also would assist her mother, Margaret told Dixon everything about what she had learned.

"It has, Dixon," Margaret said, preparing some tea, "and you need not fear telling me the truth from now on."

"You shouldn't have been so curious, Miss, and then you wouldn't have needed to fret before your time. It would have come soon enough. And now, I suppose, you'll tell master, and a pretty household I shall have for you!"

Margaret stopped her activity and froze for a moment. Since speaking with mother, she had been deep in contemplation and had found the answer.

"Actually, Dixon, I have come to a decision."

"Oh, have you?"

"Yes. I will not tell papa."

This declaration came as an utter surprise and led to Dixon stop rolling the dough that she was going to put in the oven. Looking at Margaret, she waited for an explanation—though there was no explanation needed. This was precisely what Dixon had desired, but she did not expect that of Margaret.

"He could not bear it as I can," Margaret explained.

"Miss," Dixon said, "begging your pardon, but can you really bear it?"

Margaret collapsed into the chair, and she began to weep.

"Yes," Dixon said, rolling her eyes, "I can see that you can bear it very well."

"Forgive me," Margaret said, trying to suppress her emotion. She rubbed her eyes.

"Oh, you might as well have your cry out. I suspect that you will go into the fits every now and again, so why not now?"

"Because I said that I could bear it. So, I had best do so."

"No one is stone, Miss. Over time, you will see that you don't always have to be either."

"You sound like Elizabeth now."

"That's no insult to me, so thank you. Besides, you would do well to listen to her. There's nothing wrong with having some life in you. I curse the fool who gave you the impression that being like a statue in life is the ultimate form of sophistication."

"No one told me to be this way; it is just who I am."

"Very well, Miss," Dixon replied heavily, "just as you please."

"I despise the display of emotion. Always have."

"Really? Because you were on full display a moment ago, giving way to utter and complete sensibility."

"That should not happen again."

"It would be a poor thing if that *is true*."

Margaret didn't bother to continue that debate, for she saw that it was hopeless. Dixon, like Elizabeth, would go on thinking as she did.

Seeing that Margaret needed a kind word, or a better explanation, Dixon put the dough in the oven, to make bread, then she turned to her.

"I have to keep telling myself that you've been away from your parents for so long, that there are things that you do not know and histories that went untold, eh?"

"I would like to know the truth of things," Margaret implored, "please, help me understand."

Dixon's voice relaxed and she abandoned her traditional authoritative tone.

"Though I don't pretend I can love her as you do, yet I loved her better than any other man, woman, or child—no one but Master Frederick ever came near her in my mind. Ever since Lady Beresford's maid first took me in to see her for the first time, and I beheld her, Miss Maria Beresford... well, I was so nervous that I accidentally stabbed my finger with my needle. When seeing me hurt, your mother tore up her pocket-handkerchief and wrapped it around the wound. Then, when she returned from the ball, where she had been the prettiest young lady there, she came in to see to me and wet the bandages again with lotion. I've never loved anyone like her. Back on that evening, I thought she was going to have this grand life, where she would want for nothing. For, you see, I thought she deserved no less than that. If you would have told me that I would live to see her brought so low, I would not have believed it. But she has, and it hurts to see it. She was so beautiful."

When Dixon finished her narration, Margaret's heart

was filled with a deep empathy, and her affection now could rest in its proper place.

"Dixon," Margaret sighed, "I wish I had known all this before. How much an education and enlightenment helps understanding. And to think, how often I've been cross with you, not knowing what a terrible secret that you had to bear."

"Oh," Dixon laughed, "bless you, child! I like to see you showing a bit of spirit. Like I said, I don't much care for walking statues."

"Yes, I am learning that."

"Your spirit is that good old Beresford blood. One of your ancestors, Sir John, shot his steward down, for just telling him that he racked the tenants. Which was true. He actually did rack the tenants till he could get no more money off them."

"Well, that sounds horrible."

"The truth often is."

"Well, Dixon, I won't shoot you, and I'll try not to be cross again."

"Well, thanks for my share of the first part, but I'm not so certain about that last part, because I'm not against you lifting up your voice, every now and again. And when you fire up, you're the very image of Master Frederick. I could find in my heart to put you in a passion any day, just to see his stormy look coming like a great cloud over your face."

Margaret pressed Dixon's hand and left her alone, where both understood each other better...

Now the memory had come to an end, Margaret was back to looking around her bedroom, where Mrs. Hale had just tucked her in. Fortunately, her mother didn't notice the cut on the side of Margaret's face, for Margaret had successfully covered her hair over it.

She had seen her mother when knowing that she'd die very soon.

She imagined what it was like when her father would crumble when it happened.

She recalled Thornton's face before she protected him and fell unconscious.

She recalled seeing Elizabeth, Kitty and Rasby, laying unconsciously next to her.

All the people in her life who were falling in some way, and Margaret couldn't help but wonder: how many people in her life did she have to see fall, before it would begin to make her crumble as well?

For, no matter her desire to be like marble, even marble crumbles eventually.

Chapter 8

Musings at Marlborough Mills

"Mother, really!" Mr. Thornton had said when he faced his mother. When Darcy and Colonel Fitzwilliam had told Thornton that Margaret Hale had gone home, they were wise to give them their privacy. When going to his mother, to inquire about how she let Miss Hale go, Thornton should have been prepared for his mother to have a strong answer.

They were in the dining room, having a brief argument over the matter.

"Yes, really, John," Mrs. Thornton replied, "she went home in a cab."

"Gone home?"

"Yes. She was a great deal better. Indeed, I don't believe it was so very much of a hurt. Only some people faint at the least thing."

"She suffered a terrible blow. It wasn't so very small, and you know it."

"Very well. Perhaps it wasn't. But still, Donaldson said that she was fit to go home. I brought him here myself."

Thornton relented, grateful to her.

"Thank you, Mother."

Mrs. Thornton sat there, studying her son thoroughly. Appearing distracted, Thornton began to pace back and forth.

"What have you done with the Irish?"

"I sent them to the Dragon for a good meal for them, poor wretches. In my travels, I met Father Grady, which was a stroke of good fortune. I asked him to speak to them, to help calm them down."

"Very good. Son, will you stop pacing? You make it so obvious."

He turned to her.

"Obvious? What do I make obvious?"

"You know what I mean."

They both looked into each other's eyes, and it was as if their minds were linked, and they were able to enter each other's thoughts. So much in tune, they were.

"Yes," Thornton replied, "I suppose that I do see what you mean."

"Well," Mrs. Thornton gave way, "I suppose that we have no choice but to talk of her. I do not prefer it, but what must be talked about, must be talked about, I suppose."

"Yes, mother, it must. Before that, I must know. How are Miss Bennet, Miss Kitty, and Miss Pitcher?"

"They have woken up, and Mr. Lowe is coming to tend to them. Though, I don't know if I can get Lowe to see to Miss Pitcher."

"He will because I'll pay him to, so he better get to it," Thornton snapped, not in the mood to suffer fools to pass. "He's a surgeon, for pity's sake. But if not, perhaps I should let Plato stay and tend to his sister. He's an unofficial army medic, and he probably has more experience at handling battle wounds than even Lowe does. Either way, Raspberry will receive as much care as the rest of them. I am happy that the Miss Bennets are awake. They saved the Irish, you know. They led the resistance against my workers. The men they fought alongside are calling them heroes."

"I suppose they could be considered such."

"Mother, not suppose. They *are* heroes, and you know it. Can't you soften your heart to women who have protected me?"

She looked at him with a sternness.

"And am I so little?" she roared.

Ah, the agonies and aches of a mother who had to watch her son be saved by other women other than herself! Thornton knew this, and what was worse, was that he had been saved by women of the South—and one woman who his mother detested so very much. It must have been such a blow to her pride.

"Mother," Thornton said softly, knowing that she needed to be reminded that she was still the chief affection in his life. "So, that is the source behind your bitter words." Walking up to her, he took her hand. "Whatever these women have done, no matter how they have outshined the sun itself, and how much I owe them, what makes you think that I will ever forget all the heroism that I witnessed when you saved my life and our living?"

Hearing this, Mrs. Thornton couldn't help but give a little and hear her son speak of these brave women with less contempt.

"Very well," she relented, "they are brave. And they deserve your respect. I'll make sure that Lowe also looks after Rasby."

"Good. And Miss Hale..."

"Yes, Miss Hale."

"I don't know where I should have been but for her," Thornton confessed warmly.

"Are you become so helpless as to have to be defended by a girl?"

"Mama, there you go again!"

"Yes, there I go again. I'm sorry, son, I speak a little too meanly again. I know that you are strong."

"Yes, but I do not fear having help or admiring those who help me. Not many girls would have taken the blows on herself which were meant for me. Miss Bennets and Miss Pitcher are the epitome of courage, and Miss Hale belongs right there with them."

"A girl in love will do a great deal."

This last sentence uttered made Thornton's eyebrows raise.

Love?

Thornton went to the window and looked out of it, seeing the soldiers still in the courtyard, making preparations to set up a guard around the place.

"I shall go to Crampton after I've arranged the police," he told her, over his shoulder.

This announcement was the heavy weight that pressed down on Mrs. Thornton. She had expected it, but sometimes, knowing something might occur is very different from when it actually does.

"Why would you go to Crampton?"

"To ask after Miss Hale. She saved my life, therefore I ought to see her."

"There's no need for that. I'm sending Williams to take the waterbed there today. He shall inquire how she is, so there's no need for you to make the journey."

"I must go myself. You know that. To do anything else would be wrong and indelicate. I want to thank her for the way that she defended me."

"Fine. Do as you wish."

Mrs. Thornton began to leave the room, but her son called out to her.

"Why must you act this way?" he declared. "Do not walk away from me just now. I have a right to know why you are so upset at these women who saved me. Or is it really just Miss Hale?"

Mrs. Thornton placed her hands on her hips, and she steadied herself.

"You don't know what it's like," Mrs. Thornton said.

"What don't I know?"

"To have a son, to raise him in a way where you see him become a marvel of a man. And that son loves you, and you love him unconditionally. And you are so proud of him. And he repays it by you being the principal woman in his life. The first of his affections. And then another woman comes along, and she threatens to replace you."

"Miss Hale is no threat."

"She is. She has proven it. She has protected you today, in the way that I have been protecting you for so much of your life. I cannot unsee it."

"Mama, you have nothing to worry about." Thornton's tone was soft. After all, he was beholden to his mother, and he wanted her to always know that. "Miss Hale does not love me. Though, I suppose, it won't change the fact that I do feel...yes, I have to go see her. You know what I have got to say to Miss Hale, don't you?"

"Yes," Mrs. Thornton replied, heavily, "I do. You can hardly do otherwise."

"Do otherwise? What do you mean?"

"I mean that, after allowing her feelings to overcome her, you are bound in honor."

"Bound in honor?" He held the idea in disdain. "Honor has nothing to do with it. And again, she does not love me."

"There's no need to be angry, John. She rushed to save you."

"Aye, she did, but I dare not hope. I know that such a woman would never care for me."

"Don't be scared or foolish about it. What more proof do you need? It must have taken her time to overcome her snobby aristocratic pride and way of viewing things, but I like her the better for seeing the correct way, at last. It took her long enough. Good lord, praising her is hard to say. Son, I have only one favor to ask of you."

"What?"

"Don't go today. Go tomorrow. John, I'm asking you to not go today."

"Whyever not? What ought to be done cannot be done too quickly."

"Because I will now stand second in your eyes. Give me just one more night of being the first in your affections. Son," she said, tears filling her eyes, "give your mother that!"

"Mother," he whispered, sitting beside her, wrapping his arms around her shaking form, holding her as she rested her head against his shoulder, and he kissed her hair. "I love you. You know that."

"And I love you, my dear boy."

"You may yet be the first in my affections for many

more days. She might not have me. It would break my heart, but I am prepared."

"Don't fear, John. Don't be afraid."

They remained sitting there, in such a way.

Darcy handed a letter to Williams, to have the letter sent to the hotel to inform Bingley of what had occurred. As he did so, he walked along the courtyard, to Captain Carter.

"Have you seen Plato?" Darcy asked him. "Mr. Lowe has arrived, and I wanted Plato to know that Lowe is also willing to look after his sister."

"Really?" Carter noted. "Surprising. Lowe is a better man than I thought."

"Thornton ordered him."

Captain Carter rolled his eyes.

"Of course. Never mind. Plato is on the outside of the courtyard. He's one of the lads who's staying to overlook the area, in case the mob comes back."

"They won't. They attacked women. Soon, their guilt is going to start eating away at them."

"A byproduct of no longer suffering under mob mentality, eh?"

"Precisely. When you wake up from it, you fall back into your individuality in a hard fashion. And then you begin to think for yourself again. And that's when the regrets rise up, and you despise yourself. Unless you are heartless, then you don't feel any guilt at all."

"You've seen angry mobs?"

"London has its unfortunates, and I've happened to observe such behavior before. I'll go to Plato now."

"Yes."

Mr. Darcy went to the end of the courtyard and Plato was pacing back and forth, guarding his part of the gate. Fortunately, there was no one else near him, so Darcy walked up to him, knowing that they could speak in confidence.

When seeing Darcy, Plato was ready to hear any good or bad news.

"Your sister is doing better," Darcy assured him.

"She is?"

"Yes. I was told that you volunteered to be one of the guards for the mill."

"Is she being tended to? I saw the surgeon go in."

"Yes. Mr. Lowe was ordered to tend to them all."

"I want to check on them, but I suspect Mrs. Thornton will give me the evil eye."

"She is one of those sorts of women who are frightening to cross, I grant you that."

Plato looked at him.

"How are the Miss Bennets?"

"They are also awake. I know they will recover. They have to."

"It is best to tell yourself that. But still...supposing that this situation leads to some sort of mental or physical disability, you must prepare yourself."

"That's the frightening aspect of it. One of my tenants at Pemberley—he underwent an accident. It was a head injury. He recovered, but he was never the same again."

"A surgeon I knew had a theory. He felt that certain aspects of the human brain control certain aspects of our character. From intelligence to self-control, morality, or verbality, there are different functions. Thus, a person can recover and lose something of themselves. When the women woke up, did they look like they could see and hear properly?"

"Yes. And from what I heard of them... they sounded like themselves. Their words, speech patterns and behavior were very much as they always were. If there is any permanent damage, it will be physical and not mental."

"If they don't fully recover, physical disability is better than the alternative." Plato was not the sort who feared grave subject matter, or the offense he could cause when confronting the issue. Also, he was a man who was somewhat accustomed to the confrontational ways of the North. When looking at Mr. Darcy, he didn't see the Master of Pemberley, the famous aristocrat, the nephew of Lady Catherine de Bourgh, and thus a man that all marveled. No, he refused to live his life seeing anyone else other than that of a peer. Thus he would always address them as such. Therefore, in his natural inclination to talk with Mr. Darcy, he spoke as he would with anyone. "But, say that is the case, where Elizabeth will spend the rest of her life with a limp, or learning how to write with her left hand, or losing the use of one of her limbs, I... you must do your best to never let that affect your feelings for her."

Darcy turned to him, embittered.

"Plato, you offend me, and you have not the right to do so."

"You feel offended? Why so?"

"Why so? What makes you think that I am the sort of weak character to be so easily affected by such a thing? You do me a great disservice when I have been nothing but..."

"Accepting of me?" Plato responded, not phased at all.

"Is this where you expect me to be grateful? You don't see, do you? I'm trying to help you."

"How so?"

"You took what I said personally. But I have no choice, because it is not personal, but derived from my own history. Mr. Darcy, I've seen many soldiers come back from war, permanently injured. They lose a leg, an arm, and they spend their lives using a cane or crutches. Some wives do look at them differently. They don't mean to, but they can't help themselves. Just like I've seen some men married to women who lost their hearing, use of their left arm, or lost a leg themselves. And that did affect their marriage. They are human, Mr. Darcy. So am I. And so are you. I address this, because unless we are fortunate, our women might have lasting damage. And you might need to talk about it when the time comes."

Mr. Darcy looked ahead.

"Nothing could stop me from loving where I love. I'm hopeless in that way. I promise you; I am not such a weak person."

Pause.

"But if I were," Darcy acknowledged in the next minute, "I will talk to Colonel Fitzwilliam about it. Or Bingley."

"Good. But I would advise another corner to appeal to."

"Who?"

"Elizabeth Bennet."

"You think I should talk to her about my own weakness, because I cannot bear to see her so much altered?"

"Yes. Come now, you're not a fool. Life is full of idiots who spend their time talking to everyone else about their problems, and not the one person who the problem pertains to the most. If Lizzy does lose the use of her arm, or begins to go blind, don't talk to someone else about your fears and insecurities. Talk to her about it. She'll help you through it."

"I wish you were not so logical just now."

"Why?"

"Because I like being the one to distribute the advice."

"I'm not the one who is in love with a woman who might never walk again. I have the benefit of being the observer now."

"Too right. Well, she is my life. I suppose there is no other way. I'll tell her anything that I'm feeling. I left her in the dark on many things in the past. It didn't do me any good."

"It never does. It's a common habit."

"Yes. Please, when Mr. Bingley comes, let him know to come in when he arrives."

"Very good, sir."

"Plato. Thank you."

"A soldier's duty."

Mr. Darcy went back inside.

Chapter 9

Sisters

Mr. Bingley had accompanied Jane Bennet, but they were not alone. It was one of the days that Jane had to take Molly Gibson and Cynthia Kirkpatrick on an outing with her. The Kirkpatrick brothers were with their father, who was visiting another family. Thus, Jane was given the two little girls, and Mr. Bingley, kindhearted that he was, was willing to serve as the perfect chaperone to assist them.

A couple weeks before, he accompanied Jane to the Kirkpatrick house and made Mrs. Kirkpatrick's acquaintance. Mrs. Kirkpatrick was initially apprehensive about his presence because she viewed him as the means through which Jane would be taken from their service. The children loved her, and it would be difficult to find another governess who equaled her, so the announcement of Jane's engagement was not met very well in their household. But between Jane's assurances that she would not leave their service until she found a proper replacement, and the fact that it was very difficult not to like Mr. Bingley for very long, she grew respectful toward him.

Therefore, when Mr. Bingley accompanied Jane on the outing with the children, Mrs. Kirkpatrick was not against it. But rather she enjoyed the idea of a gentleman being there as a chaperone to her governess and her two daughters, especially since she had to attend a luncheon party at Mrs. Hamper's home, along with many other ladies.

Mr. Bingley, who had been overjoyed at the idea of being with Jane, but also at learning how to accustom himself on an outing with children who were dear to her, proposed the idea of flying kites in one of the parks.

"I never flew a kite before," Cynthia Kirkpatrick said as they rode in the carriage.

"Never?" Mr. Bingley repeated, "well, that is very good, because I happen to have done the right thing, for once."

"For once?" Jane echoed, laughing. "Are you about to be cruel to yourself, sir? If so, then I really must protest."

"I like that you do that. What about you, Miss Gibson?"

"I used to fly kites with my father," Molly Gibson said, "but I never brought them with me, when I came to England."

"Then I really did the right thing."

Next to Mr. Bingley was a box. He placed it on his lap and told the little girls to open it. They did and both of them looked merry when they found two kites in there.

"You brought us some kites!" Molly Gibson laughed.

"I did. Now, let us hope that there is some wind about this day."

"This is Milton," Jane assured him, "there is always some wind. It's not always kind, but it has the inclination to linger."

"Good. I would be ashamed if Nature was not on my side today."

The coach took them to one of the main parks, and Mr. Bingley helped the ladies down from the carriage.

Once they disembarked, a gust of wind immediately swept around them.

"Well," Jane said, "that bodes well, doesn't it? Mr. Bingley, I have a confession to make as well."

"And what would that be, Miss Bennet?" He asked, taking her hand.

"I have never flown a kite either."

This surprise amused him.

"Now, I feel foolish for not purchasing a third kite."

"You don't have to worry, if you please," Cynthia said, "you can use my kite for a while, if you want, Miss Jane."

"Thank you, Cynthia. I will only use it when you tire of the activity."

Mr. Bingley showed the two girls how to fly the kite, and all the while, Jane watched him. The joys of falling in love enhanced her beauty, as the emotion was often wont to do. However, now her appearance was even more enhanced from the pride that she felt in watching Mr. Bingley assist the two girls. He was dedicated to helping them, while also doing it so effortlessly and organically, that there was no efficacy or superficiality behind it. He was willing to help them because it was a part of his natural character.

Once he achieved his aim, the girls were able to handle the kites on their own. Mr. Bingley and Jane stood behind Molly and Cynthia and the kites soared high in the sky, along the winds.

"We're doing it!" Molly Gibson laughed. "We're doing it!"

"Yes, you are," Jane confirmed. "Yes, you are."

"Don't be afraid to take some steps forward when the wind makes the kite move swiftly," Bingley advised the girls. "Sometimes, it's fine to move with the air."

Cynthia and Molly obeyed and merrily laughed as they moved along each other, with Jane and Mr. Bingley following them.

When Mr. Bingley saw Jane looking at him, he stared back.

"What?" he asked.

"Nothing so terribly important—unless you do not mind me telling you that I love you again."

"You cannot say it enough. But I wonder, what did I do to inspire that declaration."

"Nothing so terribly trivial—except be a good man. I just...you really will be a good father."

"I have you by my side. With you, I can do anything. Oh, Jane, very soon, we might be ever so lucky. I would like to have daughters."

"You do so well with them."

"I'm happy for that. They will be like younger versions of you. Imagine if we ended up having five daughters ourselves. I would be happy, but it would be so terribly daunting."

"Five girls. Well, I daresay that I have some experience in the matter. I think we would manage very well."

"I know that you would. But it would be different. My fortune comes from trade, and I can safeguard our daughter's future. Whatever estate that we purchase together, our daughters would inherit it, because I can arrange no entailment. It won't be like Longbourn."

Jane sighed.

"To be like my mother in having that many girls, is one thing," Jane said, amused, "but to be free of her anxiety! To be married to a man and not have to worry whether we produce a male heir or not, is quite the relief. Though, nothing would swell my heart more than to have little versions of you in my life, it would still be nice for there to be no entailment hanging over our heads and our marriage. We would be spared from my parent's predicament."

"Did the Longbourn entailment ever have an effect on your parents and their relationship? Forgive me if I was wrong to ask."

"You are not wrong for asking. In fact, I am happy that you did. I like that you show an interest in them because we do miss them terribly."

"I'm sure that you do."

"Well, first, I must say that I am prodigiously proud of them, because they did everything to make sure that we had a future when they died. But I will not deny that you make a very good point. Mother and father spent so much of their marriage intending to have a son. When it became too late, and it was evident that the male heir would never arrive, it was too late for father to begin saving money. He was so certain that he would give mother a son, and she was so certain that they would have one, that all their hopes of shielding us depended on it. When that dream didn't come true, there was a—well, it would lead to a great mental undoing, in some way. It easily led to tension between them, and they both became the embodiment of the other one's disappointed dreams. They loved each other, initially, but it would be foolish of me to admit that as time went by, their initial passion diminished."

"There's no need to worry, Jane. We won't be like that."

"I know we won't be."

"No need to worry at all. That won't happen to us in the slightest."

Eventually, it was time for Jane to try her hand at the kite. Cynthia handed the kite to her, and Molly, seeing that it would be good form to make a team of it, handed her kite to Mr. Bingley.

Together, the engaged couple watched as the kites above them were set off against the clouds of the sky and were like a pair of larks that braved the provocative winds. Together, they would remain.

When it was time for them to leave, Mr. Bingley suggested that the girls would be hungry. Which they were. Therefore, he offered to have them dine with him at the hotel, and the girls were excited.

Making a full day of the event, they went to the hotel's dining hall, the girls reveled in being able to order what they wished, and Jane used that as the proper time to make them practice their public table manners.

The effects of knowing that one is in a fancy establishment was enough to subdue their spiritedness, and the girls ended up proving to be quite the little ladies.

When they finished their meal, the hotel steward came up to Mr. Bingley while he was arranging to have the meal paid for on his tab. The steward gave him a letter and Bingley saw that it was from Mr. Darcy.

Unfolding it, Mr. Bingley had expected to read a casual letter about perhaps a quick invitation to go somewhere.

Therefore, the surprise when he discovered its real contents was very apparent.

"Miss Jane," Molly whispered to Jane, tugging at her gown, "Why does Mr. Bingley look upset?"

Jane looked at Mr. Bingley and saw how disturbed he looked when reading the letter.

"I don't know," Jane responded, "but I will find out."

Walking up to Mr. Bingley, Jane took his arm.

"Mr. Bingley, is all well?"

Unable to be a creature of concealment, he lowered the letter and looked on Jane with immense sympathy and shock. Their eyes met, and Jane could easily discern that he heard grave or horrifying news.

"What's wrong?" Jane asked. "Has something happened to Miss Bingley or Mrs. Hurst?"

"No, they are well, when last they wrote to me." He wiped away the emotion from his eyes, placed a pretense of pleasure in his countenance as he rubbed his hands together. "Well, we've all had quite a day. I think it is time that we deliver you two damsels back to the Kirkpatrick's home."

"Oh," Cynthia groaned, "must we? We've been having such a great day."

"Cynthia," Jane said, to assist Mr. Bingley, "you know we must. Your mother is expecting you both to return at this hour. You both have been very good ladies, and you must continue that way until the very end. I have faith in you both."

Acquiescing, Molly and Cynthia went along with it, and they were taken back to the Kirkpatricks.

Since it was Jane's day to return back to Frances Street, Mr. Bingley offered to give her a ride, which she had already expected.

When dropping off the children, they immediately got back into the carriage and Jane was surprised when she heard Mr. Bingley tell the driver that they were not going into Princeton, but rather were to be taken to Marlborough Mills.

"Marlborough Mills?" Jane asked as they drove.

"Yes, my dear," Mr. Bingley said heavily.

"Mr. Bingley," Jane deduced, "does this have to do with that letter you received?"

Mr. Bingley rubbed his lips, nervous. He had never seen Jane when she had to receive terrifying news, and he felt the weight of having to be the one to inform her of what her sisters had befallen. He had hoped to never make her suffer again, after losing her parents, Longbourn, and having to leave her home county. But now, she had to endure another trial.

"Mr. Bingley?" Jane pressed, "Does it?"

"Yes."

"Did something horrible happen?"

"Yes."

Jane leaned back, anxiety creeping into her mind, worries etched across her features as she prepared.

"Please tell me what has happened."

"It's your sisters, Miss Elizabeth, Miss Kitty, Rasby and Miss Hale. There was an attack at Marlborough Mills. The workers stormed the factory, in attempts to attack the Irish and Mr. Thornton."

"Oh, my god! The poor souls! I trust that...was anyone killed?"

"No. The Irish and Mr. Thornton suffered no injuries."

"Oh, thank goodness. No one was harmed."

Mr. Bingley took Jane's hands, and Jane saw that there was more to the story.

"Why do you still look like that?"

"Jane, I have to tell you something, and you must prepare yourself."

"Must I?"

"Yes. You sisters, Miss Elizabeth, Miss Kitty, Rasby and Miss Hale were there at the time."

"Are you...are you about to tell me that they fell into the crowd and were set upon by them? Are you about to tell me that any of them are dead? Oh, do not tell me that my sisters are dead!"

"They are not," Mr. Bingley assured her, holding her hand. "Dearest, they are not dead. But they are heavily injured. I'm taking you to Marlborough Mills to see them."

Mr. Bingley told her the entire story of what Darcy wrote, and Jane was horrified.

Mr. Bingley abandoned his opposite seat in the carriage and sat down next to her. Instinctively, he wrapped his arms around her, and she fell into his embrace, weeping a little as she rested her face against his neck.

"Why!" she exclaimed, "Why must this keep happening to my family? I am tired of it, Charles. And I cannot bear it. How much will life take from me—from them! We lose our parents, we lose Longbourn, and each time, I tell myself that it is the way of the world. I make a life for my family up here, and they have to endure so much conflict and knowl-edge of how far we have fallen from the life that was so kind to us. And so, I tell myself that I did the best I could. I tried the best I could, but what have I done? I've saved no one."

"You've been brave, my dear."

"If I had found a way to persuade you of my love for you, we would have been married by now, my sisters would have been safe, and they would have been spared all these horrors. I saved nothing!"

"You plague my heart by thinking ill of yourself! For the guilt must inevitably be mine. I was the fool who didn't propose when I knew that I should have. I allowed myself to be persuaded to ignore my own heart. The blame really belongs to me, if that be the case. However, we cannot hold ourselves in contempt for unlived actions, of errors of judgment, for we never saw the future. We had no way of knowing."

"I cannot lose them, Charles. Life has taken my parents from me, my home, and separated us sisters. All I had left was knowing that I was doing right by them. If I lose any of them now, I would never forgive myself. It would be too much. I can't endure any more loss. I cannot endure it."

"Darcy said that they all woke up. There is a strong chance of them fully recovering."

"May God spare them. May they be spared."

The carriage arrived at Marlborough Mills, and they were shown into the house immediately. When they entered the sitting room, they had arrived no more than a couple minutes before Denny, who brought Lydia with him.

"Jane!" Lydia cried.

"Lydia!"

Both sisters embraced each other, Darcy met Bingley, and Mrs. Thornton showed the sisters upstairs to see to their wounded women.

Bingley and Darcy remained at the door as it opened, Jane and Lydia rushed in and saw Elizabeth, Kitty, and Rasby awake while Mr. Lowe saw to them.

"Oh, my god," Bingley uttered, seeing the bandaged bruises on their faces and arms.

"Yes," Darcy sighed. "The villains did well."

"Tell me that some of them have been arrested," Bingley hissed. "I must know."

"Some were caught. Others will be by the end of the week."

"Good."

"Precisely."

"Jane and Lydia!" Kitty cried weakly.

"We're here, dearests," Jane said, sitting down next to Elizabeth while Lydia pressed Kitty and Rasby's cheeks. "We're here."

"We knew you would come," Elizabeth whispered.

Rasby looked at Lydia.

"Is my brother still here?"

"Yes. We passed him as Denny brought me in. He's going to stay, Rasby. He volunteered to be a guard for the place until there is no hint of the mob returning."

"They won't come," Rasby replied, her eyes tired, "they are too scared now. The worthless cowards."

Mr. Lowe looked at the two sisters.

"Are any of you equipped to be a good nurse?"

"I should wish to stay," Jane said.

"You work," Lydia said, "I would like to stay and see to them."

"You would want to do that?" Kitty asked.

"Don't need to sound so surprised. I've learned a thing or two since becoming an officer's wife. Mr. Lowe, show me what I must do, and I can look after them."

When hearing this from down the hall, Fanny Thornton was very bitter. She rushed into her room, closing the door passionately, and she hissed to herself.

"Are we to receive every Bennet in the country? It's too much to be born!"

Chapter 10

Heartache

Since the room was crowded by the addition of the two other Bennet sisters, Mr. Lowe declared that only they were allowed to remain, while the rest must leave the room, to give the ladies air, to assist their recovery.

Before doing so, Mr. Darcy gave a fleeting look at Elizabeth.

While Lizzy hugged Jane, she looked at Mr. Darcy from over her shoulder and they both locked gazes. Their eyes said so very much once more, without saying anything at all. The link was forged, and both spoke from their hearts. They would miss each other, whenever they would be severed from the other's company.

Mr. Lowe closed the door behind the men, and they were left to sit in the hall.

Now that it was just them, Mr. Bingley had time to inquire after his friend's state of mind.

"How are you, Darcy?"

Darcy looked back and forth, in the hall, and was more secretive. After all, hallways had ears.

"Come, Charles," Mr. Darcy said, "let's go to Miss Thornton's music room."

"Very well."

Mr. Bingley followed Mr. Darcy there and sat on the music stool while Mr. Darcy closed the door behind them.

"What was it like?" Bingley began to ask immediately. "What was it like to have witnessed that?"

"It could have ended worse."

"That's not what I asked, man."

"Yes, it wasn't. Forgive me if I'm a little short on words —it's just...when you witness an event, or when you take part of it, there is a strange sensation that occurs immediately afterwards. You underwent something, but you don't have the words for it. I saw the crowd. Plato and I entered the courtyard in time to see the mob throw a clog at Thornton and it hit Miss Hale instead. I saw her fall. I saw Thornton hold her as he told me that Elizabeth and the other ladies were in the factory, defending the Irish. I remember going in there and losing my self-control as I saw Elizabeth lying limply on the floor. I remember this demon taking over me. I almost killed a man, Bingley."

"You did?"

"Yes."

On the table, Bingley saw a decanter of wine. He poured some for Darcy and handed it to him.

"Thank you, but I can't drink just now."

"A glass of wine will calm your nerves."

"I don't want them to be calm. I want you to know how I feel. Wine will diminish the sincerity of it all."

Bingley was all attention, thoroughly engaged by the

gruesome tale. It is always through tales of woe that there is the most adept listener.

"I grabbed one of them," Darcy continued, "content to get the revenge for what they did to Elizabeth, oh my Elizabeth! I pummeled the man."

"And? What happened to him?"

"Plato stopped me in time. He held my arm down and looked at me. In that moment, he didn't need to say anything, but I knew it. I knew what he was feeling—or rather, the effect it would have on me. I can't explain it better than that. I just think he knew that it wasn't a proper risk for me to turn into a killer. He could do it. He's a soldier. But I am a gentleman. It could always have a lasting effect on me, that he knew could go in either a positive or negative direction. I don't need to take that risk. I am not saying that, in the future, I will not be capable of being that way if anyone threatens Elizabeth again, but for the moment, maybe I wasn't ready to take a man's life. Though, I wonder if maybe I would have been happier if I did send the man to face his maker."

Bingley sat down next to him.

"Go on," Bingley said, "I have the feeling that there's more that you wish to say."

Darcy gave him a look of feeling exposed.

"Don't worry," Bingley assured him, "I'm not judging you. I'm not judging anything that you felt."

"Thank you. Because I feel ugly now. Or unprincipled."

"What are you talking of? Darcy, what you speak of is self-defense. Any man or woman has the right to do that."

"No, it's not that. It's something else. Bingley, it's something awful."

Awful?

When Darcy said the word, Bingley wondered how Darcy could ever use that word to describe himself. No man was perfect, and that included Darcy, but he never thought Darcy would ever feel 'awful' about something. His inner pride usually did not tolerate such a sentiment.

"What makes you think that way about yourself?"

"It was something Plato Pitcher said. Or rather, it was a subject that he thrust upon the forefront of my mind."

"What was it?"

"He mentioned the possibility that Elizabeth might suffer some permanent damage from the fray that she encountered. Bingley, you didn't see Elizabeth when I first came upon her. She was defending the Irish with her very life. And she was knocked about so terribly. If there is any internal bleeding, or complications, then it might permanently scar Elizabeth. Her mind is still intact, and that is very good. However, what if her body never recovers?"

"She will be a permanent invalid."

"I am used to regarding Elizabeth as the liveliest woman, and it augmented my own character. To have her lose all that! What if I am not the strong sentinel that I pretend? What if I am frightened by this all? What if seeing her like this affects me, and I can't ignore it?"

"You are afraid that if she becomes infirm, it will affect your love for her."

"Yes. I love her now, but what happens years from now, and she has to always be lifted from her bed? Or she loses the use of her arms? What if her mind begins to shatter from an invisible injury that cannot be healed? And I would be helpless. It is too ungenerous not to go and see her every now and again. I know that I love her, but what if I am not strong enough? What if I am a coward, Bingley? I cannot bear this, I cannot!"

Seeing his friend give into despair, Bingley did something that he had never done before. He held Darcy, as Darcy collapsed into him, shrinking to the floor. Bingley sat on the floor, holding his strong friend the entire time, wondering how they had come to this.

Darcy was an oak. Therefore, to see an oak lose so much of its control was a new experience.

"Darcy," Bingley began to assure him, "I know you, and you know yourself. Your love for Miss Elizabeth is so strong that there is no doubt what would happen if that was the case. Your instinct would be to help her, to care for her, and be her protector. You will rise to the occasion. You're just afraid now, because this is a time of fear. Don't be afraid, all will be well. I promise. You will find a way."

Both men lay there, like that, with the one of oak being coaxed and comforted by the one of water. Eventually, they would rise up, and remember the sturdy gentlemen that they were, falling back into the generalization that was placed on them. But for the moment, they were the boys that remained within them, no matter what their age entailed.

In another part of the house, Fanny Thornton had rushed into her room, belligerently shutting the door behind her. When she was alone, she gave way to her fiery side of sensibility and she kicked her foot against her cabinet chest, and rested her hands on the dresser, steadying herself as she wept.

Mr. Darcy loved another woman! How devastating, how cruel, and how unkind life could be.

Fanny felt the injustice of once more, not being the one that anyone preferred to have for their company. While it could be surmised that the reason for her not being a favorite among those closest to her could be attributed to her peevish manner and inconsiderate speech, it was always difficult to contemplate what quality came first.

Was she a creature who people did not initially favor because she was so very disagreeable and of weak understanding?

Or was she a creature who was not allowed to be useful to her family, was born sickly, and therefore was never allowed to be given the chance to aspire to any level of importance, so she felt her worthlessness keenly and it led to her being of weak and shallow character?

Was she once a likable girl who was not given the attention she deserved, so she became something unlikeable as a result?

Or was she unlikeable because she made herself so?

These were questions that could never be answered in Fanny's life.

But what could be answered is that she was a young woman who felt everything so very keenly, as one is inclined to do at that time in their life. Every offense, no matter how small, feels like grand things. Time heals and mellows all, however, it neither changes nor alleviates the agonies that pry at the young red heart.

It is hard to pity a woman like Fanny Thornton, but everyone has a right to feel like they are worth pitying in one time or another. All that Fanny knew in that moment was that she had been catering to, flattering, and doing everything to endear herself to Mr. Darcy. He represented everything that she dreamed of: a handsome, rich gentleman, who liked ladies of accomplishment.

While some of her affections to him were shallow ones, it was no different than how many educated women of small fortune were trained and educated to view men as. It is not often their fault that they are trained to be mercenary in their views. For it was a sad theory, generally unspoken, that a lady or gentleman can only achieve their own marital heroism by being villainous in some way, shape or form. For one must always make matches that advance them and their family, but they also should not be mercenary. Where does discretion end and avarice begin? Maybe it really is impossible to know.

All is conjecture and guessing. All are questions that might never have an answer.

But what is fact is that Fanny Thornton, either through true feeling or through her own imagination, was heartbroken. Looking at herself in the mirror, she was filled with self-contempt.

"Why must you be such an ugly and imperfect creature?" Fanny asked her reflection. "Why do you speak, and no one listens? Is that all there is to your life?"

She threw one of her trinkets against the wall and it smashed and fell against the carpet.

Crying, she leaned against the wall and collapsed onto the floor. Folding her arms over her chest, she continued to weep until her body began to shake.

Hearing footsteps outside of the door, Fanny knew that

she didn't need to conceal her emotions, because she recognized the footfalls.

The door opened and Mrs. Thornton entered, seeing her daughter sitting there, in despair.

"What do you think you are about, Fanny?" Her mother asked. "I heard something break."

"It's nothing."

"That's not what it looks like. What do you have to be crying over for? It's all over, and nothing even happened to you."

"Of course, nothing happened to me. Nothing ever happens to me."

Mrs. Thornton closed the door, shaking her head.

"Whatever imagined offense you feel you have to suffer under, is all in your imagination, Fanny. We've got three ladies who are injured downstairs, frightened Irish, a mob almost attacked your brother, and a stubborn woman who had to throw him in harms' way, and now she's trapped him. And you're the one who's crying? I'm almost ashamed of you."

"What else is new?" Fanny Thornton cried. "You're always ashamed of me. Do you ever have any other emotion in you besides that? Do you ever see how tedious it is to have a mother that does not love you?"

"Hush, child!" Mrs. Thornton said. "You speak nonsense."

"Do I? Do I really? John is the one that you love."

"Is that really what you believe?"

"I know what I know."

"And I know that you know me better than that. Just like I know that's not why you are lying on the floor, like a wounded creature." Mrs. Thornton folded her arms over her chest. "Fanny, this is ridiculous. After all that's happened today, from the strike to the riot, and all you can care about is your wounded heart."

Fanny looked at her mother, alarmed. She had no notion that her mother suspected the attachment that her heart had made to Mr. Darcy, because they had never mentioned it. Romance was not Mrs. Thornton's province, so mother and daughter were never to have the important relationship that they ought to have, and Fanny had no outlet to her frustrations.

"Yes," Mrs. Thornton answered, "I've known for quite some time. And I don't presume to understand why you thought in that direction. Mr. Darcy never regarded you in that way, so it was foolish to think about."

Fanny winced, bitter. Her mother was offending her and didn't even notice.

"Don't you know anything?" Fanny hissed. "Love has nothing to do with the mind. It's all about the heart!"

"And your heart exposed you to falling for a Southern man of landed gentry. Pemberley may be in the North, but Darcy has Southern ways and rearing. If you want to look somewhere, you should be looking to the manufacturers that are here. Sturdy men of industry, that's what you ought to be doing."

"Don't you understand anything?"

"I tell you what I do understand. I don't see the logic of loving a man that is inconvenient to love."

"You speak like that, showing that you don't understand your own hypocrisy. Who are you to preach to me? You married a man who lost all our fortune, drove us into debt and then abandoned us to his shame. How can you laugh at my heart when you married father?"

Mrs. Thornton didn't respond to this, because she was aware that there might be some veracity to it.

"Do you know what your problem is?" Fanny asked her, grieved. "You are my mother, and I can never come to you for anything. I can't talk to you about how I feel, because how dare I feel anything? I can't talk to you about my dreams, because you don't know what those even are. I can't have any other perspective in life than the perspective that you lay down for me. You are my mother, and I can never confide anything to you, because all you know how to do is scoff at it. I'm tired of it."

"There's no use in us talking. I know that you will feel like you are the wretchedest creature in the world."

Mrs. Thornton went to the door and turned the knob. For a split second, she realized that maybe she ought to say something kind.

"You know that I don't like to show emotion, even when I feel it," Mrs. Thornton said.

"So, I have to be the same way?"

"Fanny. I do want you to be happy."

Fanny rested her head against her knees, and her mother left. That was perhaps the only way that Mrs. Thornton knew how to show emotion.

Chapter 11

The End of the Day

When I opened my eyes again, it was nighttime. Jane had to leave an hour before, but Lydia remained. She was sitting in a chair, changing Rasby's bandages, and I saw her outline, in the candlelight.

"Lydia?" I whispered.

"You're awake," she said.

"Yes." I marked her ease at being a nurse. "When did you get so good at this?"

"Time, Lizzy," Lydia answered. "Everything's all a matter of time. Besides, when I was home, in Longbourn, what chance was there for me to grow and expand? Think about it; how can you ask for enhancement of character, when there are no chances to expose you to that. Also, I'm older now, and have more to care about. Can you entertain the possibility that that's enough to alter a person?"

"Lydia, I'm in a bed from fighting a crowd of people who are also my friends. I've learned that anyone is capable of almost anything. We all needed time, didn't we?"

"Not just time. We all needed a larger acquaintance with the ways of the world. I was given both. And it also helps that I was given a good husband. And to think, there was a time where I found Mr. Wickham to be the one that I wanted to marry."

"You did?" I asked, raising an eyebrow.

"Yes, I did. The only reason I abandoned all hope was simply because you fancied him. And, from what I saw, he fancied you. So, I figured that there was no point on waiting for a man who was not coming. Now that was a happy thought. It led to me appreciating Denny and seeing him for what he was."

"You saw more clearly than we did."

"Now that is the best compliment you've ever given me."

She finished bandaging Rasby's arm and Rasby fell back asleep.

"Lydia," I asked, "can you do me a favor? If Mr. Darcy is still awake, can you get him for me?"

"Oh, I know he's still awake. At a time like this, men have a hard time resting—well, men who have an ounce of compassion in them have a hard time sleeping. Apathy, oddly enough, is very fashionable nowadays."

Lydia went to the hallway.

"Hannah?" she called. I heard the servant, Hannah, come down the hall.

"Yes, Miss?"

"Be a doll and fetch Mr. Darcy, will you? Tell him that Elizabeth wants him."

"Yes, Miss."

She went and soon Mr. Darcy returned.

When he did, Mr. Darcy appealed to Lydia to take

some time to rest and see Mr. Denny, who was outside, guarding the courtyard. Never being one to avoid being near her husband, she took ahold of this opportunity. Lydia kissed me on the cheek, told me that she would return in half an hour and Mr. Darcy, and I were left alone.

"Alone at last?" I asked. "Well, somewhat."

"Yes."

Reaching my arm out to him, he slowly walked up to me and took my hand, sitting down on the floor, next to the bed.

"It is so strange," I noted.

"What is?"

"Seeing Mr. Darcy, Master of Pemberley, Derbyshire, sitting on the floor."

He chuckled.

"Did I make you laugh?" I asked.

"Yes, you did. Even when you have just been set on by a mob of ruffians, and you still find a way to make me smile. How does Elizabeth Bennet do it?"

"By not thinking about it," I informed him, "truth is, if I were to think about being witty, I wouldn't be. So, I don't think."

"That is the trick?"

"Simple, isn't it?"

"Yes. I never would have known."

"Sometimes, there has to be something said for following one's instincts. Instinct is not always an enemy to logic." I smiled. "And I just realized that I am preaching philosophy at the end of a bizarre day."

"And now you trivialize. Lizzy, bizarre is the word that you use?"

"You can think of a better word?"

"Yes, I can. Horrendous, tragic, overwhelming, violent, belligerent, savage—but you use bizarre."

"And you are sitting on the floor. We both are showing a different sort of way, aren't we?"

"Yes, I suppose that we are." Darcy dropped my hand, and he raised up his arm, bringing his hand near my cheek. "Forgive me, unless you don't mind..."

"I don't mind."

Lowering his hand, he pressed my right cheek. I smiled, through his fingers.

"That feels nice," I said.

"I'm not hurting you at all, am I?"

"Even if you were, your affection is a pressure that I can bear. But somehow, this one cheek managed to escape the abuse." In the firelight, Mr. Darcy's skin began to glow, and I felt the magic of the evening. There is something sprite-like, almost like that of a fairy, when light illuminates a person at the right sort of time. "Do you know what, Mr. Darcy?"

"What?"

"You are quite the handsome man, aren't you?"

His cheeks turned red.

"And now you blush. I never knew that blushing was the province of masters of estates, landed gentry, and magistrates. Now I am enlightened."

"My brave love. I just..."

"What?"

"I wish that I was there. I wish that none of this had happened."

"I know that. But you came for me. I appreciate that. And all this time, I just realized, what was this all like for you?"

spend the rest of my life with you, walking at your side, then I must think of you, from time to time. Now, mind you, I prefer you to be the sort to treat me better than you treat yourself, but still."

"Oh," he chuckled, "is that what you wish?"

"Yes. And I don't deny it. Many a woman often says that she wants a man to treat her as his equal, and more for her, I say. But no, I am different. I want you to treat me better than how you treat yourself. Call me wicked, but there it is."

"I admire it. Lizzy, you must always unfold yourself to me as you do now. I love it when you tell me what you are feeling. For, in that way, I always know where I stand. I want to make you happy."

"And you better," I stressed. "When you do that, I promise, I will always think of you. And I will always fight to make you smile again."

His eyes turned even kinder.

"Elizabeth, please tell me earnestly. Because I need to prepare myself. What sort of pain are you in? Do not hide or conceal anything from me on that. When you look on me, do you see me, or is your eyesight a little impaired? Can you hear me well? Do you feel your feet and legs, or does a part of them feel as if they are breaking and will continue to do so? Does the feeling in your arms feel intact?"

"You are worried that I will be a cripple? What would happen if I was? Darcy, how would that make you feel? After all, the Master of Pemberley wants a woman to come to him complete, wouldn't he?"

137

Mr. Darcy rubbed his cheek, nervous. With men such as himself, the little quirks, the small gestures, mean so much. I was prepared to hear something that was not very pleasant for him to confess.

"Elizabeth, you must forgive me and listen to everything that I tell you before you pass judgment. I just wish for you to understand me, and for there to be no secrets to come between us."

I continued to hold his hand.

"I am braced for the truth."

"Elizabeth...my life has been a pretty clear sort of thing. What I mean by such is that, at an age, we men are meant to be solid, sure of ourselves, and impervious to the sensibilities of life."

"But you all aren't, are you?" I guessed.

"No, we are not. Within every single one of us is a little boy, who is very scared at the constant trials of life. Of the uncertainties that fate thrusts upon us. You look on me as if you are not confused."

"You discern properly. It's because I'm not. We men and women are not the same creatures, though we both belong to humanity. But one similarity holds. In the eyes of the earth, the skies, the cosmos, no matter how old we humans get, we are very young to life's generalities. Within all of us women and men, will always be that frightened infant who feels very alone. And when we lose our parents, we become more alone than ever. We are children without our protectors."

"We feel very lost," Darcy added, "and as if we shall never find cheer again. I suppose, when my parents died, I didn't smile as much. Or maybe I forgot how to. That's probably why I clung to you—and why I was right to."

"Why?" I implored him. "Tell me."

"I can't explain it, but for some reason, whenever I was around you, I felt less alone. And then it reached a point where I never felt lonely at all unless you were not there."

"That's why you sought me out in London, but when you never had much to say," I realized, "I thought you did it because you had little else to do, and it was simply boredom that you were trying to overcome. Then again, it was London, and there are diversions everywhere, therefore, I do not know what I was thinking."

"I left you in the dark for way too long, didn't I?"

"Yes, you did. But we are here now, and that's all that matters."

"Just being in your company erased all sense of loneliness. So, words weren't needed, but I see now that they were. And so, now I give you an answer. Elizabeth, I admit, there was a part of me that was scared at the idea of your injuries becoming grave. Not just them being mortal injuries that could eventually and slowly take your life, but what if it led to you having internal injuries. What if you couldn't conceive a child? What if you would spend your life being an invalid? Would you eventually go blind and no longer see me, or be deaf and not be able to hear my voice? It was selfish and cowardly. I was a frightened child who wanted to run away and hide."

"And what do you feel now?" I asked. "Do not be afraid. I am here for you."

"It was just a moment. And like many moments, it faded away. Elizabeth, no matter what happens, I will be here for you. And I will never think you are lovelier than you are now."

"I am happy that you no longer hate yourself," I said,

"remember this: children are capable of great courage. The child inside of you will always find its way back, if you will it so."

"You do not hate me?"

"You were scared. Don't be afraid of telling me your fears, because we will always get the better of them. You must always find your way back to me. Promise me that."

"I promise."

"Then we can begin."

"Mr. Darcy," Lydia said, coming back in, "it's time that you gave my sister some rest. Sleep is the best way for them to recover now."

"Yes, Mrs. Denny."

Darcy kissed my hand once more and then he had to leave.

When he did so, he gave Lydia a look.

"You heard me," she responded, "shift!"

I could not conceal the amusement I felt in seeing that. I chuckled slightly, but my gurgles were not long-lasting, because it hurt to laugh.

When Mr. Darcy walked out, the servant Jane entered with a makeshift bedding that was going to be placed on the floor for Lydia to sleep on. After Jane left, Lydia closed the door behind her.

"What part of your body is not in pain?" Lydia asked me.

"My left shoulder. Why?"

Lydia walked up to me, cackling, and poked my left shoulder.

"My sister is going to be the mistress of Pemberley! Ha ha ha! Oh, you must definitely invite Denny and I there, or I will scold you like a Fury."

"Thank you, Lydia. Who would have thought that Pemberley's mistress might have to be wearing plaster casts under a wedding gown?"

"Now that would be quite the twist," Kitty said, "I'd laugh, but it hurts to do that."

"Yes, it does hurt, doesn't it?"

"I can't even begin to try," Rasby added, "because I can barely speak as it is. Congratulations, Elizabeth, you will be a lovely bride."

"Thank you. Unless Death takes me first. If that happens, my ghost will haunt Death for all eternity."

"Elizabeth, Death is Death."

"But *she's* never met me before."

Kitty and Rasby laughed.

"Oh, that hurt," Rasby groaned.

"Yes, that hurt a lot," Kitty added.

Lydia looked at us as she arranged her bedding.

"Imbeciles."

After a while, we all fell asleep, knowing that we were safe.

At Crampton Crescent, Dixon informed Margaret that the waterbed had been delivered. But Mrs. Hale had already gone to bed, so it would have to be assembled the next day.

Happy that something had gone right for her efforts, Margaret lay in bed that night but found it difficult to rest. Her mind couldn't help but go over the events that had occurred. And she couldn't release Mr. Thornton from her mind. She had finally released the cares of gossip that would occur at her expense, but the fear of the attachment that happens when you help save someone still lingered. Her apprehensions were heavy when knowing that there would be a reluctant new sort of connection between them.

As her mind began to rest, it was at the image of him on his steps, hearing the jeers of the mob, and knowing that nothing would ever be the same.

———

Eventually, the guard was changed around Marlborough Mills and Plato and Denny had to leave with Colonel Fitzwilliam, so that they could be given some rest. Before their departure, Denny spoke with Lydia, who confirmed that all three wounded women were stable, and that they would easily live through the night. All three men were able to leave with a sense of relief.

When they lay down to bed in the militia's headquarters, sleep came to them easily, due to all the physical exhaustion that they had endured.

Denny fell asleep, swelled with pride at how far his wife had come in her maturity, while still retaining her childlike spirit. He never was the tyrannical sort of man who ordered his wife into a more sober way of being. Her character development was a result of natural growth, and an inclination to be like water, and adapt its course to accommodate any new surroundings that it found itself in. Lydia adapted all on her own. How could Denny not be prodigiously proud of her?

———

Plato went to bed with an immense sense of self-assurance. He had to spend the day in three different roles: as protector, advisor and concerned brother. All three roles proved to reach satisfaction, and his hopes were not in vain. He had protected Rasby, as any older brother had the right to. No matter how the world viewed individuals such as himself, Darcy did not despise him for offering his own words of wisdom, and he had been the officer and ran into the fray to maintain the chivalry that a man ought to when in her Majesty's service. Peace found him as he rested.

Colonel Fitzwilliam could not release Kitty from his mind. When seeing here there, so broken under the cruelty of the world, awakened every special emotion that he had specifically for her. If he had been born rich, he could have married her already and shielded her from the horrors of life.

However, seeing her like that, so courageous, was a treat for him. It confirmed why he loved her, and that she did not fear the world, nor the darker elements of it. Also, she was a working woman. At this point in life, he knew he could not marry her, because he needed an heiress. However, for so long, he had been of the mindset that any woman he married needed to provide a dowry, because she would have no profession.

How blind he felt he had been! He fell in love with a woman who did not feel demeaned in the world for choosing work. She was the sort of lady who could adapt to wherever he was and find a way to earn income. She could bring her own wages to the marriage, and they would just have to learn to economize. She did not fear living modestly either, because she proved that she knew how to do it, and not fear the words of others, or being the center of jokes.

He would marry her. If she would have him—but he knew that she would. After all, it was only his hesitancy, his static stance, that had prevented him from proposing. He had made a decision, and now he felt the comfort that came with no longer denying himself one of the great pleasures of life. He would patiently wait a few weeks after she recovered, till she was fully stable, and he would ask her. After all, it was best to do things properly, rather than hastily.

For the first time, he slept in the only way that can be obtained when you achieved a pleasant sort of peace.

Fanny Thornton's rest was not pleasant, but it was ultimately obtained. She had cried herself to the point where her mind and spirit were exhausted. Her heartache was, by all accounts, complete, with a knowledge of lost affection, of disappointed hopes, and knowledge that the woman who was in the place of where she wished to be was now sleeping in her house. The pounding of her heart was so intense that she even covered her ears, thinking it would drown out the noise. Naturally, it didn't.

When her eyes did finally close, around the stroke of midnight, dreams did not come to her. But rather it was intense nightmares that were the likes of which she did not ever have before.

Mrs. Thornton went to sleep that night in a similar fashion as her daughter. Irony found its way into their relationship, and they would never learn of it. Mrs. Thornton didn't realize that she was suffering the similar sentiments as her daughter, because she wasn't always possessed with the best sort of inner reflection.

Fanny realized that she would never win Mr. Darcy's heart. She had lost him, and it cast her into a *state of despair*.

Mrs. Thornton realized that she would soon lose her place as the ultimate woman in her son's affections, and it cast her into a *state of despair*.

For the next day, there would be a new Mrs. Thornton who would replace her. Her son would go to Crampton Crescent, propose to Margaret Hale, she would accept, and she would be the love of her son's life.

Despite that it would make her son happy, Mrs. Thornton had it in her nature to be selfish as anyone else in the world when it comes to maintaining a great love in her life. Her son was everything to her. Even though he always would be, even though he always would do right by her, protect her, and admire her for her fortitude, things would never be the same.

She fell asleep, crying, in the same manner that Fanny had. For she was aware that the next day, she would have to move aside, make way for a new woman in her son's life, and endure it. Either way, she had to reconcile herself to the grave reality: tomorrow symbolized a great loss.

Jane Bennet went to sleep in her house, and for the first time, she was afraid.

First, she was uncertain of if her sisters would live through the night, and it tugged away at her strength. As she told Bingley, she was not ready to lose any more than she already had. Her spirit could not endure it.

However, there was another unforeseeable agony that ached. She was *alone*. Ever since coming to Milton, Jane never spent the night alone in her house. First, there was Kitty as her constant companion, then Rasby would spend the night. Then Elizabeth came. The house never had only one person sleeping in it.

As the night wore on, and there was a harsh wind that swept along Frances Street, Jane felt the isolation. What is unfamiliar is always daunting, but we never are aware of it until it occurs. While she ate, it felt like every corner of the house had an invisible phantom that was there, out of the corner of her eye, taunting her.

Eating dinner quickly, Jane took a bath, washed her hair, rushed into her room, and pushed things against the door, as a useless way of keeping the specters that haunt the night at bay.

Sitting in her bed, by candlelight, she pulled out her copy of *Rachel Ray* by Anthony Trollope and began to read it. The adventures of the heroine helped remove her from the apprehension of being alone and the phantoms that she feared were just an inch away from her.

But one thing was certain. As fortune as her witness, she was resolved: she would never be lonely again. The words eased her into making her eyelids heavy, and she fell asleep at last.

Mr. Darcy could not rest at all, not out of distress, but only animated concern. It was the result of knowing that you were a man who faced the darker sides of yourself, wrestled with it, confronted it, and overcame it.

What was more was that he and Elizabeth had reached such a profound understanding, that he was too restless to fully find sleep, because he found something that he longed for: ultimate happiness. Thus, he lay in bed, and though his mind was awake, he still was dreaming. Of all the days that would come. Of all the new experiences that would be achieved. Of finally being Elizabeth's husband, and knowing he deserved it.

Thus, came the end of the longest day.

End of Book I

Book II

The Shortest Month

Chapter 1

Visits

The next day, Margaret Hale woke up with many missions to undergo.

First, the evening rest had done her a great deal of good. She was not unrefreshed, but she was well rested. All the occurrences of the day before had led to her body and mind giving way to slumber with the greatest of ease.

After she dressed, she went off to assist her mother, and her mind ran over the incidents of the day before. However, it was brief. Between the mother, son and daughter, Margaret was content to attempt to banish all recollection of the Thornton family from her mind for the moment. She truly felt that there was no need to think of them until they absolutely stood before her in flesh and blood, or she was thrown in their way again, due to her association with the Bennet sisters.

After assisting her mother, eating breakfast, and Dixon making it evident that it was her turn to be Mrs. Hale's nurse, Margaret was released from her duties and could answer to Bessy's wish to see her.

Going to Frances Street, Margaret was apprehensive. For when she had gone before, she had achieved an easy camaraderie with the street's inhabitants. But now, it was different. Rumor would spread, and soon all of Frances Street would be aware that she was the woman who was the means through the strike failing. They would either view her as the woman who vulgarly displayed herself to the world, or they were embarrassed. After all, she was the woman who the mob had attacked, along with the Bennet sisters and Rasby. These people, who they had befriended, had turned on them. And now that their ugly sides were displayed unto the world, they were ashamed...shame can lead to someone wishing to avoid you for the rest of their natural lives.

When moving past the Goulden Dragon, Margaret Hale's apprehensions were well-justified. People avoided looking at her, but not out of contempt. It was out of pity or a feeling of being disgraced. Wondering how long it would be before they looked her in the eye again, Margaret sojourned on. As she turned down the road, up ahead, a figure halted immediately and looked on her with horror.

Boucher!

When seeing him, Margaret saw his face turn white with fright. She took a few steps forward, to appeal to him, but he misinterpreted. Fearing the reprimands and thoroughly scared of what his actions led to, Boucher turned around and ran away.

There was nothing that Margaret could do but regret that he would not ever face her for a long time. She wondered what his fate would ultimately be.

As she walked down the street, she passed the Bennets' house. Knowing very well that they were not there, she stood there for a time. And that was when it all became so terribly real to her. Mr. Bingley had come and would soon marry Jane and take her back to the South. Margaret had braced herself for that, but now Lizzy! Mr. Darcy was in love with her. Margaret always knew this, but over time, she had to witness Mr. Darcy slowly find his way into Elizabeth's heart. Then Colonel Fitzwilliam was finding it harder to deny his affection for Kitty.

And now these women proved themselves to be the worthiest women in England. And Darcy would take Lizzy back to the South for periods of time, Kitty would go back down there as well, perhaps, or travel with the regiment like the other army wives.

First Edith, next Helstone, the South, her mother, then Jane...but now Lizzy and Kitty?

'Am I to have nothing?' Margaret asked herself. 'Must everything be taken from me?'

For then, the Bennet house was empty, but it foreshadowed when one day, no Bennet sister would live there. And Bessy was so ill as well. Margaret had to brace herself for the reality that all women in her life would soon be gone. When the day came, where all left her, she would feel that loss. And she would weep over it.

Tearing her eyes away from the Bennet residence, she kept going and knocked on the Higgins door. It opened and she was met with Mary.

"Oh, Miss," was all that Mary said, "thank yer for comin'. Bessy's been in a bad way."

Margaret went inside and immediately approached

Bessy, who was lying in the bed, with a violent and whooping cough.

"Oh, Bessy," Margaret said, "forgive me for not coming yesterday, but I had no choice."

When looking up at her, Bessy's eyes were heavy.

"I thought I should never ha' seen yer again," she professed, saddened.

Margaret knew what that meant.

"Oh Bessy. Must it really be so?"

"Fraid' so, miss."

"I was afraid that you would be much worse. That's why you sent for me."

"Yea. Yer must have thought so heav'ly by me sending Mary to fetch yer. And then, when I heard all those cries and loud voices, stompin' feet as they were makin' their way to Marlborough Mills. And father was gone. Have yer heard of the riot? It happened yesterday at Thornton's factory."

Margaret was happy in one way. Bessy and Mary clearly didn't hear about the part that she played in that event, and that gave her hope.

"Yes, I heard of it. Your father was not there, was he?"

"Not he," Bessy replied, shaking her head, and coughing a little. "This was ev'rythin' that he did not want. It fairly knocked down his mind when he discovered that it happened. It's no use tellin' him, fools will always break out of bounds. Margaret, I fear for him. You didn't see him. He looked so downhearted by it."

"Why? He didn't cause it."

"But he's a committee man on this strike. The Union appointed him because he's reckoned by all to be a deep chap, and true. He and the other committee-men laid their plans out, and they though' they had a real good chance this time. They ordered everyone that, above all, there was no going agains' the law of the land. And this riot was enough to break the strike. Margaret, I've never seen him so low. I fear what he will do."

Compassionate, and happy that the situation was not centered around her, Margaret held Bessy.

"Bessy, your father is knocked down now, but he will recover. I've never seen a stronger and sturdier man than Nicholas. He will recover, no matter how bleak it all looks now. Don't let this affect you. It will only take you into the grave sooner."

"Sometimes, I hope it will. At least I will rest."

"And I will miss you. Selfish as this is to admit, Bessy, please, let me have more days with you as a friend."

Bessy smiled sadly.

"I'll give it a go."

Margaret left the Higgins house, never getting the chance to see or talk to Nicholas. Then again, he was a strong man, and stubbornness was attached to his qualities. Even if she did implore him not to be angry, he would be so.

Initially, Margaret had decided to go to Marlborough Mills, but she had another thought. Turning around, she made her way to the Boucher's home, and she knocked on the door.

When going there, she saw Mrs. Boucher look at her through the window and then disappear immediately.

There was no response.

Resolute, Margaret knocked again.

"Mrs. Boucher," she said through the door, "please, I know you are there. Do not forsake me."

At last, she heard the latch raise, and Mrs. Boucher faced her.

"I know why yer here," she said.

"What?"

"Yer came to find him and hand him over to the police. He's not here, and I want yer to know that he hates what's happened."

"I am not here to destroy him," Margaret pleaded, "I want you to know that. I am here, because if he returns, I want you to tell him something. Tell him that I do not hate him."

Her eyes shifted to wonder.

"Yer don't?"

"No, I don't."

"But everyone else does. Everyone else hates my husband now, Miss Hale. I can't bear it."

"Time will help it."

"Yer don't understand. Yer... Miss Hale, I must know somethin'. I heard that someone struck women. That's what broke the strike. Violence happened to women. I also heard someone say that yer were there. Did yer see it? Did tha' really happen?"

Breathing heavily, Margaret nodded.

"Was it Boucher? Was he one of the men who hurt them? I was too 'fraid to ask."

"I know that he didn't attack three of them, but as for the fourth, I don't know. I never saw who threw the clog at the fourth woman. I'm sorry, Mrs. Boucher, but I cannot tell you."

"Well, as long as I know that three of them didn' suffer under my husband's hand, tha's somethin'."

Margaret bid her a good day and then proceeded to Marlborough Mills.

When going to the Thorntons, she found out that Mrs. Thornton was not there.

"Mother and John are not here," Fanny Thornton said, when she met Margaret in the sitting room. "John is making arrangements with the Irish, for some of them have decided to go home. Mama is seeing to their comfort, and I know that she will be angry if she is pulled away from the factory. Unless you want me to fetch her?"

"No, that will not be necessary," Margaret Hale assured her, "I just came to see Elizabeth, Kitty and Rasby."

Margaret, always willing to observe, detected that Fanny looked down when hearing Elizabeth's name. Her cheeks also were changing color.

"Miss Thornton," Margaret commented, "are you well?"

"Yes," Miss Thornton said, "I may be delicate, but it's not as if I was the one who went down there and tried to face some rabblerousers who clearly were too much for me."

Margaret raised an eyebrow. Having already been familiar with Fanny Thornton's strange perspective on situations, as well as peevish temper, she was accustomed to her ways. But this was different. She seemed to lack any compassion for the women who came to her aid. If she felt such a way about them, then what did Fanny feel about Margaret's own actions? After all, when entering, Miss Thornton made no mention of her getting struck by the riot the day before.

"They were protecting the workers," Margaret added, "Miss Thornton, I thought you would have been happy in their assistance to break the strike."

"All those workers," Fanny groaned, "and the sound that the factory makes when I'm trying to practice my music. Sometimes, I wonder if I should care."

Something was wrong. While Margaret and Fanny would never see eye to eye on anything, and their tempers were so entirely different, Margaret still knew when Fanny was just being typical of her character, and when something was aggravating her.

"If you could be so kind as to show me to my friends," Margaret continued.

"Right. Come then."

Margaret followed Fanny up the stairs.

"How have you been since the experience?" Margaret asked.

"I still hate to think about it. It's one of the many things that make me wish to leave Milton."

"Thank you and Mrs. Thornton for delivering the waterbed to Crampton Crescent. This morning, Dixon applied it in my mother's room, and she expressed great joy when she laid on it."

"You're welcome. Of course, you cannot keep it," Fanny said, when they reached the door.

Margaret blinked. This was not something that she expected Fanny to say, or that she expected to do.

"Of course," Margaret said, "I never intended to."

Fanny made a strange sound with her throat that indicated that she wanted to say something else but was prevented. It was as if she was stopping herself in some way.

"Well, they are in there."

"Yes," Margaret said, "Did they suffer through the night?"

"I know that they woke up this morning. But their sister and mama are the main ones overseeing them. I'm not built for the sickroom. Well then..."

And with that, she left Margaret Hale at the door.

Unable to ignore how Fanny met her, Margaret held the doorknob, but didn't enter it yet. What could possess Fanny so?

But she was certain of one thing: it was more evident now than ever that she and Fanny would never be friends. Not only were their characters not recommended for each other, but Fanny had done everything to make it hard to ever sympathize with her.

Accepting this fact, Margaret dismissed any hope of there being peace and compassion between each other and knocked on the door. When hearing Lydia's voice say, 'come in', it made Margaret's heart lighten. While Lydia was the least dear of the Bennet sisters to Margaret, for Lydia's exuberance was not to Margaret's taste, she also was aware that Lydia had a way of alleviating certain situations.

When going into the room, she found all the wounded women awake, lying in bed, and they were not alone. Lydia was overseeing them, but Colonel Fitzwilliam was also there, speaking with Kitty.

Chapter 2

Assurance

Margaret Hale had come to visit us, as I knew that she would. When seeing us there, still confined to the bedroom, her empathy gave way, and she rushed to me.

"Oh, thank goodness you are awake," Margaret said, coming to my side. "When a wounded person's eyes close, the largest fear will always be that it stays that way."

"We will always be of one mind when it comes to compassion," I voiced weakly, but cheery. My throat was a little sore.

"Yes. We do have that in common—thank goodness." Margaret smiled sadly at me.

"There might very well be nothing to fear, once all the pain and scars subside," I added, assuring her. "We all still have our mental faculties, and somehow, we did not get a broken bone. Did we, girls?"

"I won't say that I was fit as a fiddle," Rasby grunted, "but I've stopped seeing double of everything. That's a small kind of accomplishment. But once I know that I can laugh again and there is no pain, then all will be right in the world." Rasby looked at Kitty and the Colonel. "Is love working there?"

"Yes." Kitty laughed, then she coughed. "Oh dear, laughter; my enemy now."

"I am happy about that," Margaret said, "I was worried about you three."

"Well," I responded, "we were worried about you as well. You decided to suffer a head injury, and then you chose to be Margaret Hale, and take a cab home."

"I had to," Margaret responded, "and you know it."

"Yes, I do. You and I must have our way, mustn't we?"

Margaret smiled, gently.

"Yes, I suppose that we must."

"Did your parents ever find out what happened?"

"So far, they are not aware of there being any violence at Marlborough Mills. It will be a matter of time before they learn of it, but hopefully, they won't hear all of it."

"But why?" I asked, not in the mood to let the Hales remain in the dark. "Now that they see that you have suffered no real damage, then you don't need to worry about any response."

"On the contrary, there is something to worry over," Margaret said, and she didn't lower her voice, because it was evident that she didn't feel any concealment mattered. "I have had to accept the reality of what my actions will incite in a world that is run from gossip."

"What do you mean?" Kitty asked.

"She means that she was caught, in public, holding a man," Colonel Fitzwilliam said. "And talk has no choice but to follow, and a perfectly innocent action is rendered guilty by those with guilty minds, who pretend to be pure."

"Ah," Margaret said heavily, "you've noted it as well."

"I make it a habit to keep my ear to the ground, or just to the air, in this case."

Kitty looked at the Colonel.

"People are misconstruing her actions?"

"A woman can't defend a man in such a way and fully escape any gossip."

"People think that you have shown a romantic love for Mr. Thornton," I stated clearly, "don't they?"

"Yes, they do. And word may spread, and I worried that father and mother would hear of it soon. But then I had another thought."

"I hope it was a refusal to care about how the world perceives things that it knows little about."

"It was," Margaret assured us all. "I did what I did, and I am not going to apologize for it. Especially since I have come to accept that I would have done it all over again. And what does it matter that people talk of such things?"

"That's the spirit," I confirmed. "Curse all those who wish to think erroneous things, because that is how they justify their own existence."

"Most of the time, people come to such conclusions," Rasby added, "because that's all they have to talk about. Eventually, their biting ideas become harmless, because after their suspicions come to nothing, they must and inevitably find something else to talk about."

"That is a happy philosophy," Margaret said, "and I never thought of it that way. Well, all that I can say is that I am happy I give them a moment of reprieve. Because now, I see the pointlessness of sitting around and feeling bad for myself."

"There you go," Colonel Fitzwilliam confirmed. "I

cannot control what my officers say amongst themselves, but Plato and I will do a very good job at implying the falsities of any rumors that will continue to reach our ears. I just needed your presence here to confirm that you and Mr. Thornton are not..."

"Precisely, we are *not*. And we *never* will be."

Since Kitty and the colonel had much to talk about, and Lydia had ordered Jane and Hannah to help her take Rasby to the washroom and put her in her bath, this gave Margaret and I time to speak to each other. We quieted our tones so that we didn't interrupt Colonel Fitzwilliam's courtship to Kitty—for that's what it was. They were courting, but they knew better than to put the words to it.

"Well," I continued, "you promise me that you are not allowing any potential gossip to affect you?"

"I promise," she assured me. "I was weak for only a moment. But my apprehensions rose and fell in the course of a couple hours. It occurred to me, very quickly, that no one else was worthy of my concern, regarding the truth of my own actions."

"It is well. You can't live your life worried about someone who would die of fright because they fear any true sentiment. If you do that, you'll never get anything done."

"Was this how you felt when you stood up to Lady Catherine about certain things?" Margaret asked. "Or when you walked three miles to Netherfield Park to look after Jane when she was sick?"

"Ah, those good ole' days," I sighed, falling back into the serenity that is our happy memories, "yes, that might be how I felt. Even doing something so small as to be the only one in the room to like something that everyone hates, to prefer a meal that everyone says you are mad to do—any lack of fear of integrity is scandalous. But I know very well that people like us, exist for a reason. We are designed to break the monotony of life. Like Rasby said, thank God for creatures like us. We give people things to talk about, where they had nothing to fill up their conversation."

Margaret chuckled gently and looked at the floor.

"I wonder what Fanny Thornton is saying of us."

I squinted, preparing for a tale of envy and unquiet tempers.

"What croakings of discontent did she have?" I asked.

"Nothing so little or large. It is merely that she was very cold when she received me. It was as if nothing I did the day before happened. Or what you all sacrificed, for that matter. In fact, I cannot help but wonder if she was annoyed by us."

Rolling my bottom lip between my teeth, this was a conversation that I should have anticipated but didn't.

"I do not think she was annoyed by you, personally, but rather, you were guilty by association."

"How so?"

"She hates me. And you and I are friends."

"Hate?" Margaret questioned, "are you certain that you are not exaggerating? You and I do have the inclination to throw extreme judgments around as if they are bags of groceries."

"I know that I am right."

"I know that you and I disagreed with her when she visited Crampton, but was it really enough for her to despise you?"

"That's not what kindled her contempt. A more recent development has occurred, and from her perspective, she is the victim of a situation that her heart has put her in."

Margaret didn't speak, but there was no need. Having prided herself on not being the sort to pry into personal affairs, she was torn between the sense of secrecy, but also the curiosity that tugs at all of us.

"Do you care or not care?" I asked her.

"You put me in a strange place. I have not the right to pry into the hearts of another woman, but if she has decided to be contemptuous of us, then perhaps I ought to know."

"Would it help if you knew that she would not hesitate to pry into your affairs? She already has talked to the servants about it?"

"How do you know that?"

"Hannah and Jane talk, and Lydia is very good at over-hearing when servants speak. Fanny Thornton is encouraging that rumor."

"I should not stoop to her level then."

"Very well. I shall tell you nothing."

Margaret was silent, for a moment.

"Oh, very well," she gave in, "I should know why she is mistreating you."

I smiled slightly, but did not triumph over her. Allowing her to accept the reality of the situation was success enough, by and by.

"She is heartbroken," I whispered, "and I am the cause of it."

My announcement had no choice but to alarm Margaret and draw her into the dramatic elements of my life.

"The cause of it?" Margaret repeated, "how?"

"She is a woman who is in love with a man who does not love her."

Margaret breathed in.

"And he's in love with you," she continued.

"Yes. And she knows it now. She may have suspected it before, but it's clearer now than ever. Maybe what stopped her fully despising me was the fact that nothing was certain. But now things are certain. Our love is confirmed, and so the happy event that she might have dreaded is now set. She has lost him. She cannot forgive me now, and so her tragedy is complete."

"Complete? Then...Lizzy, I know that Darcy loves you. But by the way that you talk, it sounds like you fully reciprocate his feelings."

My eyes grew misty, I could sense, as I leaned back and confessed everything.

"I do. Darcy and I are now engaged."

When I finished telling her everything that happened, Margaret's exhilaration was complete. But it will never be in the way that one would recognize. Between her refusal to give emotional outbursts, and having a naturally composed disposition, Margaret combined strong feeling with a heavy serenity. Therefore, she was happy for me. Within her eyes, it was so obvious, even when her tone never raised higher or lower than casual conversation.

She expressed her joys and her promises that she knew I would be happy. She confessed a bit of an apprehension of me falling in love with a man that I once despised, but she also knew that I was not the sort to enter an engagement unless I really loved the man. Therefore, she wished me joy.

"When you are not at Pemberley, he will take you back

to the South," Margaret said, at last, "and you will be happy there."

"Yes, the beloved South." I looked on her, concerned. Then I realized that maybe she was sad. And there could be only one reason why. "You are afraid that I will leave you."

"I am happy for you," she said, "but to pretend like I won't miss you, Jane and Kitty, would be irrational. You helped me adjust to this life, and now you are going back."

"Whenever we go to town, you can visit, you know? Besides, we'll spend most of our time in Pemberley, which is very close to Milton. You can always come down."

"I know. And as strange as this is to say, I know that nothing will ever be the same. Change is inevitable, I have learned. But the changes in my life have been so extreme. If change is to enter, and everything is to be taken from me, then let it be taken slowly. But it's all too fast. And with mother..."

"What about your mother?"

Margaret grew pensive.

"I'll tell you about it all on my next visit. But for now, no, I won't make this about myself. This is your time, and it's about you. Elizabeth, you have been—you are one of the greatest friends that I've ever had. I am happy for you, and if I am going to lose you to a happier place, I will not weep. You deserve this. You deserve it all."

"Thank you," I said, truly moved. For I knew that it was difficult for her to say that. After all, she was right. In more ways than one. "Whatever happens after this all, thank you, Margaret."

We shook hands, cementing our bond. Eventually, it came time for her to return home.

Chapter 3

A Proposal Worth the Reconsideration

When leaving Marlborough Mills, Margaret Hale was resolved that once her friends recovered, she would never go to that house again.

And, when walking up the steps to her home, she was also under the assumption that she would rarely see the Thorntons either, unless they were attending a dinner party that Mr. Darcy or Mr. Bingley arranged. Even Mr. Thornton might not desire to be in her company. After all, he might not have been an ungrateful man, but he was a man of business. He certainly would have heard people talk, and rumor spreads quicker than wildfire. As a result, he might not wish to be near her, for fear of confirming those rumors. It was best for them to be away from each other, at present. However, Margaret was like the rest of humanity, and didn't always take into consideration that perhaps other perspectives existed, in this case.

Therefore, her surprise was immense, the shock was paramount, and the alarm was not so very little, when she came home, and Dixon informed her that there was a visitor.

"Miss Margaret, you came just in time," Dixon said, helping Margaret remove her coat and hat.

"Time for what?" Margaret asked.

"He's been waiting for five minutes. Mr. Thornton. He is in the drawing room."

Mr. Thornton!

Margaret felt her chest tighten. Apprehension, discomfort, unease, and all the other anxieties that came from facing the last person that you expected to see! They were descending upon her countenance and inner desire for solitude.

"He's here?" Margaret asked.

"Yes. When I told him that you were out, he said that he would wait."

Margaret looked at herself in the mirror, checking where the scar was on her forehead, and luckily, it had been along her hairline and was covered by the way she had pinned her hair.

"What is it?" Dixon asked.

"Nothing. It's just that time has taught me that, when coming from off the street, one should check oneself. Dirt has a way of finding itself everywhere." Margaret straightened her dress and then had a thought.

"Did he ask for me? Isn't papa come in?"

Dixon's face was a little annoyed, disgruntled by Thornton's presumption.

"He asked for you, miss. And master is out. And your mother is sleeping on the water mattress."

They were to be all alone in the drawing room. This unnerved Margaret greatly, but another part of her was relieved. Since they would be alone, Margaret could address what happened and ask Thornton to not tell her parents about the event until it was necessary. Perhaps she could even learn of what had happened to the Irishmen who they had successfully protected.

"Very well," Margaret confirmed, "I will come."

Breathing in heavily, Margaret walked to the drawing room, and she entered it quietly. When she did so, she was met by Thornton's back. He was facing away from her and was looking out of the window, at the passersby who were walking along the street. Standing there quietly, Margaret was able to analyze the Master, Manufacturer, and Magistrate as he remained there, still as a statue. She wondered what he was thinking. But if his feelings were anything like hers, he must have been filled with a strange sort of dread, but also a binding tie of compassion. Margaret understood the paradox of her emotional state. 'We mortals are such strange things!' Margaret thought.

Thornton was indeed distressed, but it was not because his heart was filled with unease. Rather it was because it was filled with romantic anxiety. The very thought of her touch on his neck when she clung to him so, awoke every passion that beat within him. His heart was awake, and it would never rest again.

"Does the street fascinate you?" Margaret asked, gently.

Her sudden voice shocked him, he started, and he turned around with a jerk. This unnerved him immediately, because this was the last way that he wished to begin. When coming to propose to a woman, a man cannot help but have a dream in his head of how he wished for the scene to occur, but reality shall always have other plans and make

171

other schemes that thwart the dream that one tries to achieve.

"I have startled you," Margaret said heavily, her eyes drooping, with her head thrown a little back, in the old proud attitude that Thornton had seen before. "Forgive me. I thought I would attempt wit. It is best to leave it to others."

"No, it was well done," Thornton responded, "I was simply preoccupied."

When he analyzed her appearance, not only did he take in her posture, but her expression. Altogether she looked like some prisoner.

"You look at me strangely," she observed.

"I see a woman who feels obligated to be here," he noted, "as if she stands before someone, accused of a crime that she loathed and despised, and from which she was too indignant to justify herself."

"You see all that with my silence?"

"Do I see wrong?"

"You must stop misunderstanding me, Mr. Thornton. It will help neither of us."

"Yes. Forgive me. I am beginning this all so terribly wrong. I will rectify that now."

"Never fear. I will not condemn you for one false inter-pretation of my expression. Besides, I have been told that my face does give off a feeling of pride and superiority, but I can assure you, that is not my intent. I suppose that it may very well be how my face is structured."

"Yes, I know a little of that habit. I am told that I have a scowl and stern appearance that makes me appear unap-proachable. Our features have quite betrayed us both, haven't they?"

Margaret sat down.

"Mr. Thornton," she began, "I feel as if we talk of such things, because we dread to talk about what must be talked about."

Thornton felt his passion quicken. She wanted to get to the heart of the matter. She had been the one to bring up the notion of them becoming engaged. Now his courage was rising with the encouragement that he assumed she had given him.

"Yes," he said eagerly, "we ought to talk of it. I long to talk of it."

"I am glad of it," she replied, "we ought to talk of the riot and the effects that it had on the strike and the rioters."

With the rise of his expectations, came the fall, and disappointment took its place. She didn't want to talk of them getting married. No, that thought had never even entered her mind. She wished to talk of the incident. But Thornton now had his dander up, and he did not want to be deterred. She had mentioned the strike, and he would find a way to get back onto the subject that he wished to confront.

"Yes. Speaking of that, Miss Hale, I was very ungrateful yesterday—"

"You had nothing to be grateful for," Margaret refuted, finally looking at him again.

"I do not?"

"No, you do not. You mean, I suppose, that you believe that you ought to thank me for what I did."

"Are you saying that I should not feel grateful to a woman who fought to protect me?"

"I see how I am belittling your sense of gratitude. That is the last thing that I wish to do, for that is a good quality to have. It is just that I wish for you to know me better. It was only a natural instinct. Any woman would have done just the same. Compassion and protection of those in danger is a quality of our sex. Also, I have to take into consideration that I was the one who was responsible for you almost getting hurt."

"How so?"

"I was the one who encouraged you to go down and stand facing them, man to many. My thoughtless words sent you down to danger. I apologize to you for that."

"No apology is necessary nor right to administer," he assured her, desperately. "It was not your words. It was their actions alone that endangered me. No more and no less. But you shall not drive me off upon that, and so escape the expression of my deep gratitude, or my..."

He stopped talking abruptly, and Margaret was not in the mood to remain in awkward silence for long, because this interaction grew heavier by the moment.

"Or your what?" Margaret asked. "What are you trying to say?"

"Forgive me," he said, "it is just that, at times like this, one must weigh every word carefully. I wish for no mistakes to be made."

"Very well. If you need help, I will remind you that you were speaking of gratitude. I will listen because I can tell that interrupting you might cause you distress."

"Yes. What I meant was that I do not want to be relieved from anything. Fancied, or not fancied— I question not myself to know which... I choose to believe that I owe you my very life."

Margaret smiled gently, looking at her lap. Thornton took this as encouragement.

"Aye, smile and think it an exaggeration if you will. Oh,

Miss Hale!" His tone turned tender, and Margaret soon realized this was the exact same expression and tone that Mr. Lennox used when he first proposed to her!

Oh, no, she thought, *not again!*

And thus, she had to embark on hurting another man. And he did not see it coming at all.

But there was hope, Margaret prayed. *Hope that I misinterpreted Thornton's words.*

Hope that she was seeing romance where there was none.

Hope that Thornton's words were spoken out of general gratitude.

Oh, give her indifferent merriment.

Indirect camaraderie.

But not direct passion.

Not emotional fire!

Thus, Margaret did not speak at Thornton's declaration, but let things unfold where they would.

"All this gladness," he continued, "in life, all honest pride in doing my work in the world, all this keen sense of being, I owe to you. And it doubles the gladnesss, it makes the pride glow, it sharpens the sense of existence till I hardly know if it is a pain or pleasure, think that I owe it to one—I owe it to you."

Margaret had heard enough. Her hopes had been in vain. So unnerved by this unwanted proposal, she stood up and walked to the window.

"Please," Thornton urged to her back. "You must—I need you to hear me now. I owe all of this, to one whom I love." Slowly, Thornton walked up behind her. "To one who I have been developing a deep passion for. In ways, that I do not believe any other man ever loved a woman before."

When he finished, he reached around and placed his hand on Margaret's.

Filled with disgust, Margaret moved away from him.

"Please," she urged, "do not speak in this way. And never speak in this way again."

"I beg your pardon?" he asked. "What do I say that makes you react such as that?"

"Your way of speaking shocks me. It is contemptuous."

"Contemptuous?"

"I cannot help it if it was my first feeling. Very well, I acknowledge that it might not have been, if I understood the kind of feeling that you describe. But I do not. For your whole manner offends me."

"How? What did I say that could cause offense?"

"I do feel offended," Margaret stressed, "and I think I am right to do so. You seem to think that my actions, the way in which I attempted to protect you yesterday, was a personal act between you and me. A gentleman would not act in such a way."

"I know that I am very much not a gentleman," Thornton responded, his brow becoming stern once more. "But if being a gentleman means such, then I do not wish to be one."

"Then I cannot agree there. A gentleman would not have immediately assumed, that just because a woman behaved in such a way, that it must mean that she now must be his wife! Mr. Thornton, think! I save your life, so now we must marry. No, a gentleman would perceive that any woman, worthy of the name of woman, would come forward to shield a man in danger from the violence of numbers."

"So, being a gentleman who is rescued is forbidden the relief of thanks! Don't you see the extremity and irrationality of that? I am a man. I claim the right of expressing my feelings."

"And I am a woman. I claim the same. Your habit hurts me, because you assume that..." Once more, her emotion betrayed her, and her eyes grew wistful. "My actions were prompted by some particular feeling for you. I felt no more or less for you than I did for any other in that crowd. I felt as much sympathy for them as I do for you."

"You do me too much injustice on that score. But yes, I am aware of these misplaced sympathies of yours for them," he replied, bitterly. "I know that you despised me for how I was the master of them. But I daresay it is because you do not understand me."

"I do not care to understand," Margaret stressed.

"No, I see you do not. You are unfair and unjust."

"Your pride is not what I believe in!"

"You are too much prejudiced toward me!"

Their harsh words each hurt the other.

Margaret did not respond against such accusations. Her pride had been too much affected and all she could do was stare at him, in silent despondency.

"Have you nothing to say, Margaret?" Thornton asked.

"No, I don't."

"Very well." Thornton picked up his hat. Suddenly, he

was stricken with the desire to have the official last word. After all, when heartbroken, having the final say was the only triumph that could be obtained.

"One more word," Thornton responded, "you look as if you thought it tainted you to be loved by me. You cannot avoid it, and I would not force you to feel anything else but how you choose to. I have not that right. I very well comprehend your feelings, but I will not be ashamed of what mine have been. Toward myself, I will be kinder than how you have been to me. I have the right to love where I love, as you have the right to not love where you don't. So, I say this now. I have never loved any woman before. My life has been too busy, my thoughts too much absorbed with other things. Now I love, and I will love. Do not be afraid of my feelings, or that I will oppress you with them. I say this now, so that I can be silent on it from this moment onward."

"I am not afraid," she responded. "No one yet has ever dared to be impertinent to me, and no one ever shall."

Mr. Thornton moved to the door, but Margaret called after him.

"Mr. Thornton," she sighed more than spoke, "you have been very kind to my father." Her tone was soft and kind. "Don't let us go on making each other angry. Pray, let us be kind to each other."

He took no notice of Margaret's words but continued to the door and opened it, preparing to leave.

Humans can be such surprising things!

Even those of us who are consistent in manner can be surprised at their own instinct.

Margaret, who by all accounts, was mostly still the entire time during the proposal, suddenly was driven by rash action. She moved to the door and closed it before Mr. Thornton could leave out of it.

With her back pressed against the door, she faced Thornton, who was no more than a foot away from her. The closeness of their bodies did not go unobserved by him. Oh, rather he felt the intensity of the proximity of their figures and the heat rose within him. Despite all the angry words that they cast at each other, his desire for her was as strong as ever.

"I heard you," Margaret said, "and I realize that you had a right to speak as you did. Maybe I was rash in not letting you speak as you wished. Maybe your version of proposing to me was out of your belief that you were doing the right thing. I confront that I did willfully wish to misunderstand you. But you do yourself no honor by willfully misunderstanding me. I mean what I say. I do not want us to hurt each other anymore."

"But you hurt me with your little opinion of me. Can you not see how it hurts, Margaret? Can you never see that the extremity of your judgments is not something that is delightful to live under? You have spent so much of our time always casting aspersions upon me, of choosing never to understand my side of things. And yet you want me to change everything I am, to suit you. But you never accepted me at all. That is very unfair."

"When I see wrong, and when I see cruelty, how can I turn away?"

"You turn away from your own cruelty very often. In the future, be kinder to me, and just maybe you might see me for what I am."

"But if your belief leaves me in a place where I can never speak my mind, what is that worth? Where will my freedom go?"

"And where will mine go as well?"

"How can you propose to a woman who, by mere association, lead to both freedoms being oppressed? I have done the right thing, and I cling to it now."

"What do you want from me?" Thornton begged, his eyes becoming wistful, and tears began to swell within them. It never reached the pitch where they flowed down his cheek, however, they were close enough that Margaret could see every emotion in them. This led to an ultimate metamorphosis of her opinion from dislike into something kinder.

"I do not want to hurt you," she uttered. "That was not what I wanted to do. I have never... I have never been very good at learning how to refuse a man when he comes to propose to me."

"This has happened to you before, hasn't it?"

Margaret looked down at the floor.

"I see," Thornton uttered, "I'm just another man who's offered you his heart, and it meant nothing. There is nothing special about me."

"Stop having me hurt you."

"As you ascertained before, we have no choice but to hurt each other."

Thornton looked at the door.

"You are still in my way."

"Because I will not allow you to leave with you feeling like you are unwelcome. You are my father's favorite pupil. He spends his days quoting you, proud of you, and your friendship is one of the joys in his life. I will not allow him to lose you."

"You think that I would be so unkind, so unfeeling, to sever all ties to your father, just because of what has happened between us?"

Unafraid and ignoring all that happened a moment ago, Margaret grabbed his hands and held them up, close to her heart. The very touch of her unraveled his resolve and his strong demeanor. Thornton felt his will crumbling at the mere touch of her.

"Then promise me," Margaret stressed, "always come here to see him. Soon, tragedy will reach him, and he will need support. Your friendship will help him recover and it will be a foundation for him. Please, Mr. Thornton. You call me unjust—well, I am not such now. I know that you are important in our lives. I just cannot love where I do not love. But I will not ignore you, and I will never look away. Do not look away from me now. Promise me!"

Thornton's heart was too overcome.

All sense escaped him, and the feeling of her fingers along his, and the beauty that he faced when looking down on her was too much. Her words fell to the wayside, and her touch was all that mattered. He must touch her more, and obtain a moment of peace in this world, where he was perpetually faced with so much conflict. Sometimes, passionate savagery gets the better of human nature. Thornton was human, not a saint. A human. Great and small all at once.

Therefore, no matter how often she had refused him before, how she had willfully chosen to not understand him, all was forgot. And with that forgetfulness, all logic was abandoned as well, fallen behind him, to be temporarily ignored and done away with.

"Margaret!" he cried harshly, grabbing her by the waist. Before she knew what he was about, he closed the space between them and kissed her rashly.

———

When one party welcomes a romantic act, and the other rejects it, a kiss has two reactions to it.

For Thornton, it provided a pleasant relief from all the rapture that he had swelled up within him.

For Margaret, it was shock. Pure and overwhelming shock.

Despite this, however, she was so blinded by the suddenness of it, that she didn't initially push him off her.

Rather, the interaction was as thus:

For Thornton:

> The joys of embracing the woman
> That he desired was finally achieved.
> Never mind that the next moment
> Would bring utter agony to his heart.
> Forgetting the fact that soon, she
> Would push him off her, and recall
> How much he was not now, nor ever,
> A gentleman. But the rapture, the passion,
> The agony, and the ecstasy was so
> Very overwhelming, that he did not
> Care for the effects that would come
> Afterwards.

For Margaret, it was thus:

'The alarming surprise of it all!'
Never had she experienced anything like it,
In the whole of her life.
Why could she not tear him off her?
Even in that moment, it was unwanted
Undesired.
Unappealing in every way.
After the shock of it fell away,
Her mind rushed back to her,
And she felt sickened.
Her first kiss in her entire life,
And it was with a man who she
Had refused.
It was with a man who did not take
No for an answer.
Even as he continued to kiss her,
She despised him.
For he had taken the most important
Moment of her life from her.
If Margaret did marry someone,
She would have wished him to be the
First man she was intimate with.
But no, she had been robbed
Of that important experience.
Thornton had taken it.

She must stop this!

At last, after what must have been half a minute of the

kiss continuing, she managed to remember herself and she pushed him off her.

When being shoved backwards, Thornton's expression changed from blissful to shame.

"And you expect me to trust you?" Margaret spat. "Now you know why I don't call you a gentleman. Do you know what you just did to me?"

"Yes, I do," he responded. "I don't regret it. But I am sorry. Margaret, please forgive me."

"You will never understand what you've just taken from me. You will never understand."

"Then help me to."

Margaret opened the door. "Get out."

"Margaret...please, forgive me."

"I know that forgiveness is something I must do. But I will not forget. You took my first kiss from me."

His face deflated, under the weight of this discovery.

"I did?" he asked. "Really, I did?"

His tone was so gentle and so innocent that it disconcerted Margaret.

"Yes," Margaret responded. "Please get out and only come back when you are prepared to never do that again."

"Do you forgive me?"

"I said leave."

Thornton sighed.

"I suppose that both of our hearts are broken now."

"I have no heart to break, in this case," Margaret refuted.

"Yes, you do. I see it in your eyes."

With that, Thornton left.

When he was gone, Margaret rushed upstairs, to her

bedroom, collapsed on the bed and finally wept into her pillow.

Chapter 4

Ring the Bell

A h, the blessings of the day. Mr. Darcy remained mostly by my side. He had spent a great deal of the morning buying three self-propelling chairs[1] for Raspberry, Kitty, and me to move around in until we could recover.

"Kitty," Rasby said, "what are we to do? We're supposed to work today."

"I had not thought of that," Kitty recalled, as Colonel Fitzwilliam picked her up from out of the bed and placed her in the self-propelling chair. Next, he lifted Rasby up and placed her in the other one, while Darcy echoed the same action to me. "How quickly the mind goes when one is only thinking of when they can walk again."

"Will Mr. Creevey dismiss you both from the service if you miss days?" I asked them, placing my hands on the wheels.

"Oh, Cringing Creevey will always look for a way to

---

1. Wheelchairs.

throw a woman from his service," Rasby said, "especially since there is always a woman who wants to be a chambermaid."

"Lydia," Colonel Fitzwilliam called, "can you go downstairs and tell Sanderson to go to the hotel and tell Mr. Creevey why Kitty and Rasby won't be coming to work for the next week? Tell him that they were injured in the line of doing a regimental service, and that their positions are to be held for them, until further notice. Also, tell Sanderson to make it very evident that if they are unceremoniously dismissed, then the police will make inquires."

"I wish I could deliver that message to Creevey myself," Lydia said, leaving, "it seems like it would be a good joke to be allowed to intimidate someone into submission."

"Lydia," I said, "in another life, you would have been a very good Tudor monarch."

"Oh, yeah. I'd behead my own cousin if they pushed me far enough."

With that, she left. Colonel Fitzwilliam and Darcy looked at us.

"Lydia was joking," Kitty said.

"Ah," both men said in unison.

Colonel Fitzwilliam ordered Hannah to assist Rasby, and they began to steer our chairs out of the room so that we could finally leave. After all, when in a sickbed for a long time, your limbs begin to hurt and you need fresh air— well, as fresh as the air can get in an industrial town. When we reached the steps, Darcy and Colonel Fitzwilliam picked us ladies up and carried us down the steps. While doing so, Jane and Hannah rolled our chairs down the steps and we were placed in them again, just when the doorbell rang.

The doorman opened it, and we were met by a pleasant surprise.

"I brought someone to cheer you up," my sister, Jane said, her arm linked in Mr. Bell's.

"And I can see that I was timely met!" Mr. Bell said, with flowers in his other hand.

"Mr. Bell!" all three of us ladies said as we were steered toward him.

"You found your way to us," Kitty said as he gave us each a rose.

"Yes. I have a habit of getting gossip quicker than most people in Milton, even when I don't come here for many years."

"You have spies, don't you?" Rasby asked.

"Was there ever any doubt?" He pressed Rasby's chin, then he did something a little unsettling: he actually looked serious. "You both really have suffered a great deal, haven't you?"

"Worried about us?" I asked, with a raised eyebrow.

"I have a right to be."

"Yes, you do. Concern is a lovely trait. And I have a duty to ask you to perform."

"Ah, Miss Elizabeth commands me to do something?"

"In the only way that you can do it."

"What is it that you desire?" he asked.

"Can you please, in your travels, go to Granger Hall and tell Mr. Hanley and Mr. Hunnicutt what has happened to me? Tell them that I will not be able to work tomorrow, but I shall be able to work the day after next."

When hearing this, Mr. Darcy looked down at me.

"The day after next? Elizabeth, you have to recover. You are not fit to work."

"Hard labor, no, but my arm is better, and I can write. Besides, I won't be alone. I will need your help, Darcy. I shall tell you later, but right now, Mr. Bell needs to promise me."

Mr. Bell smiled, sympathetic.

"And I was worried that the favor would be something difficult. Once I leave, I will visit Hanley at his home and let him know everything. He will understand."

"Good, because I can imagine Mr. Dennison rolling his eyes, complaining about female incompetence."

"Ah, that fool! He had his heart broken many years ago, and he's been blaming women for it ever since."

"Oh," I marveled, "really? That's the reason."

"Disappointed affections are often used as an excuse for blind prejudice. It's simply that no one ever talks about it."

"We were taking the ladies out for a bit of fresh air, Mr. Bell," Mr. Darcy responded. "Would you care to lend us your assistance?"

"Which lady am I to have the honor of rolling along?" Bell asked.

"That would be me," Rasby announced.

"Ah, Miss Pitcher." He came up to her and took her chair from Hannah. "Perfect arrangement. This way, you can tell me everything that happened from your perspective."

"About time someone asked, is all I can say," Rasby said as he rolled her to the door. "People look at me in silence, as if they are spooked animals who are afraid of making any noise."

"Ah, the tedious fools! Things were better when I was younger. Yes, yes, they were."

"He always talks about those better days from his

youth," Mr. Darcy whispered to me as he led me to the door, "and forgets all the other problems that existed in that time. The Prince Regent was a waste of space, the abolitionist movement still was not fully successful in Britain yet, the Impressment was a great joke, we were still constantly at war with France, and Queen Victoria was still very young."

"You cannot remove nostalgia from someone, my love," I argued with him, gently. "That's the main sense of security that we humans have to us. Take our present, take our future, but never take our past happy days from us! That is how you drown someone. Even though we ought to care for the present, and for our future, but the past—no, that must remain intact. Come now, would you take our history from us?"

"All we did was argue," Darcy half-smiled.

"And you liked it. If you didn't like it, then you wouldn't have proposed."

"Oh, very well. You have a point."

"Yes. Remember when we danced together for the first time at the Netherfield Ball? Remember when I walked three miles to see Jane and was not fit to be seen? Many years from now, when we look back on those days, no matter how good the future will be, we will say nothing compared to those days when we first met in Hertfordshire. Even our disastrous first meeting at the assembly lends sparkle to things."

"Yes, it does." The men lowered us down the steps, with Jane behind us. "Who ever thought that I would look back on those moments with such immense pleasure?"

"And did you feel pleasure at the time?"

"No, I teetered from one logical thought to a foolish

one. Then I would be out of spirits one day, then agreeable in the next. I wanted to talk to you, but then I didn't know how to endear myself to you. I wanted to propose but knew that I could not. It was a nightmare, in some ways."

"See? Nostalgia."

"Elizabeth?"

"Yes?"

"You make me happy now."

They rolled us along the courtyard, and all the while, I overheard Rasby telling Mr. Bell the full story of all that had happened to her. No one can fully resist hearing such a delicious tale of woe, strife, rioting, and grief. The human spirit is ironic: the more horrible the tale, the more enthralled we are to hear it. Thus, Rasby and Mr. Bell were fully in their element: one as the teller and the other as the eager listener.

As we rode along, we came upon some of the Irish workers. They were in the factory, and they were looking at us through the windows. Unabashed, I stared at them, and then Kitty called out to me.

"Lizzy and Rasby! Look through that window. It's Liam and Colin!"

We turned and, sure enough, Liam and Colin were looking down on us from the windows.

We waved to them. Smiling they waved to us, and then their faces disappeared.

"Are they Irish workers?" Jane, our sister, asked us.

"Yes," I answered. "They were the ones who stood with us when the fight began."

"No one told us what happened to them when we were knocked unconscious," Rasby realized.

"They probably protected us when we fell," I informed her. "I remember, before my eyes closed, they stood over us."

"Did they?" Jane asked. "I must thank them. Can I go in and speak to them?"

She did not need to have the opportunity. Soon, the front door to the factory opened and Liam, Colin, Robert, and John emerged.

"You're all well!" Kitty called to them.

"Aye, we are," Robert said, coming up to us. "Went about the twist for a bit, but we're none the worse."

"We were told you were awake," John said, "but no one was going to let us visit you, and all."

"That was our only reason," Liam stressed. "We don't make it a habit to be ignoring those who look after us, you understand."

"Don't worry, we know," I assured them.

"Brought here to work but not brought here to be allowed to express much else," Colin added. "We should have been allowed to see you. It's not fair, is all."

"You really were worried about us," Raspy said.

"Aye."

Kitty, Rasby and I looked at each other. It was difficult to say anything because they were right. They were not brought here because they were believed in; they were brought here because they were laborers and were replacements. Any feelings they had would never be taken into account.

"Might I have the pleasure of introducing you to my sister, Jane?" I invited, in hopes that it would lighten their darker thoughts. This change of subject seemed to suit them, and I made the introduction. Naturally speaking to such a beautiful woman, who lacked all pretension or prejudice, was enough to endear her to them immediately. I saw all four men's brow lighten when she spoke to them. She thanked them for protecting us, and then asked if they would not mind what the experience was like for them, and what happened when her sisters had been knocked out. Since the men were not currently working, they were happy to speak to her. As a result, they walked amongst Jane, each telling their tale, while the men rolled us along the courtyard.

Rasby and Mr. Bell were also interested in what they had to say, so he steered her chair along the Irishmen, and they listened intently to their perspective. While I was interested, I was like Kitty: we had men we loved, rolling us along, and we rarely got the chances of being alone with them. Therefore, we stayed on the outside of the group, moving along.

"Now," Mr. Darcy said, "what is the favor that you need from me?"

"Mr. Darcy, I thank you very much for getting us these propelling-chairs. They are delightful. And you do not have a woman who will spend her life always asking the world of you. This is merely me trying to do the right thing."

"What is the right thing?"

"I have to work at Granger Hall. It would be wrong not to."

"You suffered an attack."

"I know. But the fact is that I cannot have the last memory of everyone there being that a woman was not able to work when she promised. Believe me on this, it will lead to them having any excuse to not have a female notetaker again. But if I come to work, in my chair, and I write at the desk, they will know that we can weather anything, and that we are not all fancy creatures who cannot recover from things. It is not a good impression to leave. Can you help me? Ride me to Granger Hall, take my chair along, and pick me up at the end of the day."

"But I will not be able to look after you?"

"Well, if you are willing to sit in classes all day, then you can stay with me."

Darcy smiled.

"Loving you would take me back to my studies. That was not in the marriage bargain."

"Many things are left out of marriage bargains. You will spend the rest of your life figuring that one out."

"Very well. If those professors give me the evil eye for lingering, believe me, they will live to regret it."

"Oh, I am sure that they won't. Wo' betide anyone who finds themselves on the other side of your scowl."

"Is my scowl really so terrifying?"

"I thought that was an intention of yours."

"Maybe it was once upon a time." Mr. Darcy looked down at me, concerned.

"What is that look for? I have the feeling that you are about to say something very serious."

"I am. Elizabeth, if you really wish to marry me, you must understand what that means."

"What am I ignorant on?"

"Well, you must quit your job and come to be the mistress of Pemberley. I am not meaning to be oppressive."

Oh, the fear that gripped him, when he did not know

the joys that I found at the idea. He thought that I was feeling abused under his insistence.

"Oh," I replied, chuckling—and the laughter didn't hurt anymore. "Darcy, while I am very happy that you are taking my feelings and freedom into consideration, I understand. I love the life that I have created here, but for our lives to coincide, of course, I must resign from my work. I am happy to return to Pemberley with you. I never got the chance to see this lovely home of yours. Tell me, is Pemberley really all that Miss Bingley said about it?"

"Ah! I was wondering when her name would come up in conversation."

"It had no choice but to. I have fallen in love with a man who was chased after by some very determined women. In the South, there was Miss Bingley. In the North, there is Miss Fanny Thornton."

Darcy looked down at me and his expression betrayed him.

"Ah," I said, "I see that I was not allowed to know that."

"It is not that. It is merely that I was unaware that you knew of Miss Thornton's preference for me. There is no need for alarm. Her fancy is merely derived from me being a novelty, and no more. When I leave Milton, she will forget all about me."

"Is that what men tell themselves when they meet a woman whose feelings for him are very inconvenient? There is no need to feel criticized, I am being merry, and no more. Perhaps you are right in some cases, but not this one. I can assure you that Fanny Thornton's feelings for you were as sincere as Miss Bingley's. In fact, I saw her fully heartbroken."

"She was?"

"Yes. But as is the case with Miss Bingley, it is not your fault. In fact, I daresay, that when one falls in love with someone who does not love them, it's no one's fault. It is just one of those things that happens, and time has to either cure them of the fever or the indifference."

"I guess I should try and pity her."

"I wish you luck. Fanny Thornton and I have never gotten along. I'm not saying that she is very foolish. I am just saying that one of us is being foolish, and *it isn't* me."

Darcy fully laughed at this.

"Either way, the best thing for her would be to hardly ever see me again. When I'm working, she is free from the sight of me, and I would recommend making yourself scarce in her presence. When a person is bent on trying to obtain someone who does not love them, they lose their control, somewhat, and that's when the madness takes hold. Love: the pill of insanity. And yet, would we want it any other way? I don't think so."

"No, perhaps we don't. For maybe, the madness leads to a bad moment in our past, but it makes a great story in the end."

As we circled the factory and soon came back to the place that we began, I realized that I didn't tell Darcy my full plan.

"Darcy, I have an idea of how I can part ways with the professors and end my time there respectfully. This may not be what you wish, but I want their last memory of me to be professional."

"Are you going to make a suggestion that might hurt me?"

"Yes, because it might prolong our wedding."

"Oh, dear. Elizabeth, do not break my heart this afternoon. I could not bear it."

"I firmly believe that it is best to leave a place that I had such a good experience in, by not leaving it until I have secured a replacement. And I have just the person who I think might be good at being a notetaker."

"Who?"

"Charlotte Lucas."

Darcy raised an eyebrow.

"Miss Lucas?"

"Yes. It's because of her loyalty to my family. She chose to reject Mr. Collins's offer of marriage, to show respect for us. She has been repaid by Mr. Collins moving into Longbourn, marrying another woman, removing us from it, and he lords it over her the entire time. I actually think, despite the lesser living conditions, the adjustment of transforming from a country lady to an urban working-class woman, might be difficult. But Charlotte also has notetaking skills. And personally, I think Mr. Hanley and Mr. Hunnicutt liked the idea of having a female notetaker. I think it was refreshing to them to see a female face in the chair."

"But would Charlotte wish to come up?"

"She might welcome the change. Especially if the other part of my plan works."

"What part?"

"While Charlotte learned notetaking, it was not the only skill she learned—nor was she the only Lucas daughter who was taught skills. She and Maria Lucas were taught basic governing skills. Maria was the chief one who special-ized in being a governess."

"Oh! So, Maria Lucas would come up as well, and she would take Jane's place at the Kirkpatricks?"

"Yes. And they would live in our home. It's already paid for. They will pay no rent, and they will be together—away from Mr. Collins. Whatever I feel about Milton, it is a place that gives a person an adventure. Maybe, that's precisely what Charlotte Lucas and Maria need. Of course, I could be wrong, and uprooting to a Northern industrial town in Darkshire might be the last thing that they would want. But it won't hurt to try."

"Well, better to ask than not. Will you tell Jane?"

"As soon as the moment allows it." I looked at the Irish-men. "I get the feeling that they would hate me interrupting their time with her."

"I wonder if she told them that she is spoken for."

"Yes, I wonder."

"Then again, some men have been known not to care about that small technicality."

"Yes, some men perhaps just view it as another obstacle in life that must be overcome."

We both chuckled, until we saw Mr. Thornton.

He had entered the courtyard from the street, and he looked out of sorts.

"Darcy," I said, "look, it's Thornton."

Darcy turned and saw his friend nod quickly to us, his face hard, his eyes heavy, and his scowl was even more disturbed than ever. He walked up the front steps and entered the house without saying one word to us.

"While I am not such a friend to him as you are," I acknowledged, "I get the sense that something is wrong."

"It's because there is," Darcy responded, his brow furrowed. It was not out of anger, but curiosity. I could see it in his eye; he was wondering what new development had upset his host. There is always something going wrong in Milton, it seemed.

Eventually, Liam, Colin, Robert, and John had to return to work. As we were being wheeled back inside the house, I told my sister Jane my plan. She was excited for it, and she offered to write the letter and send it by express. After all, the sooner that Maria would agree, the sooner that she would come to Milton and be interviewed by the Kirk-patricks. In the letter that I dictated, I told Jane to expressly ask the sisters that we would meet them at the railway station, show them around Milton, and see if they could imagine themselves living in such a place. When it was finished, she sent it, Mr. Bell left to report to Mr. Hanley, and there was a sense of everything being put in order.

Except for Mr. Darcy, who had gone off to see Thornton and discover if there was anything amiss. I wondered what could be troubling him.

Chapter 5

Mother & Son, Friend & Friend

When entering Marlborough Mills, Mr. Thornton had to do everything in his power to overcome the anguish that ate away at him.

He had positive bodily pain—a violent headache overcame him, which was a natural reaction to suffering such a passionately resentful rejection. As far as proposals could go, he wondered if one had ever gone so utterly wrong as his had.

As he had walked along the street, everything had antagonized him. From the insufferable noise on the street, to the passersby who appeared light and carefree, which seemed to provoke every bit of pain that rested within him. Every smile, every laugh, seemed to be manifested for just one purpose: to provoke him. To remind him that he was the most miserable creature in the world, for not earning the love of the woman that he treasured.

This thought process was a common one when left alone with one's pain, and then time reminds all that usually, deep down, everyone is crying inside.

A part of him rejected the torment that plagued him.

Another part of him embraced the torment. For, by doing so, it reminded him that he could still feel; that his love was a genuine thing.

Suddenly, movement became unbearable. There, in the middle of the street, he suddenly stopped.

Meanwhile, all the world moved around him, and yet, he barely noticed it. Everything seemed to move at a slow pace and the rush of his heartbreak pushed him into his own realm of inner thoughts. The world outside was now a blur, with people walking past him, and not even noticing that they had come near him to begin with.

What prompted his mind pushing him into a higher plane of reality? Love!

He loved Margaret and would love her in spite of her desires for the reverse. His affection was in defiance of her, and that was the way it would be.

As he remained standing there, an omnibus passed by him. His still and solitary state led the conductor to assume that he wished to get on. So, the driver slowed the bus down and stopped in front of him.

"Wishing for a ride?" The conductor asked.

"I..." Thornton said, beginning to explain that he had not intended to ride. But looking at the conductor, who had an honest-looking face, and seeing this as a means that was symbolic of escape—of miraculously coming in, the last second, and rescuing him from his pain, offering to take him far away from the provocative masses, he realized that maybe this was precisely what was right.

"Yes," Thornton replied. "Why not?"

The conductor looked at him strangely but thought no more of it as Thornton got on, sat in the back of the bus, and allowed himself to be taken anywhere and everywhere.

Through the streets, the bus rode, passed home, passed factory, passed business, and transported Thornton to the edge of Milton and into the country.

Due to his lifestyle, Thornton rarely had time to experience the woodlands, the country gardens, and the hedgerows.

Suddenly, Margaret came back to him in a flash.

This was the sort of world that she came from. That she belonged. Whereas, with him, he belonged to the smoke and industry that was the industrial town.

Now, looking back on it, what was he thinking ever entertaining the notion that she would have him?

But he loved her still, and there was nothing he could do about it.

Eventually, the bus rode into a small country town and when the conductor saw him at the back of the bus, he called for it being the end of the line.

Thornton walked up to the front, paid his fare, and then said that he would just sit there, in the back of the omnibus. Then he would take the ride back home.

"Right," the conductor said. As Thornton turned around to move to the back again, the conductor called out to him. "So, are you running from something? Or running to it?"

Thornton turned back to him.

"I'm not sure," was Thornton's answer.

"Well, whatever it is, it gets better."

"I'm not sure," Thornton said again.

"Well, I am. It always does."

Thornton nodded to him, appreciatively, and sat back

Ney Mitch

down. Looking out of the town as they rode through it, he turned around and headed back to Milton.

All the while, his mind was directed to Margaret. There was no hope for him. His heart was lost to her.

When he finally did return to Milton, he thanked the driver again, and it was a heartfelt and heavy sort of thanks. He paid his fare, then walked to Marlborough Mills. When he entered the courtyard, it was to see Darcy, Colonel Fitzwilliam and Mr. Bell rolling the Bennet ladies and Rasby around in the chairs, and they were speaking with the four Irishmen. He nodded to them quickly and then entered the home.

When he was alone in the vestibule, suddenly, he froze again. The large house that he aspired for all his life, now felt very empty and possessed a coldness to it that he knew was exuded from his own inner musings and torment. He would have to go on with his life, continuing to work and live as if nothing within him had broken. Steadying himself, he walked along the first floor of his house.

Hearing the familiar sewing sounds, he walked into the drawing room, where he saw his mother, sitting down. When she saw him, she looked up at him, and her expression was grim. Thornton was aware that she was both eagerly and dreading awaiting the news of him now being engaged to Margaret Hale.

For a moment, they only just stood there, looking at each other and then looking away.

This waiting antagonized Mrs. Thornton. She was made of strong stuff and knew how to bear such hard news.

"Well, John?" she said, "if you are silent to spare my feelings, then I am prepared. I know that...well, I have had a full day to prepare to change the initials on our handkerchiefs. I can withstand hearing the reason why."

Thornton opened his mouth, and wished that he had better news to give, or at least a clever way of distributing the truth, but there was none. This was his mother. And though he had a hardness to his nature, he found himself breaking like the little boy that he once was so long ago. Then again, what is the worth of being an adult if you are not allowed to become a child once in a while?

Walking up behind her, he leaned down and kissed her stony face.

"No, Mother, your son does not return with a fiancée. Margaret Hale will not have me. No one loves me—no one cares for me, but you."

He stood up straight again, fighting back the tears that were in his eyes.

She stood up suddenly and turned to him. Thornton tried to move away from her, to hide the anguish and sadness in his face, but Mrs. Thornton would have none of it.

"No," she said, her stern demeanor giving way to a sympathetic and ultimate maternal figure, "do not look away. Look at me and see nothing else in me but a desire to be there for you. Do not be afraid of any of it. I am here. I am here!"

Wrapping her arms around his neck, she hugged him. The warmth of her embrace undid all of Thornton's strength. He collapsed in her arms, and she had to sit down as he rested his body against hers and cried into her neck.

All his agony.

All the words spoken.

Every image of Margaret Hale.

It all flashed through his mind in a quick succession.

For a brief moment, Mrs. Thornton felt as if all the years had fallen away, and she was holding her seven-year-old boy again, when he came home crying when a child had bullied him.

And he was such again.

After a moment of her rocking him as if he was a baby, she began to offer him all her reassurance that she could bestow.

"A mother's love is strong and immovable. It holds fast forever. A girl's love is like a puff of smoke; it changes with every wind. And she would not have you, my boy, would not she?"

Suddenly, the truth really began to affect Mrs. Thornton, and her speech of solace now turned to resentment toward the woman who had broken her son's heart. It was strange because Margaret Hale had indirectly given her what she wanted. John was still her son, and not Margaret's, which made her happy—internally. She didn't want to lose her son to a wife, but that meant nothing. For Miss Hale rejected John, and that was as bad as accepting him.

If Margaret chose him, she would be uneasy.

If Margaret didn't choose him, she would be enraged.

Now her anger could be unleashed.

"She wouldn't have my son!" Mrs. Thornton declared, irate. "The foolish proud and insufferable prig!"

"I am not fit for her, mother. I knew I was not."

"Yes, you are. You are worth ten times what she is."

"Mother," Thornton said, recalling the kiss that he shared with Miss Hale, and the pleasure that he got from it,

"I do not want to hear a word against her. As sad as this is to admit, my heart is weak now, and it hurts to think of her, as well as to think ill of her. In truth, I love her more than ever."

"And I hate her. I tried not to hate her when she protected you, and because I thought she would make you happy. But now I hate her, for your sake. You cannot tell me to do anything else. No true mother would do less. Your sorrow is my agony, and if you don't hate her, I do."

"You must not talk of her that way, for me. Because I love her, and hearing of your hate only rings my heart more. She does not care for me, and that is enough. Please, spare me, and let us never talk of this again. Be there for me now and let us never speak her name again."

"With all my heart," Mrs. Thornton vowed, "I only wish that she, and all her family, can be swept back to the place they came from."

They spoke of the strike, of men who were arrested, and they returned to where they used to be like again.

Later that evening, Mr. Thornton found Mr. Darcy in the library, writing a letter. When he met his friend, he poured himself some scotch and inquired of what he was doing.

"Making arrangements," Darcy said. "I'm writing to my sister, Georgiana."

"Oh, how does she do?"

"She is well. She wonders why I have been gone for so long. But now that I might return with a bride, I want to inform her that I will be returning to London very soon."

This announcement made Thornton start.

"What do you mean?" he asked.

Darcy turned to him, comprehension dawning on him that Thornton had been quite ignorant of the goings on in his life.

"Thornton, there has been so many changes lately, that I had no time to tell you everything. But Miss Bennet..."

"Elizabeth..."

"Yes. She loves me. And she's finally consented to be my wife."

Darcy unfolded everything that had occurred. While he listened to his friend's happy news, Thornton was quiet. He so much wanted to be happy for Darcy, but their experiences were so different. He was marrying a woman that he loved, while Thornton just returned from being rejected by a woman he loved.

For a time, envy overtook him and he, once more, coveted the life that his friend had. But he did his best to suppress these feelings and continued to listen. When Darcy finished telling him about how he would give Elizabeth more time, in case her feelings sprung from a place of gratitude from helping save her, rather than out of true love, Thornton's emotions thoroughly betrayed him. Sadness swelled up in his eyes, and perhaps tears might have begun to form.

"I am...very happy for you. Elizabeth and you will make —a splendid pair."

Darcy was not one to ignore when his friend had been overcome in some way.

"Thank you, but your expression says otherwise. Thornton, what is wrong?"

"Nothing."

"Yes, something is wrong. Come now and tell me. You would do well to confess it."

"It is a personal matter, and I do not wish to speak of it," he said, harshly. Standing up, he went to the fire and stared into it. "I don't want to talk of it."

"Yes, I can see that you evidently do," Darcy said, unafraid. Standing up, he joined Thornton by the fire and echoed his friend's actions. "Must it always be like this between us? With one having something to tell, the other too proud to say it, and then the fire makes us realize that we have nothing to lose?"

"I promised that I would never speak of this again."

"What is important to talk about is never wise to not address."

"I do not want to be the sort of friend who drowns out your happy day with my own inner distress. What sort of friend would I be if I did that?"

"I'm the Master of Pemberley, Thornton. I can have my happiest day include a distressed friend in it. Now, if you were to do such a thing on my wedding day, then I would be upset. But since that is not the case, I am here to listen."

"It's more than that. I am embarrassed."

"Why? I will not know if you do not tell me."

"I thought...that maybe she loved me, in the way that I loved her."

Even though Margaret's name was not mentioned, Darcy had a fairly good idea that she was the woman in question. Darcy rubbed his lips.

"Thornton, where did you come from just now?"

Thornton opened his mouth and then closed it, for it was too hard to say.

"Thornton, if it is too difficult, just say yes or no. Did you come from visiting the Hales?"

Thornton's eyes grew wistful.

"Did you see Margaret Hale?"

"Yes."

"Did you propose to her?"

"Yes."

Darcy rubbed his eyes. He knew where this was going.

Darcy moved away from his friend, to give him privacy, because he knew that was the main thing that Thornton needed. He walked to the furthest window in the room and stared out of it.

"How painful was her rejection?" Darcy asked.

"You knew she rejected me?"

"I didn't need to figure it out. Your expressions said it all."

"Yes, I suppose they did. Darcy, I daresay that it was the worst proposal ever, and the worst rejection perhaps."

"I do not say this out of trivializing your pain, but because I know what I know. I am sure that it was not the worst proposal or rejection ever."

"You weren't there. You didn't see it. Margaret Hale does not love me, but rather, she was repulsed at the idea of me loving her. She never desired my good opinion, and she only protected me yesterday, in a general sense. I thought it meant something, but it meant nothing."

"Well," Darcy determined, "it is strange to hear this."

"Is it? You seemed to be more aware of the truth of us, than anyone."

"No, I speak of other things. I speak of coincidence."

"Coincidence?"

"Yes. Never mind, it's not important. I just...you

proposed because you believed that her saving you indicated something else other than just general compassion? Oh, Thornton, why didn't you come to me and ask me? I would have told you."

"Told me what?"

"Margaret Hale is not the sort of woman who feels things in that sort of way. That action never meant love. I know how easy it is to misconstrue such a feeling, but I would have advised you to wait a little longer before you proposed. Time was meant to be your friend."

"Time would not have been my friend. Miss Hale does not love me, and she never will."

"Never is too permanent a word. Miss Hale simply doesn't know you yet. She needs more time to understand the sort of man that you are. She still has certain prejudices that are in its place and need to be overcome. Also, she is very much attached to her family, and sometimes, a woman cannot see herself making any change. We all think every woman wants to get married by the time they are Margaret's age, but that's not the case. Many women and men need more time to figure out who they are, and who they wish to be. Your proposal came at a time where she still does not know what to make of you. Give her time, then when she's ready, try and establish a friendship. When it feels like she's prepared for your love, try again."

"You don't understand, Darcy. She practically said that she could never desire me."

"Did she say that you were the last man in the world who she could ever be prevailed upon to marry?"

"No."

"Then don't tell me that I don't understand, because I do. For that's where I was."

Thornton turned to Darcy, astonished.

"That really did happen to you?"

"Yes. And now that woman and I are getting married."

"Miss Elizabeth Bennet."

"Yes. Miss Elizabeth Bennet."

———————

When hearing this, Mr. Thornton was enthralled. He knew sections and portions of the history behind Darcy and Elizabeth's relationship, but now it was being fully explained.

"She hated me, Thornton," Darcy elaborated, "and, looking back on our relationship, I gave her some reason."

"As I did when I first met Miss Hale?"

"Yes. That is what I mean by coincidence and that I had wished for you to have spoken to me first. I didn't want you to have to go through that. It can be...overwhelming."

"Overwhelming? Is this what this is, Darcy? You know it's not. It's as if there is a weight upon me, and I cannot be released from it. Everywhere I look, it's there. This house, this place that I fought for—oh, I fought so very hard to have it for us—and it antagonizes me now. I see where she fell, defending me, when I carried her inside. And then when I go out, this agony is always in my mind."

"It just occurred. It's going to be that way. You, like the rest of humanity, is not allowed to rush past heartbreak like it was never supposed to exist. Well, we are not given that luxury. And perhaps, it's best that we are not. You will feel this for a long time. Thornton, why didn't you come to me first? I would have told you not to pursue it just yet."

"Well, I made a mistake. And now I am suffering for it."

"Yes. I suppose that it was always going to happen this

way. Even if you give advice, people will ultimately do what they will do. Thornton, I am sorry. I know the pain you are suffering under."

"How did you continue on like this, and pretend that nothing happened?"

"Because I had to, and so will you. You will wake up and hold that anguish inside of you, but you will put one foot in front of the other, and you will find a way to keep living. But you will also still cling to hope, to a desperate hope, that one day, you might achieve that great love. A part of you wants to run, as far as you can, to escape the anxiety of it all. But it will always find you again."

"What do I do now?"

"You don't run. But you keep going. When you see her again, you must not run from her either. Rather, do the reverse. Speak to her as you did before, but instead, this time, try to take her disposition into account. In fact, I will speak to Elizabeth about this to try to ascertain how Margaret will anticipate you."

"No," Thornton refused. "I don't want her to learn about this."

"Well, I do not agree, nor will I accept that. Thornton, you are my dear friend, but there is no way that I shall conceal anything from Elizabeth again. When I did that before, I was met with a refusal, because I didn't let her see the man that I was. She and I will never misunderstand each other again. I will tell her everything that goes on in my life, especially since I know that she will hear it in confidence, not telling anyone else. She will help me, and by extension, she will help you."

"Are you that much in love that there are to be no secrets between us?"

Darcy looked at Thornton, unphased.

"If the roles were reversed, Margaret and you were engaged, and I had come to you about being rejected by Elizabeth, while she was friends with Margaret, what would you do? Would you leave Margaret in the dark, not being one together, but being separate?"

Thornton swallowed, understanding what Darcy was implying.

"Therefore," Darcy continued, "to answer your question, yes, I am that much in love. And I regret none of it."

"Forgive me. I was not being considerate of other perspectives. Of course, you would tell Miss Bennet."

"And she will help, believe me. Then, when you and Margaret have learned to get along better, have also gathered a wider acquaintance with each other, then you can try again."

"Try again?"

"Yes, John. Try again."

"But she won't have me."

"Stop talking when I am trying to give you hope. Yes, you are right. She might never have you. But you and she never gave each other time. I am trying to give you time. So, take it. Be patient with her, be kind to yourself, and believe in time."

Thornton was holding down his emotion.

"And you are going to marry soon, and leave here?" Thornton asked.

"Thornton, my sister is back down South, and Elizabeth deserves to finally go back home. You and I both know that it's time for me to go."

"But you leave now, when I am so confused of where to go and what to do."

"You will find your way. Remember, I did. Come now, Thornton, I am getting married. Be happy for me."

"I am! I can assure you. Is there any way that you will marry here, in Milton?"

"I had planned to wed in Derbyshire, so that my county could see it."

"But think first," Thornton urged, like a drowned man, "You have so many friends here. Would riding off and marrying somewhere else really satisfy you? Think on us first. That's all that I ask."

Darcy took Thornton's feelings into account and knew that it was best to at least consider it.

"I will give it some thought and see what Elizabeth thinks."

"I am happy for you, Darcy. Really, I am."

"I know," he said, patting him on the shoulder. They both looked in the fire, with one in his happiest state, and the other was in agony.

Chapter 6

Oh Dear!

T he next day brought Kitty, Rasby and I closer to healing. Lydia also remained with us during that time, and my goodness, was she a surprising help. Not only was she now fully equipped with being a nurse who tended to the wounded, but she also was animated. Her spirits were lively and busy, therefore, she was able to bring life to us.

Mr. Lowe, the surgeon, came to check on us once more, but he only ended up reiterating what Plato had said when he inspected us. Concerned for us, Plato had taken some guarding shifts, and he could come in and prescribe what would happen to us. Soon, it became very evident that none of us suffered internal bleeding, and that our wounds were all ones that would heal. There would be scars, but fortunately, the worst ones were not on our face. This was quite a relief, because I could greet the servants at Pemberley with having no battle scars along my cheek. I had one along my forehead near my hairline, but fortunately, I always believed in having bangs, and they covered it well.

The most curious thing that occurred was the day before I was working. I was sitting in the drawing room, for we had been allowed to leave the bed again, and I received a letter from Margaret Hale.

When I finished reading it, I was a little unnerved. There was something about it that felt a little...funny.

When Mr. Darcy came to visit me that day, to tell me the arrangements for when I worked tomorrow, he sat near me and I immediately began to appeal to him.

"It's the strangest thing," I began, "Margaret has written to me that she will not come and visit, because she fears that her presence here will be awkward for the Thornton family. Therefore, once we return home, she will visit us then. But if there are any developments, where our health takes a frightful turn, then she will brave their displeasure and come anyway. What could drive her to think so? After all, she was one of the principal reasons that the strike was broken."

In Darcy's eyes was something else, and I saw it.

"You know something, don't you?"

"Yes," he answered simply, "I cannot tell you here." He told Lydia that he was going to take me to the library.

"Yes, yes, I know," Lydia said, dismissively, "go off and be lovers."

I sighed at her rash manner but didn't feel like correcting it.

Darcy led me out of the room, and then to the library. Once we were there, he closed the door behind us and immediately began to explain.

"Your friend has every reason not to come and see you all," he explained, "in fact, I firmly believe that if she came here, Mrs. Thornton might want to claw her eyes out."

"Why?" I replied, "She defended her son."

"And Miss Hale also rejected her son."

My eyes widened.

"My love," Darcy began, "what I tell you, must be in confidence. Promise me this?"

"Yes, I do. But nothing you say now will make me assume any less than that Mr. Thornton made some sort of romantic gesture to Margaret—the last woman in the world who would have wanted that."

"Precisely. The day after the riot, he went to Crampton Crescent and proposed to her."

I closed my eyes and leaned against my wheelchair.

"How terrible was her rejection?"

"It was the same as your rejection to me."

I sighed.

"Yes, I can imagine that it was."

Darcy told me everything that Mr. Thornton had told him. The only thing missing now was Margaret's side of the story, which I now eagerly wished to know of. When he finished his narration, Darcy appealed to me immediately.

"Elizabeth, I need your advice on what to do next?"

"Next? Darcy, this is between them. How can I advise you? Oh, never mind that last sentence! I am willing to help if I may, especially since I like it when you tell me everything and given me a say in the matter of things."

Darcy smiled.

"I was hoping that I was doing the right thing."

"You anticipated me," I replied, smiling. "I like that. Now go on and don't leave me in suspense any longer. Or I shall be cross with you—even though I have no reason to be cross."

Darcy chuckled again; I performed another miracle.

"What we have are two friends, who have made each other quite unhappy. They had improved a great deal since they met, but there is still much misunderstanding between them. It's almost as if there is a desire to continually misinterpret one another's actions and feelings. And it has led to one loving, and the other resenting."

"Yes, their relationship was founded with a great deal of prejudice involved. And they never reached a true balance. A proposal founded on such imbalance was never going to be a good idea. Oh, Darcy, why didn't he ask you first?"

"That's what I said!"

"You did?"

"Yes. I wish he had come to me."

"They both needed more time."

"That's what I said!"

Oh, dear!

Rubbing my eyes, I smiled at him.

"How does that feel?" I asked him. "To have known how to solve the problem and then to feel so very helpless because you were never given the opportunity?"

"Well, now you know how it felt when I offered romantic advice to Bingley. It's very easy to give advice, because you worry that if you never said anything, chaos would ensue. After a time, maybe it was best that Thornton didn't come to me. Or at least I told myself that, because maybe this is a road that he needs to walk down."

"It's the same road that you walked down," I noted.

"Yes, it is."

"And what is it like to see Thornton have to tread the territory that you had to journey along?"

"Perhaps it's the same as you felt when you saw that Margaret is having the same path you had to undergo."

"Oh, yes," I sighed, "the irony is not lost on me. I wonder...did we cause this?"

"What makes you say so?"

"Well, out of our desire to get along with each other and move on from the very tense history that you and I had, our friends were constantly thrown together, to accompany us. If it weren't for us, would Margaret and Mr. Thornton have developed such a wide acquaintance? Or maybe I am giving us too much credit. Thornton is Mr. Hale's pupil, and Margaret and him would have had quite a chance to both tolerate and torment each other. As you said, it might have all ended the same way, no matter what we had done."

"But it is interesting to marvel at. Isn't it?"

"Yes, it is."

Once I realized that I still hadn't given him an answer, I realized that it was best to do so.

"Well, I will not make any judgments before I have spoken to Margaret first. That would be the best thing. For, while it is best to sometimes allow them some separation, I don't think so in this case. For when you and I parted ways after the first proposal, maybe it wasn't good that we spent so long not understanding each other. It all depends on them. And that is something that I am going to get to the better of. I'm not going to wait to return to Frances Street to meet her again. I want to send her a letter to meet me at Granger Hall tomorrow, after her father's lesson. We can escort them home, and I can discover what she is feeling, then I can offer her advice on what is best to do. I'll tell you and we can plan from there?"

"That is perfect for Thornton."

"I am happy to help. Now, can I trouble my fiancé to take dictation and begin to write the letter for me as I speak?"

"Yes, you can."

Darcy wrote the letter, and Hannah took the letter to Crampton Crescent.

"Well," I said, "it's all a matter of time, isn't it?"

"I said that too!" he declared, in his quiet but strong way.

I rolled my eyes.

"Oh dear. We've got to stop doing that. Or we will forever be losing our originality."

I took his hand and kissed it.

"Do you know what?"

"What?"

"You're quite the handsome man."

"And you better never forget it."

Coming to me, he kissed me passionately.

Chapter 7

The Painful Hours

When Margaret went to visit Bessy again, she came upon a horrible sight. As she reached the Higgins's door, she heard screaming and arguing going on, and also heard Bessy cry 'stop fightin', please!'

Standing at the door, Margaret halted, alarmed in hearing a confrontation.

What was she to do? It was always so difficult in such matters, even if a person had the ability to act at all. For, initially, one does not move when one is met with such a circumstance. Rather they are rooted to the spot, and their instincts freeze on them. Margaret was undergoing such an experience. Besides, she recognized both male voices. One was Nicholas Higgins and the other was Boucher.

"I'll give you up!" Nicholas cried, "I'll give you up, John Boucher. Everyone will know that it's you!"

Margaret heard scuffling toward the door, but still, she couldn't move. When the door was yanked open, she came face to face with Boucher.

Ah, the horror of seeing her there!

And then, behind Boucher, pursuing him like a harpy, was Nicholas Higgins.

As he rushed up to Boucher to push him out, he also saw Margaret's face over his fellow union man's shoulder.

And Margaret still did not move.

For, before her, was a sight that she could never unsee.

Boucher!

His expression was anguish, despair, a general air of hopelessness and failure. Of a man who had never wanted to be in the strike, who had no desire to have walked down this path, and he ruined the destination for everyone.

Nicholas!

His eyes were alight with fiery rage and resentment. Of a man who once was filled with a dream. A dream that, one day, he could have control over his future, and the rights of the working man would follow. And now he was ruined. And the root, the very source, of his disappointment could be personified in one man: Boucher.

But when they looked on Margaret, their faces underwent a series of expressions inspired by a variety of emotions.

First, there was shock in seeing her.

Second, there was a frozen look, where their previous altercation was forgotten by them and all other thought had quite fallen away.

Thirdly, there was shame at being overheard.

Fourth, there was the assessment that they were facing a lady as two lumps of failures.

Nicholas had firmly believed that they had a good chance of winning this time. He boasted of it to Margaret Hale.

Boucher was aware of the violence that was inflicted on

the woman who stood before him—and how it was all his fault.

Therefore, their fifth expression had become one and the same: they didn't want her to see them. They didn't want her eyes, her innocent, but removed eyes, to look at either of them just now.

"I'm sorry," Boucher uttered. "My wife told me that you came. I am sorry."

"Sorry?" Nicholas cried, remembering his hate now, "You think that changes anything!"

"Stop!" Bessy cried from her bed. "Please, there is no use in fightin' now."

However, Nicholas was too much on a rage. He grabbed Boucher, and Margaret only had just enough time to move out of the way when Boucher was shoved across the street, overcome.

"Clear yourself away from my house."

"Nicholas," Margaret uttered, "he made a mistake." Margaret turned to Boucher, but it was too late. Boucher had, once more, run off.

Nicholas followed his retreat with his eyes, and Margaret was now acting on instinct. She walked up to him and touched his arm. He turned to her, his face still filled with venomous scorn. But when he looked down at her, his anger died away, and despair took its place.

"Mistake?" he repeated. "That's the word you put to it? Mistake? He ruined the strike. He ruined every chance for us to have a better life."

Margaret didn't respond, but only still looked at him.

"You could have died, Margaret," Nicholas uttered. "You could have been killed. Along with Elizabeth, Kitty and Rasby."

"We are fine. We all will recover."

"That doesn't matter. His mistake almost cost four women their lives, and our children a better future." Tears began to fill his eyes, and he sensed it. So, he turned away from her. "Don't look at me. You mustn't look at me now!"

With that, he rushed along the opposite direction and disappeared down the street.

"Margaret!" Bessy cried. "Come in."

Unable to follow either man to calm him down, Margaret walked in the house and closed the door behind her. She rushed to Bessy's bedside—because now, Bessy was fully bedridden—and sat down beside her.

"Why didn't yer tell me?" Bessy asked.

"What?" Margaret responded.

"That it was yer? Why didn't yer tell me that the violence the riot put on the women was yer, Elizabeth, Kitty and Rasby? It was yer all that they hurt."

"Calm yourself, Bessy," Margaret said, "you are sick and don't need to be upset."

"I'm dying!" Bessy cried. "I've accepted that, and now so must yer."

The thawing of ice, the crumbling of stone, and the destruction of the emotionless! Though Margaret had always said that she despised the idea of outrageous emotional display, she could not help but allow sadness to creep over her features. Bessy's declaration had cut her to the quick and she was rendered speechless as her eyes became heavy.

"Oh, Margaret," Bessy whispered, resting her head on the pillow. "I'm not afraid. I never have been. Yer know that."

"Yes, I know that."

"Soon, my earthly cares will be over."

"Bessy..." Margaret sighed, wistful.

"In the litt' bit of time that I have left, let me know everythin'. Is Lizzy, Kitty and Rasby alive?"

"Yes," Margaret stressed. "When I last saw them, they were injured, but it was very evident that they will recover and survive this all."

"I'm sorry for what yer all had to endure because of this."

"It's not your fault."

"No, it's not. But someone has to apologize, and Fate won't, I reckon."

"Bessy, what did your father mean by saying that he would give Boucher up?"

Bessy breathed heavily as Margaret held her.

"Margaret, it's awful, is what it is. By Boucher leadin' the riot, he now makes men like papa, and I look like the very savages that papa was tryin' to avoid. The ones who attacked Elizabeth, Kitty, and Rasby have been caught and arrested, but there are others that the law is lookin' for. That includes Boucher. He was the one who led them all, and so father reckons that he is the one who is ultimately responsible. Boucher asked us to hide him, so that the police don' seek him out. They had a row, with father sayin' that Boucher was only born into this world to tear us all down with him. And that he was a disgrace to all of us. Then father told him that we would never protect him, and that he would turn Boucher over to the police. That's when they fought, and father drove him away."

Margaret listened and was attentive. While she was greatly affected by this all, she tried to remain impartial and productive. She could not go back in time and undo it all.

No one could. Therefore, all that could be done was move forward and try to offer the best solution that she could—a solution that she knew would very well be ignored.

"Bessy," Margaret said at last, "Boucher was wrong to do what he did, but he was starving, his family was hungry, and he wasn't in his right mind. In fact, when I was there, looking down on those faces, I knew what they were. They were driven mad from all the hunger, the disappointment of their hopes being dashed, and the demons that can taunt a person when they are not given useful employment. And between that, I now wonder if an angry riot was inevitable. I wish that it was not, but I cannot help but wonder if it would always arrive at that conclusion. I am not justifying Boucher or any of the others. I am disturbed and hurt by what they did to Elizabeth, Kitty, Rasby, and what they aimed to do to the Irish."

"And to yer."

"My injury was not intentional. They intended to strike Thornton. I pushed myself in his way, to protect him. I was a surviving casualty. No, Lizzy, Kitty, Rasby and the Irish were the real victims. I am angry for how they were treated. But, sometimes, when people are angry, and they come together, their minds link, they lose independent thought, and they become one mind—and that's a mind of madness and cold resentment. I think their individual voices got lost in the process and now they have it back...and they are mortified at what they did. Do you have any influence over your father? Can you persuade him to forgive Boucher and not give him up? He has six children and a wife who cannot work. Can he do it for them? Can Nicholas do it for them?"

"I'll try, Margaret. But you know how father is...when his will is set..."

"It's set."

"Precisely."

When Bessy's sister, Mary, returned from visiting a friend, Margaret felt capable of leaving Bessy in her hands. When she left, she had not gotten the chance to see Nicholas, and she probably was happy that she didn't. As Bessy explained, Nicholas was strong-willed; he would return angry and the last thing he needed to see was a guest. Sometimes, one just needs family by them.

Yet, walking is not only beneficial exercise, but it gives a person time to think, to contemplate everything, and to look at the great map of their lives and see where it all went right or wrong.

And so, the hammer came down in the hardest way. Margaret was perturbed by this report and felt pangs of empathy for them. How can there be an answer to all of this that could bring about a steady peace? But it seemed like pacifism, or balance, was not something that the Masters and Men were capable of achieving in Milton. It was as if, everywhere there was crisis. It only added to her disdain for this sort of life. It turned men into cruel beasts, and it tore the beauty and bloom from womanhood. 'If only' slowly began to become the words spoken more than anything in her heart.

If only the workers had not gone on strike.

If only Thornton and the other masters had the ability to give the workers the raise that they wanted.

'If only' the workers had maintained their practice of nonviolence.

If only father had not brought them there.

If only the church had not forced her father into doctrines that were erroneous for him to swear to, and that her mother had been given a stronger constitution.

If only the factories were not so dangerous to live in.

IF ONLY the workers and the masters could sit and talk amongst each other, like equals, and find a sturdy balance.

But all those 'if onlys' came to nothing because the reality was what it was. There was no going back. Everything that she didn't want, she now saw and experienced. Everywhere, there seemed to be nothing but loss. She lost her home, her community, all that was familiar, almost lost her life, and now she was soon to lose Bessy, her mother, and the Bennet sisters were all going to leave and return to the South, or the Northern country.

God forgive me, Margaret whispered in her mind, *if you are to take everything from me, then couldn't you take it slowly? Why did it all have to be taken all at once? No one likes losing what they love.*

But to lose so much, from one month's end to the next, could only tear away at someone for but so long before it drove them mad. But also, where was there to go forward?

Eventually, she arrived back to Crampton Crescent, and she halted. Standing in front of her house, she found that she couldn't go in.

Those were the steps that Mr. Thornton walked up to when he came to propose to her.

The drawing room was where he had spoken those

overwhelming words that caused an even greater rift between them.

And suddenly, Margaret felt a pang of guilt. While she didn't regret her refusal, she did regret the pain that she may have caused Thornton. Her guilt was like a disappearing and reappearing knife wound; it would come and go, stabbing at her self-certainty.

If only...

Chapter 8

Getting to the Heart of the Matter

T he next day came time for me to go to Granger Hall. I woke up, Lydia helped dress me, Mr. Darcy carried me down to the breakfast room and we ate with Mrs. Thornton. She didn't contribute much to the conversation while we ate, but that was well, for I knew why. My presence antagonized her daughter, and though Mrs. Thornton was not a gentle mother, she was a mother, nonetheless. Naturally, her heart would go out to her daughter, and not towards the woman who thwarted her daughter's happiness.

First, I found myself suffering the awkwardness of the Bingley sisters at Netherfield Park, where I tended to Jane when she was an invalid.

Now, I found myself suffering the awkwardness of the Thornton ladies at Marlborough Mills, where I was now the invalid.

I just could not win.

As Darcy escorted me to Granger Hall, in a carriage, I unfolded this all to him, and he was equally as amused.

"I swear, Lizzy," Darcy concluded, "whether you're in the North or the South, you are met with the same sort of obstacles."

"Yes. That trend does tend to follow me, doesn't it?"

Eventually, we arrived at Granger Hall. The first person to approach me, while Darcy rolled me along in the chair, was Mr. Hunnicutt. His jovial manner was enough to remind me of better days gone past, and even better days going forward.

"Miss Bennet!" he cried, eagerly accosting us. "We have not been in a right state since we heard the news."

"It's nice to see someone happy to see me, Mr. Hunnicutt," I said as he took my hand and kissed it.

"Oh, nonsense! Even Dennison missed you."

"I find that hard to believe."

"Oh, believe it. Some people are born with a need to hate. So, when the object that they exert all their anger towards is gone, they lose their way."

"Well, I am happy I served a purpose, other than the other reasons that I prefer to be here for."

I was pleased to see Darcy trying to be more approachable, and less stoic as he talked to Mr. Hunnicutt.

"Now, come, dear lady and noble carriage driver," Mr. Hunnicutt said, "my class awaits. But Miss Bennet, I wish that you had not come. I don't want you to exert yourself when you have every right to be home, recovering."

"I see the logic of your concern," I said, "and normally, I would give in to such a proscription. After all, one must do what the doctor orders. However, I found that I could not."

Darcy steered me into the lecture hall and Hunnicutt placed my desk down for me and prepared my paper and pen.

"Why not?" Mr. Hunnicutt asked. "You deserved the rest. After all, a hero ought to be allowed time to recover."

"First, thank you for calling me something so very flattering, but I am no hero."

Hunnicutt turned to Darcy.

"She belittles herself. What shall we do?"

"Never fear," Darcy assured him, "I will do everything to persuade her to take our praises and bear them with fortitude."

"Good man."

"Very well," I said, "you have forced me to appeal to my own vanity, and I will indulge you both for the moment. However, it was strange, but I found that if I didn't come to work, I would go mad. At first, I just laid it all at the feet of a desire to never give an unprofessional impression. I have been unprofessional before, and I didn't want to ever fall into that category again. But now, I wonder if it was more than that."

"Do tell us, what is in the heart and head of Miss Bennet?"

"I just...felt as if the walls were closing in about me and I would not be happy if I did not do my duty and work." I looked at Hunnicutt slyly. "Milton is a bad influence on me."

Hunnicutt chuckled.

"We all start off that way, and end that way, don't we?"

Darcy sat down next to me as Hunnicutt went to the front of the lecture hall, cleared his throat, did a couple of vocal exercises and students began to enter.

"Lizzy," Darcy whispered.

"Yes, patient one."

"You might have to unsay that in this minute. For I am arriving at a strange time of my life."

"And what is that?"

"I am gradually becoming jealous of every man who talks to you."

I raised an eyebrow, archly.

"Truly?"

"Yes."

"Oh, that is so wicked and wonderful."

Darcy's eyes relaxed. "Is it?"

"Yes. I see that you were worried that I would feel anxiety over your overreaction?"

"Yes, I guess that I did."

"Well, I'm not. I know what love is. I've seen real love on more than one occasion. It's a possessive sort of emotion. Tell me, does your chest feel like it's tightening?"

"Yes!"

"That's natural. Also, there is nothing wrong with feeling a little protective. As long as you don't take it to excess."

Feeling like he needed more assurance than just my words of wisdom and logic, I thought it best to appeal to his tenderness. Despite being in public, I reached my hand toward him, and he took it, folding his fingers around my palm.

"Darcy," I whispered, "I promise you, I am not going anywhere. I am by your side."

He breathed in heavily, his eyes filled with a strong passion.

"How long I wanted to hear you say that."

"Well, I am saying it now. And I hold fast to it. Now, hush, dear one, for class is starting."

The students had entered, sat down, and Mr. Hunnicutt began his class.

"Remarkable," Darcy said as Mr. Hunnicutt had finished his class, and I was sitting in a backroom, copying my notes onto another paper.

"What is?" I asked, still writing while we talked.

"I have not sat in on a school lecture for years now."

"And how did you find being back in the world of academia?"

"I find... that maybe I missed it."

"Did you?"

"Yes, I did. There was something very laborious about my time at university. However, there was also something stimulating to it."

"What's it like going to university?"

"Oh, it is an adventure, mark my words."

"One day, we women will be able to attend. That, I know will happen."

"I do not know. But the times are changing. People are still clinging to the past simply because...well, it is more comfortable to do so. Even I prefer the comfort of the way things are."

"Tradition and change are like everything else in the world: it's best to exercise it through moderation. I see the appeal to maintaining certain things and keeping certain customs. Tradition brings stability. But some changes are meant to occur, or nothing will ever happen."

"Would you want to go to university, if you could?"

I leaned back, distracted from my notetaking.

"Now that is a very interesting question."

"Yes, it is," Darcy leaned toward me, interested. "What would you do?"

"Indeed, what would I do? For, if I go, I have to deal with many setbacks, many negative looks, much prejudice, many implications that I am not welcome—would I do it? Well, despite it all, I think I would. For my courage has a tendency to rise with every attempt to intimidate me. Maybe I would let the resentment toward myself fuel me and give me more justification for why I would be there. But I do not see that I am alone there. Men have sometimes had their own inequalities to face, every now and again, in one form or another, so maybe it is a universal struggle that you might understand. As such, maybe we women must strive for things as men do, and our failures are other people's challenges."[1]

I looked at Mr. Darcy.

"Do you believe that women ought to be allowed to go to university?"

Mr. Darcy breathed in heavily. "I cannot tell a lie."

"Then don't," I said, prepared for anything.

"Well, I honestly never thought of it before. But I am not used to the idea of women attending Oxford or Cambridge."

"And?"

"And I would find the idea off-putting."

"Why?"

"First, it would be distracting. And second, they would

---

1. This line is a paraphrase of Amelia Earhart's quote: '*Women must try to do things as men have tried. When they fail, their failure must be but a challenge to others.*'

face so much opposition that it would be hard to witness. I don't wish to see women undergo that. So, a part of me is against the idea."

"Well, I did ask for the truth."

"You are mad at me."

"No, I am not. I do not agree, but I am not mad. You have been molded and fashioned from a world that is against such ideas. Of course, you were going to get their words on you, in one way or another. As to your first complaint, maybe us being there would be distracting, but that is something that you must reconcile with yourselves. You cannot blame us for being the fairer sex. You must learn to brave our bewitching ways and understand that is your own sort of obstacle to overcome. And second, you are right, we would face much opposition, and you would have to witness our struggle. That comes from the better side of yourself. Challenges, Darcy! We must start somewhere. Maybe the struggle has to happen. You men have to weather them, every now and again, therefore, maybe we women must do so as well. It would be hard, but it would be worth it in the end. At least, it would give us something to talk about. Even if nothing comes of it."

We looked at each other, long and hard.

"Now the question is, can you and I disagree with each other, and still be in love?"

"I still love you."

"Good. Because I won't change my mind, but I will still love you. And whether you like it or not, my opinion will never change."

"I know. I will never forsake you, Elizabeth."

"I know that as well."

We were interrupted by an arrival in the library when the door opened, and Mr. Hale's face appeared through the doorway.

"Lizzy!" He smiled, removing his hat. "Thank god that you are well!"

"Mr. Hale," I said, happy to see him, "yes, I have survived and now I persevere."

"If anyone could do it, it would be you. Oh, Margaret finally told me what happened. I was aghast when I learned of what you and the others had suffered. What of Kitty and Rasby?"

"They are also on the road to recovery, and they will walk again."

He sighed.

"That is a delight to hear."

"And your timing could not be more perfect. I have to copy these notes, and Mr. Darcy is proving to be quite the incredible distraction. If you both talk amongst yourselves, then maybe I could finish making this copy."

"Darcy, how are you, my boy?" Mr. Hale asked.

"I am well, sir. Now, I request we do as Miss Elizabeth bids and find a conversation that will occupy us long enough that we are not a nuisance to her."

"I shall do my best."

"Oh, before you both run to the other side of the library," I said, "Mr. Hale, can you tell me if Margaret is coming to see us today?"

"Oh, yes, I almost forgot. She told me to tell you that she was going to meet us after my class."

"Good. She and I have much to talk about."

The two men spoke amongst themselves until I finished my notes.

Soon after I was done, it was time to prepare for Mr. Hale's next class. This time, Darcy carried my writing desk to the classroom and now grew accustomed to sitting in the back of the class with me as Mr. Hale set up his notes.

"Mr. Darcy, your presence makes me quite nervous," he announced from the front.

"Never fear," Darcy said, "I say little to nothing in these circumstances. In a classroom, I am the most unintimidating person there would be."

Soon, students began to take their seats and the class began. Once more, Darcy was devoted and remained with me the entire time.

While I wrote down notes, Darcy watched Mr. Hale attentively and was probably impressed with how Mr. Hale instructed. After all, he had come a long way since his first class and had gained more confidence.

When he finished his lesson, I decided to take the notes with me back to Crampton Crescent, where I would write the extra copy and return them to Granger Hall for the next day.

Taking my notes and purse, Mr. Hale escorted Darcy and I out of the lecture hall, with Darcy rolling me to the front door. When we got to the front, my eyes brightened when I saw Margaret walking toward us.

"Margaret!" I called.

"Lizzy," she responded, taking my hand, and looking down at me. "You..."

"Never fear. I shall be out of this chair soon. And what about you?"

"Oh," Margaret rushed out, "the shock of the experience has quite done away." She leaned down and whispered in my ear. "Do not tell mama about it. Mama still is ignorant on the matter, and she needs to always be."

When seeing her speak of Mrs. Hale, all my questions about Mr. Thornton's rejection had quite escaped my mind. All that I cared about, in that moment, was Mrs. Hale's health.

"How is your mother?" I asked.

Margaret looked grave.

"That bad?" I asked.

She nodded to me heavily.

"You must tell me all about it," I said. "You've left me in the dark for too long."

"I'll tell you once we get home."

Darcy took us back to Crampton in his carriage, and I asked him if he would do me the favor of occupying Mr. Hale while I spoke with Margaret. Understanding my desire to speak to my friend, Darcy appealed to Mr. Hale, to talk of his lesson and have a discussion on Ancient Greek Comedy and Satire. Eager to have someone who shared his interests, Mr. Hale was glad.

Dixon informed us that Mrs. Hale was resting and that it was best not to disturb her.

"Ah, Dixon," I said to her as she put pillows behind my back, "still a fortress?"

"I'm a castle," she stated, and then she went to prepare some coffee for us.

When she left, we were all alone in the room.

"Finally," I said, "Margaret, tell me what is really happening here. Don't leave out any detail."

"Lizzy," she sighed, "it turns out that it has been happening for quite some time now. Doctor Donaldson has told me to prepare myself, because now he says that there is nothing that can be done. It is all a matter of time."

Sitting there, I was aware of my own woes on the subject, but what of Margaret? For there she was, sitting as still as a statue again. Quite frankly, I was not in the mood for it.

"Margaret," I said, gently, "it is perfectly right to cry. No one is here to judge you."

Her breathing became heavier and heavier.

"I've cried enough already," Margaret said, "you are sitting in a chair, and you lost both of your parents in one day. You don't need to hear my grief."

"On the contrary, I am the precise sort of person who can understand."

She began to weep, but she managed to hold back her tears.

"I cannot bear it, Elizabeth. It's not fair. All those years that I lived in London, with Aunt Shaw and Edith, and now I found my mother right as I am about to lose her. It's not fair!"

"Death never is fair, when it comes to those worth loving," I said, holding her. "Margaret, I am so sorry. At least, you are given time to get to know her, and she is still with you. And she has one child, a devoted child, who is there with her, till the very end."

"With any luck, she will have two."

I squinted.

"Two? But Frederick..."

"She knows. Elizabeth, Mama knows that her time with us is brief, and she longed to see Frederick again. So... I sent a letter to tell him of her state, asking him to come here, to Milton. She needs to see him one last time."

Large moments, terrifying moments, are always present in Milton! She invited Frederick to come back to England?

"Frederick will come here? Margaret, if he comes, what are the chances that he will be in danger?"

"There will always be a chance. But if she died, and we never gave him the chance to see her again, I do not think he would forgive us. She is so special to him."

"Do you know," I asked heavily, "if he is coming, or not?"

"He is in Spain, therefore, it will take more time for the message to get through. But I hope that he will come in time. It is not about 'if he comes', but 'when'."

I looked ahead.

"Father was initially upset when I did it," Margaret said, "but then his anxiety quickly gave way to appreciation and now he is happy to see him. Oh, I hope he does come in time. It would be devastating if he were to arrive, and she died before she could see him. Life could not be that cruel."

"It can be, but for your sake, I hope it is not so. When he comes, we must make sure that he is concealed and that no one finds out that he is here."

"We will. Secrecy is vital. I don't want to feel as if I have brough him back, only for him to walk to the gallows."

"We can help you."

"You've done so much already, Elizabeth."

"I want to help. Especially since you and I are going to be parted eventually."

"Yes. You go back to the South, or the country."

She could not fully conceal her regret over losing me. To offer her comfort, and to ease the idea of losing acquaintances while also losing her mother, I held her hand. It was impossible for me to even begin to understand what grief she was feeling, even when I had experienced such a similar tragedy. However, I had my sisters and aunts and uncles to be like a comfort—a balm for me. Margaret did have her father, but sometimes, nothing could replace a maternal feeling. Jane had that habit about her, exerting a maternal force that could ease the hardship of our loss. But Margaret, well, I wasn't so sure. For, we both had been uprooted from our Southern lives and thrown against the whims of chance. We each were given a proverbial raft, on which we were victorious over the waves that had kept trying to push us backwards. However, not all ships can last. Sometimes, we have no choice but to sink.

"Frederick will come to England, and he will leave it, safe and sound," I said. "All will be well. Margaret, regret none of your life, for it was a good one. Even when we came here, it is still a good one."

"Elizabeth, I try to tell myself to be brave and weather anything, but sometimes, regret does find me."

"Regret finds everyone, from time to time. We all wish things had turned out so very differently. But when the tragedy is over, there is a sense of triumph at the end, because we have proven that we have the ability to recover and keep going. You lived in a fancy home, where you had an aunt and cousin who loved you and gave you the best of city life. You've been proposed to and have had to learn your strength and not to give in to empty affections. You went home, reconnected with your family, chose to be part of provincial life, and you became your father's strength.

You've found your voice, you've regained your mother, and then you did not despise your father for bringing you all here. You tried to understand, then you tried to adapt, you've made friends with the very poor here, have dined with the wealthy, have met masters and men, and all this time, you did it as a Southern woman in an industrial town in the North. All of this...is life. It's a part of the journey. And you endured it all. Your mother could not have had a better daughter."

Dixon brought the coffee in.

After she served us, she looked down at us.

"Now, I trust you both are not the flimsy sort of useless totties," she announced, "and won't need me?"

"You want to go and see to Mother," Margaret said.

"Yes, I do," Dixon said, sincerely.

"Thank you, Dixon. Go to Mama."

"Ring if you need me."

Dixon left us alone.

"It took me a long time to find the perfect balance between her love for mother and mine," Margaret explained. "I sometimes could be short with her."

"She is a devoted servant who your mother has spent so much of her life sharing all her feelings with. It is only natural to wonder how to find your way into that same level of intimacy. But you managed it."

Margaret looked at me.

"I am happy for you, Lizzy. I know that I will miss you, but I am happy for you."

"I am sorry that we might be far apart. But you can visit."

"You know that I can't. When...the inevitable happens, father can't be alone. It will be too much for him. I have to stay and look after him."

"I understand."

Scratching my chin, I didn't know how to prepare for what I needed to speak to her about. However, it had to be said.

"Margaret," I began, "when I received your letter, saying that you could not visit me at Marlborough Mills, I wondered why that was. After all, you acted so bravely. You must imagine why I was curious."

When I said this, Margaret's cheeks changed colors.

"I suppose that you knew this conversation was coming," I encouraged.

"I do not wish to talk about it, Elizabeth."

"Perhaps not, but you need to talk about it. Margaret, believe me, you *do* need to talk about it. Am I correct in assuming that something happened between you and Thornton?"

Thinking it best not to let her know my knowledge about the proposal, I allowed her to unfold as much as she wished.

She did not respond, so I took it as confirmation.

"And am I correct in assuming that he came here, and proposed marriage to you?"

"How do you see that so easily?" she asked, simply.

"Because I am aware that he feels deeply for you."

She looked at me, startled.

"You did?"

"I had an inkling for some time, but I had no certain

evidence. I didn't want to tell you something just because I had a theory and also, well...time has taught me not to make statements on things that I don't know for certain. Does that upset you?"

"Not at all. That was the right thing to do."

"Also, when you did grab hold of him, to save him from the riot, that could easily lead to a man assuming that maybe the woman returns his affections."

"I do not regret anything that I have done."

"And you shouldn't. But Margaret, please, tell me what fully happened. Help me to understand."

While being content to keep it a secret, she found it was easier to allow her inner feelings to pour forth. The joys of expressing oneself! She gave me the whole history of Mr. Thornton's proposal.

When she finished, I had a strange sensation.

Now I knew what Darcy had endured when Thornton had confessed it all to him. I looked at Margaret and felt as if I was seeing a pale reflection of days long past.

I could imagine the coldness or anger that she expressed when rejecting Mr. Thornton, for it was the precise manner in which I had initially rejected Darcy. Oh, to see two people fall into the same trap that you had done.

But there was one difference. One chief difference that I began with first.

"And he kissed you?" I asked. "He truly embraced you?"

"Yes," Margaret said, sighing. "He did. In that moment, I really despised him, Lizzy. He robbed me of my first kiss. I have no intention of marrying, at present, but when I do, I had intended it to be to the man I would marry. And that's not going to happen now. My first true kiss, passionate and personal, was taken, out of my power, by a man who I rejected."

"I understand the importance of a lady's first," I said. "I know that it feels as if you have lost something. But if you do marry, there will be many firsts. What I mean is that there are still other happier moments that you can have with that man, whoever he may be. But as for first kisses— again, I know that it is hard to think of it as anything else but sacred—but you will soon understand that you have lost nothing. My first kiss was not with Mr. Darcy, and I am quite certain that his first kiss was not with me. But we are still special to each other."

Margaret perked up.

"Mr. Darcy was not your first kiss?"

"No," I replied, simply and unashamed. "I am in my twenties. You think I spent my entire teenage years without any of the rash and reckless passions that overtake one at that age? I was not stone, and not all men in the country want to marry the first woman that they kiss. In Hertford-shire, there was a young man, from Norfolk, and he was visiting his relatives. One day, at a ball, we found ourselves walking onto the balcony together, and we kissed. I am not ashamed of that. I was young, and I ought to have been allowed to have that experience without sullying every other encounter with the man who I eventually would choose to marry. No. There are more special moments to come, and I aim to appreciate all of them."

Margaret looked ahead at the wall.

"Very well, you have convinced me. I just...why did Thornton have to do that? He knew that I would not accept him."

"He is in love. When that happens, you become like

that of a drowning man, who is clawing his way to get to any surface and take refuge."

"I did not mean to break his heart."

"Nor did I when Mr. Darcy proposed to me."

"But Elizabeth, that was different."

"How so? He and I often passionately disagreed with each other."

"Yes, but you and Darcy come from the same sort of world. You are country folk."

"And what difference does that make? Why must it be that people can't fall in love with difference?"

"I just...it makes things easier."

"Perhaps it would. But at the end of the day, one just has to love who one loves. It's a very blind emotion, and sometimes, its blindness is in its favor."

"Whatever has happened between us, I don't want him to despise me," she elaborated. "Just as I didn't want to initially cause him injury. This was not what I wanted."

"And you told him that."

"Yes, I did. But it didn't stop that we both have gone to do nothing more than make each other angry, again. And you should have seen him, Lizzy. When he left, there were tears in his eyes. I don't know why I am so unnerved at hurting him."

"It is right for you to feel so. It shows compassion. It was wrong of him to kiss you, but he knows that now. And it cannot be undone. And the question is not what you have done, and what he had done, but what must happen now. First, I need you to understand something. When you said that he offended you, Margaret, I really don't think that's what he intended. I really think he proposed to you because he cared. No more and no less."

"For him to assume that I saved him because I felt for him…"

"He was wrong to think so, but he was seeing things from a different perspective. I know it's not very easy to see things from other perspectives than our own, but it will help us in life to try. I really don't think he regarded his feelings as being offensive. From his perspective, he thought he was being just…and I daresay, romantic. Also, there is nothing wrong with being flattered."

"Flattered? How can I feel such when I have never liked him?"

"You don't have to be in love with someone to be flattered that they noticed that you are worthy of being loved. For that's what Thornton did. He showed that you are worthy of being loved. Even if you don't want to be loved by him. He deserves credit for having such a great preference when it comes to ladies."

"You tease me, Lizzy," Margaret said, blushing as she looked at her hands.

"No, I do not tease you. If you were a lesser creature, I would say it. This is just me being frank. He is not offensive for preferring you to any other woman, Margaret. We are trained to be offended by anyone thinking we are worthy of notice. I do not know where that backwards way of thinking has come from. But think, Margaret, is that logic really sound? You must harden yourself to the notion that you are worth looking at."

"Lizzy, you know it's not my way."

"I do. But I tell you this now, so that you understand Thornton better. And here is the one moment where I admit that I am about to give you pain. There was one thing that I think was too hard of a thing to say to him."

Margaret looked at me, but she was not made of weak stuff. When it came to my criticisms, she was always prepared.

"When he said that you do not understand him, and you replied that you did not want to understand him, Margaret, that was wrong to say."

"Was it? I could not help it."

"At the moment, you couldn't. But now, in the cold light of day, you can. With reflection, and considering his side of the situation, how do you think it feels for someone to say that they don't want to understand you? That they will always be a little prejudiced toward you and never consider you in the process. Margaret, you come from a devout man. Don't you see the cruelty of that comment? And the unholiness of hardening yourself against camaraderie, and choosing willful bias in its place?"

"Are you determined to make me quite ashamed of myself?" she asked, hurt.

"No, I am not. I am trying to ask you to remember that not wishing to understand other people, and not respect their views and feelings, is not becoming. Intentional misunderstanding leads to bitter ignorance, a fall from enlightenment, inequality, even personal segregation. Is this what our Great Redeemer preaches? You are worth more than that."

Her eyes turned serious.

"You sympathize with him? You think I should have accepted him?"

I was flummoxed at her coming to such a conclusion.

"No," I stated harshly. "Of course, not. Do me no dishonor by assuming that I mean that. Don't marry where you do not love. I am simply saying that you do not help yourself by turning away from people when they try to explain who they are and why they feel as they do."

She stood up and walked to the window.

"I don't say these things because I want you to feel wrong," I said, urging her to understand me, "I say these things because I have been precisely where you have been now, and I am trying to spare you all the days, weeks, and months, of self-doubt that follows such actions. There is nothing so very startling like waking up, one day, and realizing you were blind to so many things. I am trying to save you from that. Margaret, at least let me try."

"I know," she replied, simply and quietly, still looking out of the window. "That's the painful thing of it all. I know that everything you said makes sense. What frightens me is that I didn't act like that at the time. And I am upset with myself over it. Why did I behave so coldly?"

"Because you were in an emotionally heightened encounter, and it triggered all your vexations and animosities. Like it or not, Margaret, you're as human as the rest of us. Emotions come out every now and again."

"I wish that I was above that."

"Well, you are not. Welcome to the world."

At last, Margaret turned back to me, her eyes gentle, but sad.

"Help me again, Lizzy. How do I triumph over this? I don't regret refusing him, but I regret how I did it."

"I am going to offer you a solution. You will not like it. But please, consider it, before you reject it."

Nodding, she sat down beside me again.

"You need to talk to him," I began.

"Talk to him? He and I probably wish the other were on the other side of the world."

"You would be surprised. Sometimes, men do not want to ignore us after such an event. When I turned down Mr. Collins, he immediately did ignore me and set out to woo Charlotte Lucas. When I refused Mr. Darcy, when he saw me again, he sought me out. Not all men and women are the same. When you accept that, it prepares you for anything in life. Sometimes, men want to run when a woman refuses him. Some men are the reverse. They want to be beside you, then more than ever."

"I don't think I can bear to be near him now."

"This is where I need you to be brave. So very brave. If you ever see him, talk to him. Ask him how he is. His work, his thoughts on things, and when the time comes, ask him how he is feeling. In particular, talk to him about the proposal, and tell him that you are sorry if you caused him pain."

"He would think that I was encouraging him."

"Then tell him that you are not."

"I should not do that."

"Why not? Again, where is the logic and reason in allowing yourself to not be understood, as well as to willfully misunderstand? What will you gain by this? Margaret, you will see him again. That's the tragedy of this all. You both cannot ignore each other forever. You will have to establish peace and compassion. You are capable of this."

"I need time to think."

"Time. Yes, it helps everything."

Soon, Mr. Darcy joined us again and it was time to return to Marlborough Mills.

Margaret saw us off, with a good-natured attitude, and she and I arranged for us to soon visit Bessy Higgins together.

As we headed home, I unfolded everything to Mr. Darcy.

"Did I do right, I wonder?" I asked him. "Sometimes, friends don't need advice like that. Sometimes, they just want a friendly shoulder to weep on."

"I think you did the right thing," Darcy acknowledged. "Miss Hale doesn't really strike me as the sort to be upset over hearing reason. Besides, it's only Thornton who has the largest emotional disturbance."

"When you spoke to Thornton, was that how it felt when I rejected you?" I asked, curious. "What he is feeling now, is that how you felt?"

Darcy looked away from me, but not out of disdain. Rather, he was thinking of the recent past, and our tumultuous relationship.

"Yes," he answered, simply, "It was. And so, I must ask you, what Margaret is feeling now, is that how you felt when you rejected me?"

"I'm not so certain. After I rejected your proposal, I was upset with you, but not for you proposing to me. When I had time to think about it, I actually found your affection for me to be gratifying."

"You did?"

"Yes. I was angry with you for all the reasons that I said I was, but it didn't eradicate that I felt flattered by your attentions. And yes, after the proposal, I was happy to not see you again. But as you recall, that didn't stop me from communicating with you when you were willing to speak. And then, when you finally were able to explain yourself, I felt so utterly ashamed and embarrassed. But I was willing to understand you. In fact, I was eager to know the truth of everything. With Margaret, I am not so certain that she wants to know the truth of Thornton. Our rejection was equally as wounding, and like me, she does not regret it, initially. But the thing is, Margaret and I are similar, in the sense that we are not afraid to give either you men pain when we talked to you, but I did open myself to you, even when I didn't know it. I can see what drew you in. But with Margaret, how well does Thornton know her, I wonder? Is it really enough for a marriage?"

"Oh, I hadn't thought of it that way."

"She was right to reject him. If they ever have a chance of feeling affection for each other, they are not ready now. Also, Mr. Thornton...what is similar is that we both felt that you hurt someone that we felt protective over. I thought you hurt Mr. Wickham, and then I found out that you hurt Jane. Mr. Thornton runs a factory where there is a carding room, and people can die from the fluff on their lungs—and that's what's killing Bessy. You both represented a wounding of someone that we worried over. Remember when I found out that Wickham lied to me, and you never hurt him. My concerns for him immediately disappeared, and it got transferred to you and Miss Darcy being the victims. Right now, Thornton still antagonizing to Margaret. Her lack of care for manufacturers was already set within her, but also, he represents men who allow their workers to die, he did not listen to his workers, so they all went on strike, he called the police in—"

"That's not all Thornton's fault."

"I know, but that's how Margaret sees it. Recall, that's what I experienced. Everything that Wickham said was so obvious a lie. But when we have prejudices, we will allow ourselves to demonize anything that feeds to our preferences. Margaret was right not to accept him. They are not at a stage where they understand each other."

"That is true. Even if I had warned Thornton, he still would be where he is."

"You wrestled with your feelings for me, and you proposed anyway. If someone had tried to convince you out of loving me, would you have listened?"

His eyes smiled. "You know that I wouldn't have, because I clearly didn't."

"Precisely. We humans will do what we want, no matter how good the advice."

We arrived at Marlborough Mills.

"Go to your friend," I said to Darcy. "Something tells me that he needs someone to be by him."

"You complete me."

"I'd better."

As he wheeled me into the house, I saw Robert and Colin walking into the factory. I waved to them, they smiled and returned the gesture, and I began to copy my notes from Mr. Hale's class.

Chapter 9

Routine

As time progressed, we began to return back to our ways of being.

Over the next four days, the pains in our legs dissolved, our wounds were fully closed, and we felt that we had trespassed on the Thorntons' hospitality for long enough. Naturally, I didn't care very much, because it gave me the chance to always be near Darcy, and it was at a time where we needed to be near each other. Also, I very well knew that we were not causing any expense to the Thorntons at all, because Darcy was very good at being an unofficial tenant to them, and assisting them on all our plaster, bandages, and surgeon visits.

But when remembering that your company can upset a household, that Jane had no one at home with her, and that my very presence antagonized Fanny Thornton, it was time to remember ourselves. Also, even Lydia missed being at the soldiers' headquarters with Denny. As she had put it, she had a hard time waking up to a bed where he wasn't next to her.

Also, Margaret could not come and visit.

However, it ought not to be assumed that she and I were estranged to each other over those next four days. On the contrary, I received a letter from Margaret, and the contents were not only sanguine, but she showed no indication of being slighted from my advice. Instead, she impressed me:

Dear Lizzy,

After having thought about our last parting, I can see that maybe I might have been a little intolerant. You were probably more patient with me than I would have been if I had been the one in your predicament.

You, of all people, understand what it feels like to have been in my place. And between your experience, and the wisdom that can come from the passage of time, you probably could see things from a clearer perspective.

I don't know if I am ready to speak to Thornton about the incident. However, I am willing to try. Please inform him that I am sorry for any pain that I may have caused him. I do not regret my decision, and I will ask that he does not throw himself upon me so again. But, if he ever wishes to talk about our past, and try and gain a wider acquaintance with me, then I can supply it, as a friend. I will try to understand him. I can give him forgiveness, compassion and understanding. But no more than that.

I can't wait to see you when you return to Frances Street. Not being able to have more personal interactions with you has greatly affected me. Remember,

*when you return home, visit Bessy and Nicholas. They
need to see you.*

Margaret

When I finished reading it, I went to Mr. Darcy. Since it
was the day that Kitty, Rasby, and I were to be returned to
Frances Street, I thought it was best to show Darcy the part
of the letter that pertained to Thornton.

As he saw it, I saw his expression shift from apprehension to ease.

"Now that is a start," he uttered.

"Also, Margaret has given me authority to let Thornton
know this," I said, "but I think it would be better if it came
from a friend."

I gave him an arched look and it did not escape his
notice.

"Never fear," he deduced, "you are right. It ought to
be me."

"Good."

As he stood up to leave, to make preparations for taking
us back home, I called out to him.

"Yes?" he asked.

"Thank you," I said.

"For what?"

"For giving me time. You have not pushed us into
getting married so quickly. How did you know that I
needed to get to court you more before anything was
confirmed?"

He sighed.

"Truth is, I didn't. Perhaps I might have rushed into it all, if I had not had some very good advice."

"Who advised you?"

"Let's just say that I have a very logical cousin."

"Ah," I said, knowing that he referred to Colonel Fitzwilliam. "The joys of having logical family."

"Yes."

The hour of departure came, and we returned to Frances Street. When doing so, Jane was still at the Kirkpatricks, so there was no one to greet us.

When we stepped down from the carriage, we stood in front of our home—well, Rasby lived elsewhere, but she was going to spend the night with us again.

"Strange, isn't it?" Kitty said, "we're back, and yet, everything feels different."

"Yes," Rasby noted. "Hopefully, we will settle back in when we get inside."

We did so, and when we entered, it was to see our house all over again, and there was something about it that had a coziness to it.

I could not explain it so very well. However, a rush of different feelings overcame me. Immediately I felt my spirit soar and rush back to the place where Mr. Darcy was, but another part of me felt the comforts of being back to the familiar.

Kitty, Rasby, and I walked around our sitting room and then I went back to our kitchen, to make us some tea.

"It's strange," I overheard Kitty say to Rasby, "tomorrow, we go back to the hotel, we work our shift and then we go about our lives again."

"Yes. It's like all that we did never happened. Or it did, but life goes on. The question then becomes, how can we go back after so much has happened?"

I entered and stood in front of them.

"We have to entertain the reality that there is no official way to go back," I said. "But we will anyway."

I told Kitty to mind the tea as I left to see the Higginses.

When I knocked on their door, it opened to me seeing Nicholas Higgins. His face was hard, heavy, and I could see the disappointment that swelled up within him. Sometimes, you don't need to hear the whole history. For some of us, the history is written in our eyes. This was the first time that I had seen him since the riot. Now I was glimpsing the after-effects of that tragedy. It never occurred to me to think that the first victims of the mob were the committee men who really thought they had a good chance. They must have felt quite betrayed. Nicholas's eyes said it all.

"Nicholas," I said, concerned.

"Oi, Miss Bennet," he greeted me, "you've come back to us."

"Yes, I did. How is Bessy and Mary?"

"Mary is out, and Bessy is sleepin'. She would be happy to see yer, but I don' want to disturb her."

"I understand."

"Is Kitty and Rasby..."

"They are here with me. Do you want to see them?"

"I'm 'fraid to."

"Nicholas, they would want to see you."

"I know. And I want to see em'. I am just..."

"Nicholas, what happened to us was not your fault."

263

"I know, but it still feels like it is."

He looked at me, his eyes so lost and overwhelmed with regret.

"I'm sorry about the strike. I know that you felt like you stood a good chance."

"We did. And now I don't... I don't know how we will ever get what we deserve again. This feels like our last chance."

I touched his arm.

"Can you get work?"

"I'll try, but it will be hard. They know who I am."

"The Masters?"

"Yes. And they will blame me for it all, even though I had nothin' to do wi' it. If one of us is guilty, then all of us is."

"Is that Elizabeth?" I heard Bessy's voice from the inside. Her voice was weak, and I could hear the mortality dripping from her words.

"Yes, it is," I said. Nicholas allowed me to come in and I went to Bessy.

She was so weak that she couldn't leave her bed. I sat down next to her, and I touched her shoulder, affectionately.

"Oh, miss," Bessy sighed, her eyes barely open.

"Bessy, I am so sorry."

"Say none of that. When I heard what happened to yer all... Elizabeth, we were so scared for yer lot."

"We're fine. Can I bring Kitty and Rasby to see you? Or do you not want to see anyone?"

"I can see yer all before I go, but I can't talk much anymore. But bring them here for a minute, then leave me. I don't have the strength to have yer remain."

Anguished, I looked up at Nicholas, who looked heavily down at us. In his eyes, he knew it. We all knew it. There was no point in arguing with Bessy because she embraced the reality that we were too scared to do ourselves.

I went off, retrieved Kitty and Rasby, and we went to visit her. We sat with her, but truly, Bessy was not able to hold conversation for more than a minute.

After watching her rest for a little longer, we gave kind words for Nicholas, and then we left.

When we went back into our house, we sat down and had our tea.

"I wonder what it's like," Rasby said.

"What?" Kitty asked.

"To lose a battle. We don't look at it that way, but it's evident that there is a bit of a war between the masters and the workers. Nicholas must have felt like they lost the battle. And while this is all happening, he is losing his daughter. What's it like to lose so much?"

"Yes," Kitty said, "home sweet home."

When the night came, I prepared my clothes for the next day. After I finished taking my bath, it was Kitty and Rasby's turn to use my same water. So, I got out as quickly as I could, so that the water was still warm for them.

As I heard them in the washroom, jumping into the water, I sat in my bedroom, drying my hair. When recalling how we didn't have to reuse the same water at Marlborough Mills, I wondered how we could fall back into our lesser lives so easily. That was when it occurred to me how much I had changed since we left Longbourn.

I had lived a comfortable life, then I had fallen into reduced circumstances and became poor, and then I fell in love with a man who owned a large portion of Derbyshire. When I was poor, I was no longer ashamed. The large and frightening thing that we had been warned about all our lives, that we had been trained to dread, had occurred, and we had weathered it. It was in that moment that I felt like we had been tested, time and time again. Any happiness we now found was reward for endurance.

And then, Mr. Darcy's image came to my mind. He loved me. He truly did. As I marveled at the idea of him, I then began to realize all the other things that it entailed.

He had an aunt who would never welcome me.

He also was marrying a woman who once had a profession.

All the sacrifices that he had made. Then again, more and more people from the aristocracy were marrying people of trade, due to the debt that their families had fallen into. How much of life was transactions?

But with Darcy and I, it was not like that. Our union was something that was founded under something much deeper and more profound than I could have predicted. Marriage was a duty—the main duty for an educated lady with moderate wealth. But as for us Bennet sisters, none of us fully adhered to that lesson. It had to be something established under the foundation of love and affection.

Knowing that, it dared me to dream of other days. Standing up, I imagined myself soaring over land, leaving Darkshire, flying over hill and dale, and returning to the English countryside. I imagined the sweeping hills, woodlands, lakes, and streams that would be either near or on Pemberley estate. Even though I had never seen it, I allowed myself to believe that it was a land of immense beauty, and for it to uncover the beauties of human nature, augment life, and bring it to the apex of idealism. I could see myself running along parts of it, the hem of my white gown becoming dirtied in the process. But I would not care. I would feel the air sweep around me.

And Elizabeth Bennet would know who she was.

Chapter 10

A Bit of Light

"So," Thornton said, sitting in his office in his factory, with his account books on his desk. "That's what Miss Hale feels?"

Darcy had come to see him, to tell him what Margaret had written to Elizabeth. With the door closed, he unfolded everything to his heart-torn friend, and the transformation was slight, but very much present. Thornton went from pouring over his records, to looking at Mr. Darcy with interest. When Darcy finished his report, Thornton was very still.

"Yes," Mr. Darcy answered, "that's what Miss Hale feels, according to what she allowed Elizabeth to profess."

Thornton stood up and rubbed his eyes.

"How does this make you feel?" Darcy asked Thornton.

"I don't know."

"How don't you know? I thought that this would have made you feel lighter—happier that she does not have a terrible opinion of you."

"I know, but what if it is temporary? I want to hope,

Darcy, as this message has dared me to hope as I once hoped before. I don't think I can suffer her rejecting me again."

"You have to stop thinking in the direction of proposing, Thornton. It's not wise right now."

"But I'm in love with her."

"And she's not at the same place as you. You cannot force something, believe me. Things need time to arrive at the proper place. When you see her again, analyze her demeanor, and approach her when she is ready to be approached. Take her comfort into account. Also...do not let this stop your lessons with Mr. Hale. From what Lizzy tells me, your friendship with him is one of the higher points of his time here."

"Yes, I always do like speaking to him. He has an ease about him that is comforting. And he feels—he understands the desire for freedom in the way that I do."

"And if you married Miss Hale, you would have had him for a father-in-law," Darcy pointed out, his deductive skills being fully on display, "and you would finally have the sort of father figure in your life that you always wanted."

Feeling utterly exposed, Thornton looked at Darcy and knew that his friend would show no signs of feeling like he was being too introspective.

"Well," Thornton continued, "I promise, that wasn't a main reason for my proposing to Miss Hale. I saw the benefits of that connection, but..."

"I know," Darcy assured him, "you proposed to Miss Hale because you loved her. Gaining Mr. Hale as a father-in-law was simply an addition. My cousin, Richard, fortunately still has a father in his life. However, with Bingley,

Plato, you and I, we are boys without fathers. I could never begrudge you for wanting to have one again."

"They leave us too soon, don't they?"

"Yes. But in most cases, they don't mean to. Your case was different."

"It was different. It was unfair. Sometimes, I used to rail at the world, 'Why me? Why must I always be the one who suffers so?' Of course, I got no answer, so I kept going. I just feel like...it's only a matter of time before I am denied everything. Oh well, it is best to continue."

Darcy just sat there and listened. For often, some people didn't want you to speak; they just needed someone to be there while they bore their souls out. For life is a quick succession of humanity always having to put on their bravest face, hiding their heart and vulnerability away, and replacing it with severe sturdiness. One must not break— but that philosophy ultimately leads to one inevitably breaking, in the worst way. Darcy was very aware that his shoulder was the main shoulder that Thornton had to lean on when his vulnerable side was presenting itself—because Thornton had no one else to expose this side of himself to.

A boy...without a father.

When drawing back into himself, Thornton rose out of his musings and turned back to Darcy.

"You say that I should tread carefully," he summed up, "and that I ought to give Margaret time."

"And when she's ready, talk to her. See if she is willing to get a better understanding of you. Look for friendship, but don't go looking for her to fall in love with you. If you do that, you will lose any chance you might actually have."

"I understand. She might never fully love me, will she?"

"Perhaps. Or perhaps not."

"And I have to keep going on. Yes, yes, I must."

Thornton drew back into himself, reverting back to the stern and strong demeanor that he usually had. He stood tall, like an oak, and Darcy knew that Thornton's confession was over.

"Thank you, Darcy."

"You're welcome. Bingley wishes to come to dinner tonight. Do you think your mother will mind?"

"Not at all. She likes him."

"Everyone does."

Thornton grinned.

"Sometimes I am jealous of Bingley."

"We all are, from time to time. Now, I'll leave you to it."

"And you to yours."

Darcy left to speak to Mrs. Thornton while his friend went back to work, feeling lighter than he did the day before.

Chapter 11

Her Exit

I had fallen back into my work, along with Kitty. Jane eventually returned home, much to the joy of us being returned to her.

After a week of living back on Frances Street, I was becoming a little apprehensive. On my way to work on the omnibus, I was a little discomforted that I had not received word from Charlotte and Maria Lucas. A part of me now doubted myself. Charlotte and Maria were ladies, and their father was knighted. Would Sir William readily accept the idea of sending his daughters to the North to become working-class ladies?

When arriving at Granger Hall, those thoughts and doubts still occupied me when I got my desk ready. As I sat in the back of the lecture hall, Mr. Hanley entered. When seeing me, he stopped in his tracks, and I was glad to see him.

"Yes," I said, smiling, "I still live, sir."

His eyes, once more, were filled with emotion. It was very difficult to discern what those emotions were because there was a plethora of them occurring within him, in conflict at one time.

"When I heard about what happened," he said, "I was worried. No one told me where you were staying when you recovered. All I was told was that it wasn't at your home. If I had known..."

"I know. You would have come."

"Yes, I would have."

Once more, he just stared at me. Unable to stay firm under his gaze, I looked down at my lap and blushed. Seeing the effect his stare had on me again, he stuttered, 'Yes, yes,' a couple of times and he went to the front of the hall, preparing for his students.

Once more, he captivated them all with another class about technological evolution. He would prove to be the best speaker of them all, because I could always follow his lectures the most.

When his session finished, I went back to the library and began to work on my second copy. While I was there, Mr. Dennison entered, and we looked at each other. Of course, venom shot from his eyes.

"Still hate me?" I asked.

"Still hate me?" he echoed.

"Don't do that."

"Don't do that."

"Oh," I groaned, "get out already!"

"Very well, spirited one'."

He turned his heel and left me alone. And thank goodness for that.

As I finished my notes, I went to the storage shelf to catalogue them. As I did so, Mr. Hanley entered.

"I finished your notes," I announced, "do me the honor of checking them, to make sure that I made no mistakes."

"You know that I will."

"Yes, I do. Sometimes, we humans say obvious things because we have no notion of what else to say. But we also feel obligated to fill the empty space of conversation."

"Oh, is that what you were doing?" he asked, chuckling gently.

"Yes, I was, I was, I was."

Removing his spectacles, he began to clean them.

"Miss Bennet, I need your advice on something."

"Oh, what is it?"

"I received a letter from the Kirkpatricks."

"Oh, and how is little Molly doing? Do they find her to be a satisfactory companion to Cynthia?"

"More than that. Cynthia has taken to Molly very much, to the point where she frets whenever Molly has to return home to me."

I turned to him, having a notion of where this narration was headed.

"Oh."

"Yes," he said, "and Mr. and Mrs. Kirkpatrick have requested that they take Molly in, as a ward to their household and raise her there. Of course, I would get to visit her whenever I wished, but she will be a part of their household."

"And you are wondering if you ought to accept this."

"Yes. By the look on your face, you don't seem so surprised."

"Your voice helped me hint correctly."

"Ah. Well, there it is."

"Before I tell you what I think, I want to make sure that you know this invitation was done out of no offense to your parenting skills. You are a very good godparent. This is a request done more out of the Kirkpatricks thinking of their child and giving her a sister."

"Yes, I thought of that. Of course, my pride was affected at first, but afterwards, I began to see reason. It's a logical request and was a great compliment to Molly."

"I am happy that you feel that way. Well, this is a hard thing to advise on. I shall take into account everything from many directions. First, I must ask you what do you feel? Second, what does Little Molly feel? Third, what is best for Molly? Have you thought of this all?"

"I have." He put his spectacles back on and continued. "As for myself, I love Molly, but she deserves this. If the Kirkpatricks make her Cynthia's particular companion, then she will always be around other children, she will grow up to be quite a lady, and she always can return to me, happy. As long as I get to see her often, then everything is well."

"It sounds like you already have made up your mind," I said, "and you were just waiting for me to validate them."

"Perhaps I was."

"Well, no other opinion is needed. You are right. This arrangement is entirely in her favor. You are giving Molly her best chance in every way. As long as you promise me that you will visit her often enough that she still regards you as her guardian. Don't take time for granted and tell yourself that you are too busy to go see her. Because, if you do that, she will grow up and then not know you."

Once more, he looked at me with a whirlwind of emotions in his eyes.

"I promise. She is my niece. I won't forget her."

I smiled.

"Mr. Hanley, I must stop forgetting that you are a good man."

———

The next class for the day was Mr. Dennison's class. Once more, he was an excellent teacher, and once more, I found myself grimacing at him as I copied my notes.

This evidently had no effect on him, and when he finished the class, he steamrolled past me, and I couldn't resist sticking my tongue out at him. What about him brought out the savage in me?

Putting his notes in my satchel bag, I planned to take them home with me, to copy them, when I had been given a pleasant surprise.

"Margaret!" I cried.

"Lizzy," she said, smiling as she came up to me. "Forgive me for surprising you, but I was wondering if you were meeting Mr. Darcy today? If you are not, then I was wondering if I could join you as you returned to Frances Street. I was hoping that you could accompany me to visit the Higgins house."

"Your arrival was not in vain," I assured her, "Mr. Darcy and I are not meeting this evening. Rather, I was going home, so your company is most welcome."

Helping me gather everything from my desk, we left the hall and waited for the omnibus. As we rode on the way home, I asked about her mother and she assured me that

Mrs. Hale was still maintaining, but any day, that might change.

After we spoke about her mother's illness to excess, she changed the topic and brought up the letter she wrote to me.

"Yes," I said to her, "I did pass along the message that you gave me the authority to speak on. Mr. Thornton is aware of your desire to get along with him. Are you regretting that message now?"

"Not at all. On the contrary, I wished to thank you for helping me see how severe I became. It is never right to willfully misunderstand someone who has tried to understand you. I will tell Thornton that I will not abide him taking liberties the way that he did before, but I do wish for us to reach some sort of peaceful coexistence. I still disagree with him on many things."

"And you are not wrong to. I only tell you to practice moderation, not blind conformity. Well now, I am proud of you. You are better than me. It took me longer to learn that lesson."

"Are you teasing me again?" Margaret asked, amused.

"Tease? Me?"

When we walked down to Frances Street, I told Margaret that we should stop at my house first, so that I could put my satchel bag down and put my notes in my chifforobe.

As we entered, Jane was inside with Mr. Bingley, along with Kitty, Rasby, and Plato.

"Lizzy!" Jane cried, merry, "We have a letter from Lucas Lodge!"

When hearing that, I immediately felt both elated as well as full of trepidation. Either it would be good news or bad.

"It was addressed to you," Jane said, "so we couldn't open it. But make haste."

"Oh, I intend to," I said, snatching the letter and prying it open.

"Oh," Mr. Bingley sighed, "I hope that it bears good news."

"Why?" Plato asked.

"Maria might be my replacement," Jane explained. "If she agrees to be interviewed by the Kirkpatricks, the sooner —" here she blushed, "Bingley and I can proceed to our wedding plans."

Plato looked between them as Bingley squeezed Jane's hand.

"Ah, the plot thickens."

Raising up the letter, I read it, and each word brought hope to me. Once I realized that I could tell everyone, I decided to read certain parts of it out loud.

> ...the prospect of going to the North, at first, filled Maria and I with apprehension and discomfort. After all, we had no intention of working, and the fear of the unknown will always be daunting.
>
> However, the more that we thought about it, the more agreeable an idea it became. I should like to visit Milton and at least see the sort of life that we could have there. Also, Maria and I are in need of a little bit of novelty. We also have begun to consider that maybe a change of scenery and society will offer us potential prospects.

I cannot guarantee that we will say yes to the scheme, but Maria and I are willing to come to Milton, visit you all, be interviewed and see how things shall progress.

Write to us soon so that arrangements can be made for us to purchase our railway tickets and journey to the North.

It will also be a delight to see you all!

Yours etc.

Charlotte Lucas

When lowering the letter, the reaction was immediate. Bingley and Jane were overjoyed, and the rest of us laughed at their proclamations.

As for myself, this news was perfect, and I could not wait to tell Mr. Darcy when I saw him. Oh, just to have the chance of plans coming into action, of seeing Charlotte again, of knowing that I could repay her for her devotion to our family.

Ah, hope being on the horizon! My spirits soared, and I felt that I was one step closer to being Mr. Darcy's wife.

All that I had endured.

All that I had to witness.

All the mistakes I had made.

And now, having found a clearer path, and a better way of being, fate was beginning to come together, and say to me 'maybe this time, you shall win'. With knowing that, I knew that all had the potential to be put to right. Things were beginning to fall into place and the euphoria of the room seemed to channel my mood.

There was so much joy, so much contentment, and daring to hope that all would turn out well.

It was this mentality that I had when Margaret and I walked a little further down the street to visit the Higginses. On the way, I skipped somewhat, and Margaret noted it.

"Merry mood?" She asked, laughing a little.

"Why not?" I cried. "For the moment, life is beautiful, and I will not let it be any other way." I spun around, giddy as I chose to be ignorant of those around me. "Life is beautiful!"

We reached the Higgins house, knocked on the door and were not waiting for long. The door opened and Mary was looking at us...with tears in her eyes.

Her expression immediately silenced our mirth, and we stopped smiling.

"Mary?" Margaret asked.

"Oh, Misses," she said, her tears rolling down her cheek. "Bessy...she's..."

Margaret and I entered, and we moved to the adjacent room. Our walk was heavy and slow. Even though Mary had not said the word, we felt the deadness of the air, how stagnant and stale it all weighed down on us, and we didn't know how we had the power to move. It was as if our feet were moving of their own accord, pushing us forward, provoking us at every step.

When we walked into the other room, we froze.

There was Bessy, on her bed, her eyes closed.

I told myself that she was sleeping.

Margaret perhaps had done the same.

However, as we stood there, seeing Bessy's chest not move, having no air come in and out of it, she remained frozen.

Still.

Lifeless.

Oh, no, not Bessy...not Bessy!

The reality struck down on us, with the weight of a storm cast over the land.

Bessy was dead.

End of Book III[1]

---

1. There is another afterword behind this book, if the Reader is interested in hearing more about Gaskell's and Austen's work.

Afterword

Hello and again, fellow classical readers. In this afterword, I thought it was best to explain a few things, in case the reader was a little curious.

On Book Three of the series, I admit that there was a deliberate reason for so much focus on the incident in the first half of the book. By doing so, I was able to approach the subject from many different perspectives and reveal many different sides to the situation.

And now that we are here, I hope it might interest you all to discuss what I mentioned previously before. The compare and contrast of the 2004 BBC adaptation to the 1970s BBC adaptation.

First, I shall begin with why I don't despise the 1970s BBC adaptation.

To be honest, I wonder how they obviously did it with such an abominable budget. It was very evident that the adaptation was not given much money at all.

Also, Elizabeth Gaskell's works are not like Jane Austen's; they don't lend themselves to film adaptations so

very easily. Jane Austen is a Regency writer who, interest-
ingly enough, wrote in a way that made her writing perfect
for film and tv. Since a significant part of Miss Austen's
work took place inside houses, villages, and country estates,
it led to most of the story being able to be told on a small
budget. Also, I was able to get used to the 1970s 'North &
South' adaptation, because I had become accustomed to
that formula of storytelling.

A little over a year ago, I brough the Jane Austen BBC
adaptation collection, where it gave all of Jane Austen's
novels that were adapted from the 1970s and 1980s. In the
1970s, there were some adaptations, which included
Persuasion and Emma. There was also a 70s version of
'Sense & Sensibility', I believe. But sadly, it didn't make its
way into that collection.

Either way, that version of 'Emma' and 'Persuasion'
have grown on me since then. But what could be evident is
that, on a small budget, both novels were able to be adapted
well, because Jane Austen's novel knew how to lend itself to
adaptation. Also, with her novels being set mostly in the
country, it is easier to have outdoor scenes.

With 'North & South', the best way to adapt it is to have
the budget to film historical outdoor scenes in an industrial
town. That makes it more complicated because that is more
expensive to look more historical.

This is the main thing that the 2004 version had so
much in its favor. Not only were you able to enjoy parts of
Helstone, and see why Margaret was loath to leave it, but
we also got to see much of Milton. By doing that, it added so
much to the story, enhanced the visual wonder, threw the
viewer into the Victorian industrial city life, and augmented

the experience. This could never be achieved with the 1970s 'North & South'.

However, I could be mistaken, but it seemed like the budget for that version increased with each episode. In part 1, it was so evident that they didn't have much money to do anything. Then, in the second episode, they had a little more money. In the third and fourth episode they seemed able to make things become a little more presentable.

Due to this, there were quite a few aspects of the story that couldn't be adapted, i.e. Leonard's trying to take Frederick in, Leonard's dying, and Margaret having to lie to save Frederick. Many subplots, such as Mr. Lennox's going to Helstone to propose, was either condensed or gotten rid of altogether.

Of course, there were many other parts that were very faithful to the novel. For example, this adaptation was very loyal to how Margaret and Mr. Thornton really had met, when Mr. Bell really came into the story, how Margaret wanted Mr. Thornton to know, eventually, that she was protecting her brother, and how the story really ended.

There were also some scenes that I liked:

- When Mrs. Hale died, the emotional scene that Mr. Hale displays is beautiful! I believe the actor's name was Robin Bailey, and he was obviously a good actor. That was some very good acting on the actor's part.
- When Nicholas Higgins went to the auction that Dixon gave.
- When Mrs. Thornton and her son are sitting together after Thornton has to talk about selling

the house. It was a nice scene between the mother and son.

- When Thornton bids goodbye to his workers and shakes their hands. Also, when Higgins tells him about Margaret's brother.
- At the end, when Margaret and Thornton finally get together, I will always feel something. It just had a bittersweet quality to it.
- The actor who played Mr. Hale in the 2004 version of 'North and South' was the same actor who played Frederick in the 1970s version. I love it when that sort of thing happens.
- Once more, Mr. Bell was a breath of fresh air. Yes, I will always love Mr. Bell.
- Margaret's line at the end 'It is not places that matter...but people'. Beautiful line.

Overall, the acting was not bad at all. The only major defect is that, due to the quality of film in that time, it's hard to always understand certain actors. But the show acknowledges this, and that it wasn't the actors' fault. It is simply that, in that time period, recording wasn't as good as it is now. Fortunately, the DVD had subtitles, because due to the recording conversion and the colloquial language that was often used in the adaptation, it was difficult to understand sometimes.

I've often heard people criticize the actress who played Margaret, Rosalind Shanks. I guess I have strange standards. I thought she did a very good job in the part, because it was how the character was written. All the Hales were well-cast, along with Dixon, and they had the clearest diction out of the lot.

Patrick's accent was perfect for Thornton, and Fanny was wonderfully peevish and annoying. As such, she did a good job of it. Mrs. Thornton was the difficult one. Sometimes I like her performance. Other times, I find it slightly satisfactory, but that could be prejudiced because of the 2004 version. Though I don't deny that she is a good actress.

Now it comes to the Higginses. This was a drawback because of how close they kept Bessy's dialogue to the books, and the dialect was difficult. However, as the story unfolded, you find yourself caring for Nicholas. It is simply that the first episode did the Higgins family no favors.

When it comes to the 2004 version, it had so much in its favor: better budget, a fantastic director, a screenwriter who knew how to be loyal to the book while also adding touches here and there to augment the story...and Time.

The fact is that the 1970s was tackling an author who, when it came to adapting her novels to screen, was still a bit of a tough nut to crack, for financial reasons, as well as experience. 'North & South' does work on tv, of course, but it was not as familiar to the screenwriting world as the likes of Miss Austen, Dickens, and Charlotte Bronte. As such, I view the 1970s North & South as the beginning of how Miss Gaskell's works could be tested and tried. And then, when 'Wives and Daughters' was adapted, as well as 'Cranford', it became more evident than ever that Mrs. Gaskell's works were obviously ready for the world to see. So, when the 2004 'North & South' adaptation was released, it was at the point where television writers had cracked the case and knew how to adapt Mrs. Gaskell to perfection.

So much of what made the novel interesting was the

change from the Southern country life, to the Northern industrial town life. From the environment, even to the sky, the change is palpable. The best way to have us feel that is to show it, and this version does it well. Also, this adaptation gives us more reasons for Margaret not to initially prefer Mr. Thornton, and the root of prejudice becomes so very cemented.

And the ending...oh, my god! Every time I see the ending of that, where they find each other on the train station, one going to Milton and the other from it—yes, the subtle storytelling is so nuanced there. And then when they hold hands and kiss, it's like a wonderfully pleasurable wrenching of my stomach. Then Thornton says 'coming home with me?' and they ride off together. Does it get any better than that? I just don't think so.

And then the casting...oh, the delightful casting. Once again, all the Hales are exquisite. I love Daniela Denby-Ashe as Margaret Hale. I liked both actresses who played Dixon, but the 2004 version is my favorite. She just has that natural authoritative demeanor that works.

And the Thorntons...first, Fanny Thornton is sometimes hilarious. When she fans Margaret, when Margaret was unconscious after being hit, makes me laugh each time. But Fanny, in this version, also displays signs of either being snobby—but maybe that snobbishness might come from the fact that she is not often listened to. Is she antagonizing or is she a woman who needs more attention every now and again, to help her improve? I'll never fully know.

Like I said before, I liked the 1970s version of Mrs. Thornton, but I will always prefer this one. In this version, we see her prejudice for the Hales, but we also see her warmer side displayed toward her son. I liked that, even though the 1970s version might be more accurate to the character from the book.

And now we come to the man of the hour: Mr. Thornton himself. Smolder-alert! My goodness, it is hard to walk away without being so very much enraptured by that version of Mr. Thornton. If Thornton ever gets redone, under another adaptation, I doubt they will ever find someone who is on the same level as Richard Armitage. That was lightning in a bottle casting.

And now we come to the wonderful secondary characters. The main ones are the Higginses, which I find to be better than their original counterparts. The 1970s version paints the Higginses as more in despair, and it might be more accurate. Also, I admit that I grew to like the 1970s Nicholas Higgins by the end. However, the Higginses, in 2004, were not only cast by actors who you feel a kindred spirit to immediately, but they were introduced very well. The way that Sandy Welch introduced Nicholas was a good idea, for you quickly felt endeared to him, and I like that she had made Bessy's words to be more plot-oriented and common sense-like, rather than focused on going to the afterlife. It made Bessy more interesting.

And I was so glad that Mr. Bell was brought in earlier than he was originally supposed to be. The actor was like a bit of light in a dark room, and you were drawn to him.

Therefore, in conclusion, yes, I do prefer the 2004 version. It has everything to recommend it. However, I shall still, every now and again, tread toward the 1970s adaptation, because it has the nostalgic feel. Therefore, I shall enjoy it from time to time, as a diverting time of the beginning when Mrs. Gaskell's works began to really become known to us, from an adaptation-perspective.

What do you think of one adaptation, or both? We all can admit that it's a fun experience to think about it.

Thank you so much for reading, and sorry for the delay in publication. But I'm a working-class little snip, and these last couple of months, I've had to cover more work shifts, because I have a simple dream: one day I will afford to have health insurance! I know, laugh out loud all that you wish, for I often do. So, that is my tedious and roundabout way of explaining why this publication didn't come out as soon as I would have wished. If a publication of mine ever comes out later than expected, it's not me being lazy, I assure you. I wish that I could release books at the time that you deserve, but my time is often not my own. But I will always focus on getting my books complete as fast as I can. Cross my heart!

Thanks again, and in the words of the show 'The Prisoner': be seeing you!

— Ney Mitch

Don't miss out on your next favorite book!

Join the Satin Romance mailing list
www.satinromance.com/mail.html

THANK YOU FOR READING

Did you enjoy this book?

We invite you to leave a review at your favorite book site,
such as Goodreads, Amazon, Barnes & Noble, etc.

DID YOU KNOW THAT LEAVING A REVIEW...

- Helps other readers find books they may enjoy.
- Gives you a chance to let your voice be heard.
- Gives authors recognition for their hard work.
- Doesn't have to be long. A sentence or two
  about why you liked the book will do.

About the Author

Ney Mitch has been a long-standing Jane Austen enthusiast, having written forty novels that were inspired by her various works. Since stumbling on Miss Austen's books after graduating from college, she has always dabbled in Austen inspired literature, ranging from writing works for teens to adults. Originally, her desire was to adapt Jane Austen's writing in a way to help young adults connect with her, however over time, she has spread her aims to other genres and styles. Having received her BA Degree at Desales University, she is a writer, both literary and dramatic, as well as being a Historic Reenactor.

facebook.com/courtney.mitchell.589

x.com/CMMitchelPsyche

pinterest.com/shebaanna

Also by Ney Mitch
with Satin Romance

Austen Gaskell Series

Curiosities & Contemplation

Resolved & Resigned

Triumph & Tragedy

Kitty Bennet Adventure Series

Vanities & Vexations

Forms & Fashions

Romance & Recklessness

Nuance & Novelty

Doubts & Difficulties

Follies & Forgiveness (*Coming Soon!*)

Romance & Revolution Saga

The First Impression

The Memory Series

Moments of Moments Past

Moments of Moments Present

Moments of Moments Future

Moments of Moments Infinite

Pride & Prejudice Reimaginings

Rapture & Rebellion

Fortune & Misfortune

Desire & Destiny

Pride & Peace

Resolve & Revelations

Hope & Hopelessness

Chances Series

Chances Are

Chances Come

Chances Fade

Chances End

Novels

The Tale of Mr. & Mrs. Bennet: A Pride & Prejudice Christmas Tale

Considerations Near Christmastime

www.ingramcontent.com/pod-product-compliance
Lightning Source LLC
Chambersburg PA
CBHW030955260626
47169CB00002B/555